the wright brother

MARIE HALL

The Wright Brother

Published in October 2014 by Marie Hall, Honolulu, Hawaii, United States of America

Cover Designed byRegina Wamba
Interior Layout by Author's HQ

Books by Marie Hall

Kingdom Series:

HER MAD HATTER
GERARD'S BEAUTY
RED AND HER WOLF
JINNI'S WISH
HOOK'S PAN
DANIKA'S SURPRISE
MOON'S FLOWER
HUNTSMAN'S PREY
RUMPEL'S PRIZE
HOOD'S OBSESSION
HER ONE WISH
A PIRATE'S DREAM

Moments Series:

A MOMENT
RIGHT NOW
THIS TIME

Night Series:

CRIMSON NIGHT
ALL HALLOWS NIGHT
HOWLER'S NIGHT
RED RAIN

Chaos Time Serial:

SABLE
SLAYDE
SYNNERGY

Eternal Lover's Series:

DEATH'S LOVER
DEATH'S REDEMPTION

DEDICATION

To my husband, Matt. I still remember the day I first saw you walk into my geometry class sophomore year of high school. We've been a part of each other's lives for over nineteen years now, it doesn't seem possible. I couldn't do any of what I do without you.

Chapter 1

Three tiny little bundles stared back at Elisa Jane. Their faces were scrunched and red as they shuddered and wiggled beneath their monkey-print blankets.

They were sorta cute, in an ugly kind of way.

Two of the babies looked back at her. Cooing and making funny noises.

"Aww." Her tiny heart melted as she reached out her hand to let one of the babies latch on to her finger, but she couldn't shove her hand through the bars far enough to get to him. "Cute."

Leaning up on tiptoe even higher so that she could get a better look at the triplets, Elisa held tight to the edge of their crib.

"Elisa." Mum glanced up from her spot on the couch. "You be careful, young lady."

"Okay, Mum," she said dutifully, wondering why Mrs. Wright's face looked so splotchy.

Sometimes Elisa's face would go splotchy too. Like when she'd fall off her bicycle and scrape her knees. Or that one time she accidentally touched the hot stove. Her face had gone really splotchy then, too. There were no scrapes on Mrs. Wright's knees, so maybe she'd gotten burnt.

Pressing her lips together, she turned back to study the babies.

They were grunting and scrunching their noses, and their fists had wormed their way out of the snuggly blanket.

"You're ugly," she murmured and then quickly glanced back at her mother. Mum would be mad if she heard her calling babies ugly. But they were.

Their faces were so red, and they had no hair. "But pretty eyes," she said as a consolation, even though their eyes weren't all that pretty. And Daddy had told her once that boys weren't pretty, they were handsome. But she didn't think they were handsome, either.

One of the babies sneezed. And that was cute. It tugged a smile to her lips.

All year Elisa had been so excited waiting for Mrs. Wright to have her triplets. And now they were finally here and that was nice. Of course it wasn't fair that they weren't girls. Because boys were dirty, and sometimes mean. But as long as they understood that they couldn't be mean to Elisa, then she'd be okay with that, she supposed.

But it would take a while before they could play with her. Elisa would be three soon. She was the biggest of the big girls and they were just really small.

Two of the babies were blinking huge owl eyes up at her. But the third baby was looking at the wall of the crib with a weird stare. Elisa had been trying for the past ten minutes to get that baby to look at her, but he just wouldn't.

It made her cranky. Obviously he didn't like girls.

"Mum?" She looked up at her mom, who was deep in conversation with Mrs. Wright.

"Yes, Elisa?" Mum asked, sounding *e-zas-per-tated.*

That was a big word that Daddy was teaching her. He said that Elisa always made them *e-zas-per-tated.*

She huffed the blonde lank of bangs out of her eyes. "What names?"

Instead of Mum answering, Mrs. Wright did. Her smile was watery as she said, "Christian. Roman. And Julian."

She dabbed at her eyes when she said Julian's name, and Mum wrapped her up in a big hug.

Elisa frowned. Grown ups were so weird sometimes. Turning back around, she smiled at the boys.

"Hi. I'm Elisa."

Christian and Roman cooed. But Julian still wouldn't look at her.

"Julian." She singsonged his name. "I'm here. Hello, baby."

But he still wouldn't look at her. Maybe he just couldn't hear her or sumthin'. She shoved her arm through the bar, but again she couldn't reach them. Annoyed, she decided the only way to get Julian to pay attention to her was to get in there with him.

It would be kind of tricky, but she was a good climber. Daddy had taught her how to climb the great big elm in their back yard. Glancing over her shoulder one more time to make sure Mum wasn't watching, Elisa stuck her shiny, black-slippered foot on the outer edge of their mattress and stepped up.

Mum and Mrs. Wright had gone into the kitchen to get some more snacks. Which was good, because then Elisa could climb without Mum worrying that she'd do something wrong.

"I coming, baby Julian," she grunted as she shimmied her way up the white-painted metal side of their baby crib.

But Elisa had overestimated her climbing abilities. Her arms were shaking only halfway up and when she went to pull her leg over the side of the crib she lost her balance and fell hard onto Mrs.

Wright's wooden floors.

Fire exploded down her side and this time it was her turn to shriek.

In seconds Mum had scooped her off the floor, hugging her tight to her breast. "Elisa Jane Adrian, what have you done? Are you okay?"

But Elisa couldn't talk because her arm hurt so bad and now her face was all splotchy. She wrapped her arms around her Mum's neck and cried, feeling bad because the babies were crying too.

Mrs. Wright was over there, picking them up one after another, patting their backs and telling them she loved them.

"I'm sorry, Loribelle, I think we're going to go now. But if you need anything at all..." Mum walked over to Mrs. Wright and gave her a side hug. "You don't hesitate to call me, got it?"

Mrs. Wright sniffed and dabbed at her eyes. "Thanks, Bethy. I will."

Mum's hand was big and warm as she rubbed Elisa's back, already her arm was feeling better. She wished she'd had a chance to say hi to Julian too.

Christian and Roman were still squalling, but Julian was where he'd always been, just staring at the wall of his crib, like he'd never even heard her fall.

Elisa decided right then that she didn't like Julian Wright much at all.

Chapter 2

5 years later

The sea was calling to Elisa today. The sky and water were so blue. Seagulls circled above her sandy playground, crying out loudly. Obviously smelling the hot dogs and hamburgers Daddy was grilling up. The grown-ups were further up shore; Mrs. Wright would occasionally cast an eagle eye in the direction of the boys, who played along the coastline.

It was the fourth of July; tonight there'd be fireworks. This was really Elisa's favorite time of year. The fireworks looked so amazing when they shone off the darkened reflection of the bay.

Not to mention no school. No homework. Just fun.

With her boys.

Roman and Christian came running up to her. Their five-year-old legs churned up the grainy sand in their wake. Roman was missing his front tooth and his smile was huge as he wildly waved his prize high in the air.

"Lisa. Lisa!" Roman jumped up and down; his turtle-themed

water shorts flopped around his legs as he did. He had a habit of dumping mounds of wet sand down his shorts. "Look what we found!"

"Well, I found it." Christian stepped in front of his brother, shoving him gently out of the way as he pointed at his little bird chest.

The boys weren't identical triplets. But the two of them still looked sort of similar. Roman was a little darker, his hair and eyes a pretty dark blue. Christian was just a little bit lighter. Looking more like Mrs. Wright with his sandy blond hair and slightly brighter blue eyes. Julian, on the other hand, looked just like Mr. Wright. Inky black hair, with the most striking and vivid set of bluish-green eyes that always reminded Elisa of the tropical waters she yearned to one day see in person.

Julian was the one that really didn't look like he was one third of the triplet gang.

Which at least made it easy for Elisa to tell them apart.

She laughed, eyes widening as she stared at the broken bit of shell. Holding out her hand for it. Once Roman placed it on her palm she turned it around and around after. The outside was dark and gray looking, full of green moss and other yucky bits. But the inside gleamed like mother of pearl.

"Oh, that's pretty," she cooed, patting their heads. "Good job," she chirped when Christian snatched it back, hugging it tight to his body.

It never really bothered her that she was almost three years older than the boys. Well, technically, she was two years and five months older, but that was a bunch older than them.

Still, they were sort of like her brothers. She loved them, kind of. Not when they were being buttheads and tripping her feet out from under her and stuff. But she was the kind of girl that loved fishing, playing down by the docks, and swimming like a little fish.

She guessed because she was more of a tomboy the boys thought she was all right, too.

"Where's Jules?" she asked, shading her eyes as she searched the cove for any sign of Julian.

Christian and Roman both sighed in unison.

"Julian!" Mrs. Wright's voice was a sudden shrill that rent the peacefulness of the afternoon. "Julian!"

She came running up, her pale face and normally artfully arranged sandy blonde hair that now tumbled haphazardly around her shoulders attesting to her panic.

Yanking them each by the arm, she gasped, "Where is he?"

Christian's eyes grew wide. "He's...he's over there." He pointed to a sharp area of rock.

And sure enough, a dark head could be seen bobbing up and down around the dangerous bed of sharp rock.

Suddenly everyone seemed to become aware of what was happening. Mr. Wright, Mum, and Daddy—all of them rushed toward Julian, who seemed completely unaware of the fact that when the tide rose and covered the rocks they became too slick and dangerous to walk on.

Elisa had lived along the coastline long enough to know that the tide had already begun to shift and in moments those rocks he now played on would be hazardous. She didn't stop to question her actions. With her heart lodged in her throat, she ran.

She was already wearing her swimsuit; she could slice through the water and make it to him before anyone else could. His parents were close to the rocky outcropping, but they wouldn't reach him in time—they'd have to step carefully themselves.

Elisa was already a champion swimmer and as capable in the water as any average adult.

She didn't shiver when the cold water rushed up the length of her calves and thighs. Instead, taking a deep breath, she dove into the almost frigid waters, breast-stroking expertly out.

Mrs. Wright screamed when Julian did exactly what everyone expected him to do. With a strange, garbled sound coming out of his throat, Julian's arms windmilled violently, and like a cartoon falling in slow motion, Elisa caught a glimpse of him crashing into the dangerous waters.

Julian could swim, but just barely. He was really only good enough at keeping his head above water. She swam harder, kicking with all her might, when she noticed he was barely moving.

Elisa knew how badly head wounds could bleed. She'd seen her dad crack his forehead open once; she just hoped Julian was okay.

Kicking her feet with all her might and with five more powerful strokes, she got to his side. He'd turned over on his back, floating with his arms spread eagle and moaning loudly. Already she could see a purple knot swelling on his head, but thankfully there was no blood.

"Get him, Elisa!" Mrs. Wright called, waving her hand as if guiding Elisa toward the spot where she stood.

Julian was heavy, but the water made him buoyant enough that Elisa was able to wrap her arm around his middle and gently kick her way back toward the rocks, where Mr. Wright waited with arms wide open.

"It's all right, Jules," she whispered as she concentrated on getting them back to safety. He was gurgling, his fingers digging like claws into her wrists as he held on to her tight.

"I've got you. Don't worry," she soothed.

Her arms trembled when she finally was able to hand him over to his father. Mr. Wright plucked Jules away from her easily, wrapping his arm around his son and smiling down at her with a proud beam to his ocean-colored eyes.

"Good job, girl. Good job." Faint lines around his eyes crinkled as he gazed down at her, but she was only thankful that she'd gotten to Julian in time. It could have been so much worse.

Arms feeling like wet noodles, she gave him a weak grin as she latched on to her daddy's outstretched hand and landed on the rocky outcropping beside Mr. Wright. Gratefully accepting the towel Mum held out for her, she wrapped it around herself twice before patting Julian's back.

"Hey, Jules, you okay?"

He didn't respond to her question, but he did respond to her touch. He had his face pressed into his father's neck, but his brilliant blue-green eyes were just for her as he nodded. As if to say thank you.

She smiled. "You're welcome," she said, even though she knew he'd never hear it.

Because Mum was a nurse, she checked him out quickly and determined that aside from the fact that he might have a bad headache later that night, he didn't need to go to the hospital.

That night they watched the fireworks in silence. She and Jules held hands on the beach. He'd moved to her side after supper, and though she knew he couldn't hear the booms or even see the colors, his eyes lit up as each firecracker danced through the air. And it made her happy to sit right there on that wet sand and listen to his happy little gurgles of laughter.

Elisa didn't know what she would ever do without Julian Wright in her life.

Days turned into weeks, weeks into months, and months into years.

Elisa was almost ten years old the day she learned the devastating news.

The day had started out like any other day. She was happy because now she was a fifth grader.

Mum had also told her she could finally go to a school dance. Next week was that dance and last week Mum had found her a pale pink dress that fell to her knees in soft waves. It looked super pretty on her. But even better, Mum had gotten her her first stick of lip-gloss. Elisa couldn't wait to wear it. Janet was gonna be so jealous too, because her mom still wouldn't let her wear makeup.

Of course her date was Christian, which totally didn't count as a date, but she was still excited, even if he was a third grader.

Elisa had been held back a year because of her father. Well, because of his training in Europe, that was. Her parents had decided to hold Elisa back so that he could concentrate on his training, without forcing her mother to stay back home because of Elisa being in school. Because of that, even though they were almost three years apart, they were only two grades apart. Which was still sort of young, but she liked Christian and, unlike most boys in school, he could actually dance.

Of course, it would have made it even better if she could have gone with Joey Crawford; he was only the cutest boy in fifth grade. But Joey had a stupid girlfriend and probably wouldn't have asked her anyway.

Brushing out her hair one final time, she slipped it into a ponytail, pulled on her prettiest purple bathing suit, and tried to ignore the nervous flutters in the pit of her stomach.

Today was the biggest day of her life. Qualifications to get to be a part of the club team—Mid-Maine Seals.

Roman and Christian told her she had it in the bag. Which she totally thought she might, and even though she was fast, she was scared she might not be as fast as some of the other swimmers trying out.

What if she didn't make it?

Or, worse yet, what if she did?

She grimaced.

There was a heavy knock at the door. "Elisa, you dressed?" Her father's deep baritone was a muffled sound.

"Yes." She nodded, still hanging on tight to her stomach.

He opened the door and she smiled when she saw him. Daddy was still the most handsome guy she'd ever seen.

There was some gray now at the corners of his dark brown hair, but she thought it made him look very distinguished.

He grinned, but the smile never really touched his eyes. "You look nervous, little bit."

She plopped onto her vanity stool and nodded. "I'm terrified. I'm not sure I'm good enough for this."

Snorting, he sat on the edge of her day bed and nodded. "Oh, I understand that feeling. I'm always nervous before a big race—"

Daddy was a professional triathlete. Mum said that was where Elisa got her athleticism from, which was probably true; the most Mum ever did for exercise was gardening. She claimed to be allergic to running, which Elisa had totally believed until she turned eight and realized "allergic" was just another word for lazy. It had made her laugh when she realized how gullible she'd been.

"—but that's how you face your fears."

"How? By failing and coming in last?" She made a sound between a whimper and a whine.

Crossing his legs, he ran a hand through his hair. "If you try your best and come in last, there's no shame in that. The only shame is if you defeat yourself by not giving it your all. No matter the outcome, we'll be proud of you."

"I love you, Daddy."

Getting up, he came to her and wrapped her up in a big, soapy-scented hug. His hug lasted a long time, longer than normal, and he kept clearing his throat. It was starting to make her nervous, but she thought maybe she was just imagining things when a second later he took a step back and smiled down at her. And this time his smile did reach his eyes. Eyes that looked a little more wet than usual. "Ditto. Now let's go."

Blowing out a deep breath, Elisa got up, slipped on her shorts and shirt, and nodded. "Okay. The guys are coming too, right?"

The grimace had happened so fast that Elisa almost couldn't be sure she'd seen it happen at all.

"Yep. Sure, they'll be there. Where else would those rugrats be? They only worship the ground you walk on."

She laughed. "They do not."

But she knew they totally did. That was okay, though, she pretty much adored them herself. Being an only child may have been a sad life for her if it hadn't been for her three friends that were more like brothers.

She leaned her head out the car window and waved just as the Wrights came tromping out of their house ten minutes later. Daddy was taking her ahead of the crowd so she'd have time to warm up before the competition.

But she frowned when not one of the boys waved back at her. In fact, Mrs. Wright didn't look well, either.

Her nose was a bright cherry red.

Elisa jumped to her knees and stared out the back window of her family's SUV as they drove off, watching as Mum walked out her home and over to Mrs. Wright before pulling her in for a tight hug.

"Daddy, is something wrong with Mrs. Wright?"

But instead of answering he clicked on the car radio and the nerves that'd been simmering in her belly now flared back to life.

All of that was forgotten the moment she arrived at the swim meet.

Elisa shouldn't have been worried—her form was top-notch, her strokes sure. She'd slid into first across the finish line, even beating out two boys from her class who'd sworn up and down they were faster than her. Blinking water droplets out of her eyes, she scanned the bleachers for Mum and the Wright boys when she stepped out of the pool.

But the only face she recognized was her dad's.

He was clapping and gazing down at her proudly. "Good job, little bit." He scooped her up and twirled her around, but his voice seemed to lack some of the joy he normally enthused when she won a competition.

With a bad feeling in the pit of her stomach, she wiggled out of his arms. "Dad, where is everybody?"

It was rare that the Wrights ever missed any of her meets. In fact, it'd only happened once before and that was because Roman had gotten a sudden case of appendicitis.

Suddenly the smile was gone. His face turned very serious and grave as he held on to her hand. "Lisa," he sighed, "baby girl, we need to talk."

She couldn't do anything other than grab her stomach. People kept coming up and clapping her on the back and congratulating her, but she couldn't respond because she knew something was really, really wrong.

She let her father guide her over to the bleachers and he sat her down and waved off her coach as he made his way over. Her father was never rude, and now she was even more scared.

With a mouth grown dry, she swallowed hard. "Daddy?" Her voice trembled.

Tipping his chin up toward the sun, Elisa knew she would never forget that moment. Never forget the way his face suddenly looked so shattered, or the way he inhaled three deep breaths, or how rough his palms felt when he grabbed her pruny ones.

"There's no way to put this that won't hurt you, Elisa. Mr. Wright died last night. It was very sudden and unexpected. Mrs. Wright is taking the boys to her family for a couple of weeks and—"

She couldn't take a proper breath. It was like her lungs had suddenly stopped working correctly. "But...but..." She shook her head, because there were too many thoughts.

Mr. Wright is dead.

The dance.

Mr. Wright is dead.

Christian.

Mr. Wright is dead.

Roman.

Mr. Wright is dead.

Julian...

He shook his head.

What did that mean, exactly?

"Daddy, have they left already?"

"I'm afraid so."

She screamed, hugging her arms to her middle. "But they're coming back, right?"

He didn't answer her, and even though she could feel the press of eyes all over her, she couldn't seem to stop the tears from falling fat and heavy down her face.

"Daddy, please tell me they're coming back."

"I'm sorry, baby girl."

He tried to wrap her up in his arms again, but she wouldn't let him. She ran for the car. Maybe if they were fast enough they could get back. Maybe they could…

"Elisa, stop!" Her father ran after her, his footsteps pounding the pavement.

"Why did you bring me here?" Twirling on him, she balled her hands into fists. "Why would you do that to me?" She swiped at the tears dripping off her nose, angry with her father, with herself for caring so much about a stupid swim meet. "I should have been there for them. Daddy, why?"

His brown eyes were sincere and shimmering with wetness. They had attracted a large crowd, but none of it mattered.

She needed to see them one more time. Needed to say goodbye at least. They may not have been blood, but they were her brothers. They'd grown up together, she'd tended to their scrapes, played hide and go seek, listened to them talk all about their stupid cartoons because she loved them. From the very first minute she'd seen the triplets, she'd fallen in love. They were her family.

"How could you do this to me?" she hiccupped.

"Because your mother and I thought it would be best, Elisa. We know how you feel about them. What finding that out would do to you. You couldn't stop them from leaving; they're already gone. All you can do now is live, baby girl. That's what this is about. Living.

Remembering that no matter how sad, or tough, or hard things get, sometimes there's nothing you can do to change it."

Her lower lip quivered. "I hate you."

"I know you don't, sweetheart." And this time when he pulled her in for a hug, she let him. Crying for Mr. Wright, crying for Mrs. Wright, but especially crying for the loss of her boys.

The Wrights returned back to Sunny Cove, Maine three weeks later to hold Mr. Wright's funeral.

On the one hand, it was wonderful getting to see them. But on the other, Elisa felt terrible. All three boys had been quiet and sullen as they'd entered the church for Mr. Wright's memorial, Julian even more so than normal.

His eyes as he'd stood beside Mrs. Wright on the stoop after the service accepting condolences had seemed lost and empty.

Dressed in bright yellow shorts, a black and green pinstriped shirt, one blue sock and one red sock, Julian looked like a kaleidoscope of color.

Elisa frowned at the snickers some of the kids made when they saw him. It was obvious Mrs. Wright hadn't been in her right frame of mind when she'd allowed him to walk out the house as he was.

Julian was not only deaf, he was colorblind, too. Two conditions which had caused him to be picked on in school.

Her lower chin jutted out when she spied both Roman and Christian standing on the lawn out in front of the church surrounded by a couple of kids from their old class. They were chuckling and pointing at their brother.

Furious that Julian's own brothers would be so cruel, she marched over to Jules's side, and, tossing the boys an evil glare over her shoulder, stood directly behind Julian to shield him as best she could from their eyes.

"Jules," she whispered and placed a gentle hand on his shoulder. Her touch caused him to look at her.

Tears slipped soundlessly from the corners of his eyes.

Julian was tall for his age. Almost to her height. With a messy shock of black hair and those bold eyes, her heart gave a tiny pang. He looked so much like his father.

Her sign language wasn't the best—she and Julian had learned to speak to one another in their own private language of finger taps and gestures—but she'd taken the time to practice a little while they'd been gone. It suddenly bothered her that in all the years she'd known Jules she'd never tried to learn it.

Tapping her pointer finger so that he'd glance at her hands, she spoke to him for the first time.

She didn't actually know phrases—that'd been trickier to learn so quickly. But she'd learned the alphabet. Painstakingly she twisted her fingers into letters.

"I'm sorry."

It took her close to a minute to spell it out. And he shuddered when she finished. His thin shoulders visibly trembled beneath his shirt.

Biting onto the corner of his lip, he nodded and did something back with his fingers. But he moved them so quickly it was a blur she couldn't hope to understand.

Shaking her head, she gave him a helpless shrug. Hating all over again that she'd never learned to talk to him properly. Julian's hearing was so bad, the doctors hadn't even given him hearing aides, for him—they'd said—the aides would be totally useless.

He relied almost solely on sign language.

He wiggled his fingers at her again, but again, she couldn't make out more than a couple of L's and maybe an A. She wasn't sure.

Shaking his head, as if to say nevermind, he then stepped into her and wrapped her tightly into his arms.

She held him tight, knowing it would be the last time she'd ever get to do it.

"I love you, Jules," she whispered and then kissed the top of his head.

Three hours later the Wrights had gone back to New York State and Elisa's world seemed suddenly grayer.

Chapter 3

9 years later

"**I** totally think Joey's gonna ask you to the dance," Chastity giggled over the phone line.

Elisa rolled her eyes. Of course Joey was going to ask her. It wasn't like it was the best-kept secret: he was a jock, she was a jock, it was a match made in jocky heaven. She snorted and crunched into the red apple. Rubbing her pink and black-striped socked feet together as she lay on the piles of pillows her father always teased were more than any one girl should need for a bed.

"I'm not sure I'm going to say yes. I have a swim meet that morning."

"Ugh." Elisa could practically see her goth friend rolling her heavily mascaraed eyes. "You are so frustrating, do you know that? You always have meets. When don't you have meets? All year you've been saying you wanted to go to homecoming with Joey, and now he's gonna ask and you're not sure! I mean, hello!"

She chuckled. "Whatever. Ms. dark, black, and deadly, shouldn't you be getting ready to do some voodoo alter chant or something?"

"Grr. I don't even know why we're friends anymore."

"Whatever, freakazoid." She laughed, swallowing her bite of apple, and then took another. "I think secretly you're tired of playing goth so you live through me."

"I am not a goth, I just like dark clothes, and you are just ridiculous."

"Yeah, you keep telling yourself that and I'll just pretend that you don't actually have a voodoo doll hanging up in your locker."

"I will stick a pin in you," she growled, "just bet me."

"Yeah, you go ahead and do that." She shook her head. Her friend might be weird, but Elisa pretty much thought Chastity hung the moon anyway.

"Whatever," Chastity snickered. "Anyway, homecoming. You going or what?"

Chastity and her family had moved from Trinidad and Tobago to Sunny Cove three years ago. At first everyone had avoided the dark-skinned girl with dreds that fell long and heavy down to her butt. She'd been like a bird of paradise stuck inside a monochromatic garden of white roses. She just stuck out. But Elisa had seen beneath the unique exterior to the intelligent, cool girl beneath and in no time the two of them had developed a tight bond.

Eventually Chastity had won almost everyone over; with her hint of an island accent and her silky, dark skin the boys had fallen prey to her charms and she'd gone from being the outcast to the girl everyone wanted on their speed dial.

"I don't know, probably, I guess. If he asks."

"Jeez, could it have taken you any longer to get that out?"

She stuck out her tongue, curling her fingers through the worn threads of the one and only afghan blanket she'd ever attempted to crotchet. The colors were a mix of black, green, and blue. Colors she'd always loved. "Well, if I'm going, you're going too."

"Nah, I don't do dresses."

Which was entirely true. Chastity had one outfit. Tight black jeans, tight white tops, and a crucifix. Always the crucifix. She was the strangest pseudo goth/voodoo priestess Elisa had ever seen.

Of course, she was the only one Elisa had ever seen, but that was just semantics.

"Elisa!" Her mother's shrill yell came up the stairs. "Please come here!"

"Oops." She jerked. "Coming, Mom. Chas, I gotta go. Dinnertime. Maybe we can go shopping for some gowns tomorrow."

"Keep dreaming, girlfriend."

With a cheery laugh and another goodbye, Elisa hung up. Slipping the cell into her pocket and holding the apple between her teeth, she flew down the stairs and skidded to a complete stop at the sight that met her eyes.

It wasn't dinner sitting on the kitchen table but the group sitting in the living room that'd made her mother call her down. Four people who'd become merely a memory to her.

Mrs. Wright was no longer as tall as Elisa had once recalled her being. Her skin was pale, attesting to the fact that they no longer lived next to a coastline. Her once shiny sandy blonde hair was cut to bob length and now had thick strands of gray between the blonde.

But she wasn't the reason why Elisa suddenly felt like running back upstairs to her bedroom and locking the door.

Three extremely tall males surrounded their diminutive mother. Realizing that she still had the stupid apple stuck in her mouth, she spat it out and rubbed it on her shirt. Which was kind of weird and dumb, but yeah, Elisa was completely taken aback.

Mom smiled. "Okay, I'll leave you guys to have your reunion." She took Mrs. Wright's hand and led her back into the kitchen where the banging of pots and pans resumed.

"We're back," Christian, or Roman, said the moment the four of them were finally alone.

It was really hard to tell the two apart. They looked almost identical. From the Hollister hip jeans to the collared polo shirts. They weren't nearly as pale as their mother, but they weren't as sun-kissed as she remembered them being once upon a time, either.

Their hair was cut stylishly short and curled around the napes of their necks. She might be eighteen and them a few months shy of sixteen, but it was obvious to her that they were turning into super good-looking guys.

The girls at school would eat them up.

Their lips twitched and then the one wearing the red polo spoke up. At a guess she'd say he was Christian, since his hair was just a little bit lighter than the one wearing the blue polo.

"We look kind of different, huh? You too, Lisa." His pretty blue eyes sparkled. "I'm Christian by the way."

She snorted. "I knew that."

"Yeah, right." He yanked her into his arms.

It felt strange being hugged by him. What had once felt so normal now felt awkward. She patted his back, but her eyes drew like magnets to the third Wright boy sitting on her couch.

Unlike his brothers, Julian wasn't the all-American boy next door. Dressed entirely in shades of black and white, his hair was long. Hanging in a kind of skater style around his shoulders. Soft and wavy looking, and it was bizarre that her heart suddenly started to pound as hard as it did. Especially when she noticed a hint of black swirls on his wrists peeking out from under the cuffs of his shirt.

Did he have tattoos?

She wet her lips, jerking her eyes away from his, hoping it might help her to breathe a little easier.

And maybe it had something to do with the intense way he was staring at her, his gaze unswerving from her face, his breathing just this side of heavy, that'd caused her heart to thump so violently, or maybe it was just the shock of seeing people she'd sworn she'd never see again.

Christian stepped back and then Roman took his place. Giving her a quick side hug.

"Jeez, I forgot how boring this place was," Christian snorted when she stepped back.

It took everything Elisa had to ignore Julian's hard stare. But she felt it move all through her.

"Boring? You're boring." She swatted his shoulder. Her legs were jittery as she made her way over to her father's favorite worn blue recliner and sat on the edge of it.

The boys sat down beside Julian and Elisa was suddenly upset that her mother had failed to warn her that company might come over today. She was in short blue jean shorts and a Minnie mouse crop top.

She brushed her fingers down her shirt; thank God it was clean at least.

"So…umm." She giggled—that was always her thing when she got nervous. It was a terrible habit. "You guys here on vacation? Can't imagine you'd be happy to trade in the bright lights of New York for Maine."

Resting his arm on the back of the couch, Roman crossed his leg over his knee. "Nope. Here for good. Yay."

She curled her nose, tossing a quick glance at Julian. Her heart thumped loudly when she realized he was still looking at her. All three of them looked so different from the boys she remembered and yet she could have picked Julian out in a crowd.

There'd just always been something different about him. Something uniquely Jules.

She gave him a little wave.

But instead of waving back, he turned his face and studied her father's running magazine on the end table.

"Ignore him, he's still just a freak," Christian said with a roll of his eyes.

She frowned. Feeling that weird need to defend him, which was ridiculous. Julian was no longer a little boy and she was no longer his sister.

They were all pretty much strangers now.

"He's not a freak," she said anyway.

Roman scratched the side of his jaw. "Yeah, and how would you know? Not like you've been around for a few years."

"Ouch. That was mean." She crossed her arms. "When did you become such a jerk, Rome?"

Christian shrugged. "He doesn't mean it, Lisa."

Roman rolled his eyes again.

Clearly things hadn't been good since the Wrights had left Sunny Cove. She glanced back at Jules. He still wouldn't look at her.

Mrs. Wright came out of the kitchen. "Okay guys, we gotta get the bags moved out of the car. You look so gorgeous, Elisa. As tall as your father." She hugged Elisa and then kissed her cheek.

It was weird how much a scent could ingrain itself into a person's brain. How even after years of not smelling Mrs. Wright's perfume of lavender and verbena, suddenly the smell of it transported Elisa back years.

Memories of seaside barbecues, birthday parties, movies under the stars in their backyards, and all the wonderful times they'd spent together.

She hugged her back hard and smiled; those had been some of the best days of her young life.

"Right, boys? Isn't she beautiful?" She looked directly at Julian as she said it.

Elisa's pulse pounded hard in the back of her throat when Julian's sea-green stare turned to her.

From the corner of her eye she could see Christian and Roman nod. Julian never answered; instead he stood, shoved his hands into his pockets, and walked toward the front door.

Mrs. Wright's smile wavered just slightly. "Anyway, it's really good to see you guys again."

"You too, Mrs. Wright."

"Call me, Lori," she said and patted Elisa's cheek. "I think you're old enough now."

And just like they always seemed to do, the Wrights walked away from her again. But this time they were back, and for Elisa it was like something in her world had changed forever.

Chapter 4

"Hey!" A loud male voice caused Elisa and Chastity to turn in the crowded hallway. It was Roman. With his stylish jeans and funky turquoise blue and orange chuck sneakers on, he was hard to miss.

It'd only been two weeks since the boy's return, and Elisa's thoughts had been proven correct. Christian and Roman, regardless of the fact that they were only sophomores, were already the big men on campus.

Girl's heads swiveled on their necks whenever the boys walked past. Jocks would high-five the brash soccer duo. Roman fist-bumped the varsity team's longhaired goalie as he sailed past to reach her side.

"Roman?" Her lips twitched when Chastity's brow rose. She was probably one of the few girls at school who hadn't fallen under their spell. "What's up?"

He shrugged. "Nuthin'. Waiting for Christian to get out of Mr. Speller's class. Saw you, decided to grace you with my presence." His grin was all teeth.

She rolled her eyes. "Gah, anyone ever tell you you're cocky?"

"Nope." He scratched the back of his head as his eyes twinkled.

"Never. Anyway, where you going?"

"Chas and I are going to lunch. You want to join us?"

He frowned and stopped at his set of lockers, resting his back against it. "Can't, we don't get lunch for another forty minutes. You coming to our match tonight?"

"I think it's ridiculous to have a match on a Wednesday." Chastity sniffed, curling her nose up at him. "Not a chance in hell I'm going."

She might dress like a goth princess, but her friend was obsessed with her grades. The only way she'd make it to college was by winning a scholarship; her GPA was something she took very seriously because of that.

"Good, 'cause I don't recall asking you." Roman gave her a little snarling grin.

Shaking her head, Elisa sighed. "If I didn't know better, I'd swear you guys were flirting."

"What?" Chastity smacked her on the shoulder and cocked a hip. "You do know the boy's jailbait, right?"

Roman stuck out his tongue and wiggled his brows. "Methinks the lady doth protest too much."

Flashing him the finger, Chastity rolled her eyes. "Suck my—"

"Now children." Elisa shook her head, slapping Chas's finger away. "Play nice. And of course I'll be there, Rome. You know I will."

"Sweet." Giving her a playful hip bump, he turned and spun the dial on his locker, opening it quickly to take out more books. "See you then. It's at five, don't forget it, lame ass."

"Oh jeez," Elisa sighed and shook her head as she and Chas headed for the cafeteria.

"I cannot believe you are friends with those boys, bunch of arrogant assholes." Chastity gave Roman one final withering glare over her shoulder before turning back around.

"Nah." She shrugged. "They're not so bad."

Which was true. The past two weeks Elisa had gotten to hang out with the Wrights a lot. Mostly because her mom kept inviting them over for dinner every freaking night, which was kind of annoying, but she was getting used to it.

One thing Elisa had learned from hanging with them was that she basically had to relearn all of them. They in no way resembled the seven-year-old boys she remembered. They were way beyond cartoons and playing wrestling matches.

Roman and Christian were hardcore athletes. But Julian... She still didn't really know a thing about him. Other than he barely ate, he picked at the food on his plate, and that he did indeed have tattoos.

Even her parents had been shocked when he'd shown up three days ago wearing a short-sleeved CBGB shirt that clearly showed the thick, swirling bands of tribal tattoos down both arms.

No one had asked about them, but she was sure her family had thought the same thing she had. How was it possible that at fifteen Julian was already so tatted up?

Chastity sighed. "Damn, we're going to have to sit in loser row."

Glancing up, Elisa realized that because of the rain almost everyone was inside today, which meant only the tables all the way to the back were still open.

"Then let us press onward to our most certain demise." Elisa shook her fist and struck a dramatic pose.

Giggling and rolling her eyes at the same time, Chastity shook her head. "I do not know you."

Turning on her heel, Chas walked over to a table to save their seats, pulling a packed lunch out of her book bag. The Debisette's weren't poor; Chas could have afforded to buy hot lunches if she'd wanted to, but Fareed Debisette was a penny-pincher if ever there was one. Chas's father believed in the merits of saving and hard work and had raised his only child to live by his same code.

Jumping into line, Elisa frowned at the day's selections. She was a swimmer and needed carbs, but that didn't mean she liked noshing on things like fried chicken and fettuccine alfredo.

With a growl, she snatched up a wrapped tuna fish sandwich, a carton of whole milk, and was digging through the bowl of fruit, trying to find one stinkin' red apple in the pile of greens and oranges.

"Excuse me." Elisa looked up at the heavyset lunch lady.

Elisa had never learned her name, but everyone in school called her Scary Mary, mainly because of the flesh-toned wart on the tip of her nose and the wild shock of purplish red hair tucked behind her black hairnet.

"Yes?" she said in the deep voice of a pack-a-day smoker.

"Do you have any red apples back there?"

"Nope." She popped the P and began snapping her fingers for Elisa to hand over her money.

"Nothing at all?" she tried to use her sweetest wheedling voice, but there would be no taming Scary Mary.

"Look, young lady, the world doesn't revolve around you. Either pay up or get out of line, there's a lot of people waiting."

When she said that Elisa glanced down the row, ready to murmur an apology when she noticed that three kids down stood Julian. His intense sea-green eyes roved over her face, making the back of her neck feel suddenly hot.

"Oh, I'm...ah..." She snapped her gaze from his. "Sorry about that." Dropping a five into the lunch lady's hand, she waited for her change and then stepped to the side, waiting for Julian to come up.

Today he was dressed in dark tapered jeans and another one of his rock band t-shirts. She was hopelessly clueless when it came to the band names. She wasn't really into rock, Dad had raised her to be a lover of jazz and blues.

Elisa was also slightly surprised that Julian wore rock shirts considering he couldn't hear the music.

His dark hair slipped over one eye and she couldn't help but want to pat it back into place. Julian was just so different from his popular brothers. He didn't seem to care about fitting in and being cool; for him it was all about being who he was and doing his own thing, and she had to respect that about him. It wasn't easy marching to the beat of your own drum, especially not in high school where opinions mattered so much.

She knew he could feel her looking at him, because his left finger kept tapping his tray in an agitated manner. But he didn't look back at her as he paid.

"Jules." She tapped his hand before he could walk off.

Glancing down at her fingers, his eyes narrowed.

She wasn't sure what that look meant, but she had been practicing some sign language in the past two weeks. Sadly, she wasn't very good at it yet, but she was determined now that he was back in her life to learn from her past.

Julian didn't talk much in school. She'd catch him every once in a while signing to his special ed teacher in the halls, but almost the moment he'd catch her watching him he'd drop his hands to his sides and saunter off.

Whether that meant he was embarrassed because he had to sign or he just didn't feel like talking anymore, she didn't know. But she was tired of pretending like they didn't know each other.

It was one thing to be five and seven and communicate with jerky weird movements that only the two of them could understand. The days of pointing to a playground and having that be enough were long gone. There was really only one way to learn him and that was to talk with him.

Back when they'd been little they had a way of talking with each other that'd been slightly different from what others had done.

Sometimes when they were too busy digging in the sand or watching cartoons to look up, Elisa and he would tap things out on each other's bodies. Two taps would be "food." Three would be "run," etc. Sort of like Morse code, but on skin. As they'd matured their taps had taken on different meanings, meanings only they'd understood. Elisa couldn't help but think that if he hadn't moved away from her their language would have evolved into having actual conversations.

It'd felt special to their relationship, like something only the two of them had shared, and feeling all of sudden like talking a walk down memory lane, she tipped his hand over and placed her fingers on top of his palm.

But instead of tapping, she used her letters.

Lunch. She signed it slowly. Her fingers weren't as dexterous as they needed to be to really have a fluid conversation, but given time she knew it would get there.

She lifted her brow, proud of herself for trying, and then pointed to herself. "Come with me?"

His hard stare always left her feeling slightly breathless. Julian was so much more intense than she'd remembered him being before.

She was pretty sure he would say no, so she was surprised when he shrugged and turned his tray toward her.

Giving him a brilliant smile full of relief, she turned and headed toward Chas. Julian dropped into the seat next to her.

Chastity was taking a bite of her *very* red apple and Elisa almost moaned. Chastity knew how much she adored red apples. The fact that she was forced to eat lunch and not get her daily red apple had obviously not escaped Chas's notice as she proceeded to groan and chew dramatically.

The wench.

"You're Julian, right?" Chastity said after she swallowed, rubbing her mouth with the back of her hand.

Elisa pointed to her ear. "He's deaf, Chas. He can't hear you."

Julian frowned, glowered at her, and then reaching into his pocket, pulled out a small pad and pen and furiously scribbled something down on it. She cocked her head when he turned the pad around.

In bold, sure strokes he'd written: "I read lips."

Mortified, and ears burning a bright shade of crimson, Elisa covered her mouth with her hands. "Oh, Jules, I'm so…I'm…"

But he was looking down at his tray and she could tell by his rigid body language that he didn't want to see anything she said.

Chastity patted her shoulder gently, telling her without words to drop it, and began chatting about dresses. But Elisa's heart just wasn't in it. Every once in a while she'd peek at Julian, hoping to catch his eye so she could say she was sorry, but he wouldn't look at her.

Disgusted with herself and beyond embarrassed, it was an effort to pretend like nothing had happened.

Halfway through lunch Joey Crawford, star quarterback of the Bay Consolidated High Mariners, sauntered up to their table. "Slummin' it, I see, Adrian."

With his short brown spiky hair and his rich brown eyes, he made her heart flutter. Every girl in school wanted to be with Joey, and right now, Joey wanted to be with her.

It made a girl feel special.

He planted his hands on the table, leaning forward until their faces were close enough to kiss. To her left Chastity snickered and Elisa's throat grew warm. The spicy scent of his aftershave was all she could smell.

"Joey?" She smiled. "What do you want?"

He took a deep breath, as if considering something important. "I'm the hottest guy in school, you're the hottest girl, bada bing bada boom." He winked. "So what do you say?"

Her brows twitched. "Jeez, that was lame. Wasn't that lame, Chas?" She turned to her friend, who was having a helluva time hiding her humor at the situation.

"Totally, straight up lame as hell," Chastity agreed and then took a huge bite out of her apple, as if for emphasis.

Joey snorted. "Fine. Come with me to homecoming."

Elisa flicked at her milk carton. "You asking me? Or telling me?"

His pretty eyes narrowed. "Whatever it takes to make you say yes."

Laughing, and very aware of the multiple sets of eyes on them, she nodded. "Don't wear brown. You look terrible in brown."

Pretending to be affronted he clutched his chest. "Damn girl, you telling me I have to go shopping again?"

"A price must be paid, Joey." She sniffed.

They sealed their date with a handshake, which was probably not at all what Joey would have wanted. For months now Elisa had gotten the feeling that Joey was going to ask her to be his girlfriend.

Which was cool. She had every intention of saying yes, but Mom had always told her guys didn't like desperate girls, so until he asked, she'd continue to play coy. But even though she got the feeling he would, he never actually had. They flirted like crazy, but not much beyond that, which had begun to make her wonder whether it was all in her head.

With a wink and an air kiss to her, Joey turned and pumped his fists in the air as the table he'd been sitting at erupted with cheers of, "Score!"

The silly smile died on her face when Julian's chair scraped back. He didn't look down at her or even wave goodbye. Picking up his tray, he turned and walked away.

She didn't see him again in school that day.

And after Rome and Chris's game, the Wrights went to the Adrian's for dinner, which she hoped would be her opportunity to talk with him. But tonight Julian didn't show.

Which made Elisa feel terrible. She shouldn't feel terrible about it. But she did. She wasn't sure what she was doing wrong, but Julian was obviously upset with her. Was it the ear comment?

Or her making the date with Joey?

Her mouth grew dry at the thought. Did Julian like her more than he should? No way.

She almost laughed at that dumb thought. Julian barely even spoke to her. There was no way that he was upset about the Joey thing, which meant he was angry about the ear thing. She sighed. Maybe he'd feel better in the morning.

But her hopes for getting a chance to apologize flew out the window when he failed to show the next day too.

It was stupid to think he wouldn't go because of her, but he didn't show up to dinner again that night, either.

She knew she needed to apologize to him for the comment she'd made to Chastity, but there was no way to do it when he continually refused to show up. When she'd asked Roman about it Thursday night at dinner, he'd just shrugged.

But it was Mrs. Wright who'd glanced up at her with a sad look in her eyes and lips that'd thinned down to slits that made Elisa stop talking about it.

She didn't ask about him after that.

It was a shock to her when she finally saw him on Friday in the lunch line. But now so many days later, it felt weird to go up and apologize for that. What if he wasn't mad at her for that at all? What if he'd been sick and she was just crazily overreacting?

Unsure of herself, she sighed and walked over to where Chas was saving her a seat.

They talked about dresses again, and Elisa had almost forgotten about Julian or her nerves when a shadow fell across them.

Glancing up, her heart jerked when Julian stared back at her with his intense, moody eyes.

"Julian, I'm—"

She didn't get to finish her apology. Reaching into his dark aviator jacket, he pulled out a shiny red apple from his pocket and set it gently on her tray.

Then he turned on his heel and walked out of the cafeteria.

Chapter 5

Dressed in black pumps, a cherry-red thigh-high dress, and with an intricately braided knotwork bun, Elisa felt a little like a pinup Barbie doll.

"Mom." She winced, glancing down at the long expanse of exposed thigh and calf. "Are you sure this isn't too short?"

Her arms were bared and the dress had a heart-shaped corset to it—Elisa never dressed like this. She was an athlete, so sexy clothes was usually the last thing on her mind.

Joey was going to arrive to pick her up in about ten minutes and there were no other dresses appropriate enough for a dance in her closet. At this point, Elisa was very tempted to just call him and cancel.

She never should have let Chastity sway her into getting this dress. What had she been thinking to take advice from a girl who'd never worn a dress in her life? Elisa's father's eyes had bugged out of his head when he'd seen her walk out of her room tonight, and he'd hidden himself away in the study and refused to come out, claiming he'd punch Joey straight in his face if the boy so much as looked at his daughter the wrong way.

But her mother only laughed. "Elisa, you look amazing. You're going to give those boys a heart attack tonight."

Her mother had Elisa backed into the corner of the living room with her camera out, locked and loaded and ready for action. She'd tried at one point to sneak away back upstairs, but her mom had barred the way and given her the upraised brow of disapproval. She was determined to put something in her scrapbook whether Elisa wanted her to or not.

Grumpy, Elisa glowered and crossed her arms, which caused her breasts to pop up. Elisa wasn't busty in the slightest, but there was something about the way the corset hugged her body that gave her the illusion of big boobs, which only made her more self-conscious than she already was.

"Where are those kids?" Elizabeth frowned and stared out the window toward the Wrights' house. "I told them to be here five minutes ago."

Muttering beneath her breath, she padded over the white lacy curtains and pulled them back.

Why her mother had decided to tell Mrs. Wright that not only should she let the boys go to homecoming, but they should also go as part of Elisa's entourage, was so completely beyond her.

Worst part of it was, Mom hadn't bothered to ask Elisa's opinion of it first. She'd simply told Lori that it was fine. Elisa loved them both, but they were busybodies. How was she supposed to get in some good flirting time with Joey now that the three amigos would be tagging along?

She sighed, belly going crazy as she thought about what Joey would say. Elisa had not yet shared that latest development with him.

The doorbell rang.

"Finally," Elizabeth growled and dropped the drapes, rushing to open the door.

Stomach a mass of swarming butterflies, she gripped her belly as her mother greeted the Wrights.

Christian and Roman wore goofy smiles on their handsome faces. Their light brown hair had been slicked back stylishly and even though they were dressed in steel-gray slacks and silk button-down shirts, they'd managed to keep it cool by wearing black Chuck Taylors with it. Christian wore a green shirt and Roman a dark blue one.

Even Elisa could admit they looked adorable.

Shockingly, Julian also stood behind them. She'd halfway expected him to bail on the offer, not because of his deafness, but because of how anti-social he was about everything.

Dressed in jeans, and his rocker-print shirt with black Chucks, he looked no different than he did for school. So maybe he wasn't going after all. But the moment he stepped through the door she could smell the soapy scent of his aftershave and it was obvious that he'd tried to get his messy hair into some sort of order. It still feathered out from his face, and she couldn't help but smile about that.

They'd not gotten to talk after the last week when he'd set the apple on her tray. Elisa was beginning to suspect that maybe Julian just didn't want to be her friend anymore. The thought bothered her, but there wasn't much she could do about it, either.

She snorted when Roman and Christian began flexing for the cameras as both moms started flashing one picture after another. Elisa tried to get into the spirit of it, but she couldn't seem to keep her eyes off of Jules. Even when she tried to stop staring, she was crazy aware of his presence. How he moved, how he breathed—it was kind of freaking her out a little bit how fascinating she suddenly found him.

Not being close to him for a week, and now he was here, her eye took in his every little detail. He had his arms crossed and was leaning against the front door and every once in a while Elisa would feel the hard press of his eyes on her too. And when that would happen her whole body would tingle with a sudden rush of blood.

The air would become a little thicker, her breaths just a little choppier. Then he'd glance down at his sneakers, nibbling on a corner of his full lips as if internally grappling with something, and she couldn't stop her fingers from feeling jittery. Couldn't stop from wondering what in the world he was thinking of that would make him look so serious and intense.

"C'mon, Elisa, smile." Her mom mimed drawing a smile on her face, jerking Elisa from her thoughts.

"Yeah, girl." Christian shoulder-bumped her. "You've got the honor and privilege of taking pictures with us, so at least pretend like you're enjoying it."

Aware that she was surrounded by a bunch of people who would probably be freaked out by her turn of thought, she plastered on a weak grin and pretended to get into it. Determined to ignore the sullen boy who'd every once in a while give her a look that made her blood hot.

The boys were so silly, though, and after a minute she no longer had to pretend to be having fun. Feeling ten times more at ease, she draped her arms around their shoulders. "Cheese!" She grinned proudly when they both draped an arm around her middle and kissed one side of her cheek.

After ten shots she began to find her rhythm, taking her lead off the boys' cue. They'd do a stupid model pose, and so would she. Then they dropped to their knees, pretending to propose and she fanned her face. Toward the middle she was laughing so hard there were tears running down her face.

The moms were happily snapping away, and Elisa knew that whatever made it into the scrapbook would probably be a cringe-worthy shot as she'd be captured in a horrible facial pose, but she didn't care. She was just having too much fun.

Until she made the mistake of glancing up to see Julian's lips were parted and his chest was rising and falling rapidly; in fact, his entire body seemed to be quivering like a tightly wound spring.

Immediately her skin flushed pink and the laughter died on her tongue. No one had ever looked at her like that before.

Elisa didn't see the coastal decorations of her mother's living room, or the pretty lace curtains, or the potted ferns her mother insisted on planting in every corner of the house. She no longer saw Christian or Roman, Lori, or her mother.

She only saw Julian.

His pale skin. His dark hair. And his sea-green eyes.

Elisa drowned in their depths, lost to his scrutiny. She didn't fight the current of it, either; she simply let herself be swept away in his heated gaze.

His hands were balled into fists at his side. His gaze roamed up and down her body slowly. So, so slowly that it felt like a physical caress against her anywhere it touched.

Her scalp tingled, her neck flushed, her breasts ached, her stomach tickled, her thighs shook, and it was suddenly too hard to swallow.

She blinked when the glare of the flash blinded her. What had felt like an eternity had barely lasted all of five seconds. Now it was no longer just she and he in the room, no longer a stolen moment in time where she could have sworn that she'd seen beneath Julian's skin into his soul and he into hers.

Everyone was still talking and laughing, and posing, and no one else seemed to notice that for a split-second her world had turned completely on its axis.

The doorbell rang again.

She jerked her gaze away from Julian's.

What was wrong with her tonight? Digging her nails into her palms until she left crescent moon imprints behind, she reminded herself that she was Joey's date, not Julian's.

And that Julian was almost two and a half years younger than her.

A kid.

That reminder helped a little. But only a little.

Her mother opened the door and this time Joey was the one to walk inside. His smile turned into a frown the moment his gaze landed on her posse.

She took a tiny step back away from the boys, pressing her spine into the stand of one of the potted ferns, needing just a little separation from all of them. Even if it was only a few inches' worth.

Joey looked nice tonight in black slacks with his dark red shirt he'd bought to try and match her dress. Determined to make this night the best she'd ever had, she walked up to him and placed a quick kiss on his cheek, and if he didn't smell like clean soap and mint, it was okay, it didn't matter that those were her two favorite smells in the world. And maybe his hair wasn't quite as long as she liked, or feathered out the way she liked, but that didn't matter either.

"Hey, you look nice," she whispered, taking the red rose from his lax hand.

His brown eyes looked stormy when he turned to her. "You never told me the Three Stooges would be tagging along."

She frowned. "I didn't know until just a little while ago, and they're fine. We're all riding together, but I'm sure they'll be doing their own thing when we get there."

His lips thinned.

And of course her mother chose that moment to come up and cheerily ask them to pose for a picture. But by that point Elisa's heart was definitely not in it. That picture would definitely *not* be going into her scrapbook.

Thankfully Joey had a truck with a huge cab. The Wright boys—including Julian—climbed into the back, while she got into the passenger seat. It was a squeeze, but they all fit.

Neither she nor Joey talked much on the drive up to the school. He was pissed and she knew it, and where she'd cared earlier, now she didn't.

The boys were laughing low and between themselves, but as if they sensed that things weren't going smoothly with her and her date, they didn't try to include them in their conversation.

The Wrights were her friends, and if Joey wanted to date her, he needed to understand they was a package deal. All or nothing.

Only once he'd parked in the gymnasium parking lot, did he finally turn to her, after the boys had climbed out. "I was surprised. Sorry about that."

Frowning, she sighed. "Don't be a jerk and maybe we can have fun tonight, Joey. They're my friends."

"Fine." He held up his hands. "But you're my girl."

Not really, but if it helped him to feel better, she wouldn't argue the point that he'd still not asked her out. Getting out, he walked around to her side and opened the truck door for her.

The night was cold and just this side of nippy. The dark sky gleamed from the soft glow of fluffy white clouds. Music thumped and blared, and even out in the parking lot she could feel the steady thump of heavy bass booming through her.

And just like she'd said, the Wrights were already walking off. But unlike Christian and Roman who were laughing and chatting it up with a group of guys from their soccer team, Julian had his head lowered and his hands shoved into his pockets as he disappeared into the crush of kids.

She nibbled her lip. What kind of fun could he possibly have here all by himself?

"You ready?" Joey asked, holding his arm out for her.

Knowing she had no choice but to stay put and be the date he expected her to be, she plastered on a fake smile and nodded. "Yup. Ready."

The dance was...well, just another school dance. The punch was awful. The music too loud, and the theme—Arabian Nights—pretty damned lame.

Two hours in Elisa was ready to go. But when she looked over to where she'd seen Christian and Roman last, the boys were dancing on the dance floor and looking like they had no intention of leaving anytime soon.

"Yeah, man," Joey snickered, "she had a rack out to here." He mimed an obscenely large set of breasts.

Mike, the Mariners' varsity team nose tackle, chortled. Heavyset, as most nose tackles tended to be, with a ruddy complexion, and small beady blue eyes, Mike Albert wasn't exactly what a girl would call a stud. "Dude, I'd have hit that thing," he snorted then sipped on his sixth glass of punch.

Elisa bit down on her tongue to keep from saying what she really wanted to say. That no girl that looked like what Joey had described would have ever let Mike "hit it," not unless he was making NFL kind of money.

"Yeah, but it took some serious beer goggles, dude. Nah." Joey swatted his hand. "I wasn't gonna touch that snatch with a ten-foot pole—too many snakes swimming in that pond, if you know what I mean."

They laughed as Mike banged his fist on the table.

She cleared her throat, giving them both a withering glare.

"Ah, come on, babe." Joey tossed an arm across her shoulder. "You know you're the only girl for me."

Mike snickered and nudged his date, a quiet, mousy-looking girl from eleventh grade. "Let's go dance," he told her and she nodded silently, just like she'd been doing all night.

Elisa was bored out of her mind. Brushing Joey's arm off her, she twisted in her seat and scanned the crowds.

She'd yet to find Julian again after he'd disappeared.

"You ready?" Joey asked a minute later, leaning into her ear to whisper it.

His lips feathered along the shell of her ear far longer than she liked. Breaking her out in a wash of goosebumps, but not the good kind.

All night he'd been grabby. His hands all over her ass and even once grazing the swell of her left breast, it had always felt like accidental contact, but then again, it was homecoming and high school guys pretty much only ever had sex on the brain. And the way he'd been talking about that rival team's cheerleader for the past ten minutes, she seriously doubted her date didn't realize what he was doing.

Beyond irritated, she vaguely wondered how rude it would be if she just begged off from that after dance party and get her own ride home. Chas said she'd probably be there, though, and Elisa did actually want to see her. Could she stomach the torture of being Joey's "date" for another couple of hours though? That was the real question.

Wetting her lips, she ignored his question and continued to the scan the crowds, looking for the one face she'd not seen since the moment they'd arrived.

Where the hell was Julian?

Had he gone home already? But if so, how? He couldn't call...

The second she thought it, she wanted to smack her forehead. Even if he couldn't talk, he could text. God, when had she become such a freaking idiot? What if she'd said that in front of him too? She'd already hurt his feelings once.

"Hey." Joey gave her a slight nudge. "You ready to go or what?" He sounded exasperated this time.

Realizing she couldn't continue to ignore him, she sighed. "Yeah, but let me see what the boys want to do first."

His eyes narrowed and he tapped the table with his finger. Clearly not happy that she continued to insist on including them in their night, but she wasn't going to just leave without telling them goodbye first, either.

Getting up from the table, she walked toward Christian and tapped his elbow. "Chris!" she called over the roar of the crowd and music.

Turning to her with a happy smile on his face, he lifted his brows. "Heya, hottie. Wanna boogie?"

She snorted. "Not really, you dork. Look, I think I'm gonna go to that after party now. You guys want to come?"

He bit his lip and glanced over his shoulder at Roman, who was dancing behind a twerking redheaded female, his blue eyes full of mischief and exuberance.

"I don't think there's any way in hell I could drag him away from that, do you?"

Chuckling and shaking her head, she patted his arm. "Yeah, don't think so. You guys have my cell, though, just call me when you're ready to go home and we'll come and—"

"We're good." He shook his head. "We'll catch a ride with our boys."

Just then a pretty blonde whom she vaguely recognized as being a junior walked up and tugged on Christian's hand, trying to drag him toward the dance floor.

"Where's Julian?" Elisa called as he started following the blonde onto the floor.

Miming like he was holding a phone, he yelled, "Texted Mom. Think he's gone."

With a sigh and shrug, she turned and walked back to Joey. "All right, I guess we can go. Jules left already and the other two are probably gonna hang out till it ends."

Jumping to his feet, Joey fist-bumped his line backer and then hooked his arm through hers.

"Good, because I've been wanting you all to myself tonight."

"You've had me all to yourself," she huffed.

"Oh no." His dark eyes gleamed under the glare of red lights. "Not really."

Ever since elementary school, Elisa had had a serious crush on Joey Crawford. Mainly because he was cute, but she'd learned one glaring fact about the quarterback tonight: the man was as dull as a bag of rocks. If he wasn't talking about football, or the size of his dick, he was making lewd jokes about girls.

Which, whatever, guys did that. But it sucked to learn that the guy she'd practically lusted over for most of her life was basically a giant prick. Tonight had sucked the big one.

On top of that, she hadn't been able to stop worrying about Julian, no matter how many times she kept reminding herself that he was none of her business.

It wasn't that she didn't feel safe with Joey, she actually did. It was more the fact that she just flat out didn't want to be around him any longer. If it weren't for the fact that she wanted to see Chas, she'd have just asked him to take her home instead.

They'd go to the party, she'd hang for a little, and then she'd go home and try to forget this night had ever happened.

But when she got into the cab and he got in beside her, Joey had other ideas. Grabbing her face between his meaty palms, he slammed his lips down on hers, thrusting his tongue down her throat and making her gag. She tasted his steak dinner, the sugary punch, and the mint he'd eaten to try to mask it all.

She was going to throw up in his mouth if he didn't take his tongue out of her throat soon. Banging on his chest with her fist finally seemed to make him realize she wasn't kissing him back.

"Get off me," she snarled, shoving him back and immediately wiping her mouth off with the back of her hand.

His breathing was heavy and labored. And even though it was practically pitch black in the cab of his truck, she could see the fury in his dark eyes.

"Dammit, Elisa," he growled, "I should have known you'd be as cold as a fucking fish. Everyone told me to stay away from you. But I thought tonight—"

"What?" she snapped. "You thought you'd get laid? Get a fucking clue. That is not the way to do it. And if you'd wanted to get laid, then you should have probably paid more attention to me then your nose tackle all freaking night long."

She glowered at him.

Turning around he gripped the steering wheel and stared straight out the window as his jaw muscles clenched over and over.

"Take me home." She looked to her right, staring at the rows of cars. No way could she handle another hour with him. She was so over Joey Crawford.

"Get out," he snarled.

"What?" She twisted in her seat.

"Out of my goddamn truck, now!"

"Oh God, you're a piece of work, you know that? I don't know what I ever saw in you." Practically kicking the door open, she hopped out. She'd barely even gotten it closed before his rubber tires squealed off.

She slipped her jacket back up her shoulder. His manhandling had caused it to almost come off. It was ridiculous that she suddenly felt the overwhelming need to cry. He'd stopped when she'd told him to, but she couldn't help but wonder what he'd tell everyone at school after this.

What lies would he spread about her?

As much as she hated him, Joey was the most popular guy in school, so everyone would believe whatever he told them. She squeezed her eyes shut. All she'd wanted was to have her senior year end with a bang. Who knew what the hell would happen now.

She was just reaching into her purse for her phone so that she could call her mom and ask for a ride home when a gentle hand latched on to her elbow and turned her around.

It was Julian. He was breathing heavy, glancing between her and the spot where Joey's truck had been. His hands gripped her shoulders and he gave a gentle squeeze.

She knew immediately what he was asking.

"I'm okay," she nodded. "I'm fine. It's okay, Jules."

His jaw was clenched and there was a fire in his eyes she'd never seen before. Hooking his finger at her, he turned and walked under a street lamp. She knew he wanted her to follow, probably because he wanted to talk. The minute she joined him he grabbed her hand and turned it over and placed his fingers along her palm. Her sign was still not very strong, so he spoke to her in alphabet, in the only way she knew how to understand him.

"Dick."

Her lips twitched and she laughed. "Did you just call him a dick?"

His nostrils flared and the tears she'd felt like crying before were suddenly gone, replaced by gratitude and an overwhelming feeling of calm. Julian might not be able to tell the school what'd really happened tonight, but at least he knew the truth.

Wrapping her arms around his neck, she yanked him in for a hug. And when his arms banded around her waist and she felt the shudders roll through him, she heaved a heavy sigh of relief.

"I missed you, Jules," she whispered, knowing he'd never hear.

The boys celebrated their sixteenth birthday just a few weeks later. Mrs. Wright had bought them an old, beat-up cream-colored Toyota Corolla. One to share between the three of them. Again, she'd been surprised to learn that even hearing impaired, Julian was legally allowed to drive.

At this point, she shouldn't be shocked how much he could do; just because he was technically handicapped, there wasn't much about him that was that different from the rest of the world. He couldn't hear and he couldn't see in color. Julian was proving to her that neither of those issues was as big of a deal as she'd always thought they were.

Now, he rarely drove. But that mostly because neither Roman nor Christian were inclined to give up their throne. Not that she minded. Because now that they had a car, she got to ride with them, and, bonus, Julian rode in the back with her every day.

The best part of the rides for her was that he'd help her practice her signing. It was a point of pride how proficient she was becoming in such a short amount of time. With each week that passed she got better and better, to the point where she could sign phrases rather than relying only on the alphabet.

Julian was finally coming out of his shell with her. He was still quiet at school, but he also seemed to seek her out whenever he could. Walking her through the halls, sitting with her at lunch, and if it looked weird to others to see them talking in sign, no one ever really said much about it either.

Other than the fact that Chas couldn't understand what Elisa saw in Julian, to her friend Jules was weird, distant, and broody. But that just wasn't the case. Not with her, anyway.

Julian, she was discovering, had a whole lot going on behind his pretty face. He was an amateur artist and wanted to go to art school someday. He still hadn't shown her any of his work, but the way his eyes would animate when he'd talk about the different styles of art made her realize just how passionate he was about it.

She'd finally gotten up the nerve to ask him about his tattoos and learned that he'd let a friend of his back in New York practice on him. Something Mrs. Wright had gotten super pissed about, apparently.

And Elisa knew that Julian was finally starting to get comfortable with her when one day he laughed.

Julian was always buttoned up, rarely letting his emotions out.

It wasn't hard to figure out why. Even as a kid he'd always been extremely private and shy. Because when a deaf person laughed, the sound was unlike what someone who could hear would make. It was a soft, snuffling kind of noise.

The moment he'd done it, his eyes had widened and he'd looked at her as if expecting her to laugh at him.

But she hadn't.

Elisa had merely wrapped her arm around her middle and laughed right back, signing with her hands that he was too silly and the joke hilarious. Once he'd realized that he could trust being himself around her, it was almost as if they'd never even been apart. It was like being with the old Julian.

Gradually he began showing up every night for dinner, and every school morning he'd walk over to the house to pick her up for a ride.

It was like the four amigos all over again and for a while Elisa was content.

But as the days marched on and winter turned to spring and graduation happened, and then to summer and her university acceptance letter came in the mail, a sad realization began to dawn.

In just two short weeks, she'd be gone.

She'd been accepted with a full ride athletic scholarship to her father's alma mater—Ashe College in Portland. Which was a two-hour drive from Sunny Cove. And as excited as she was about that, she couldn't help but worry about Jules.

He was still a loner, and while it was probably none of her business, she didn't like him being like that, either. She wanted him to make friends, to become as popular as his brothers. She never worried about those two the way she did him.

Getting up early one morning and glancing out the window, she smiled at how sunny and beautiful the day was. The sky was just beginning to turn pink, and the sea would be nice and calm and cool.

A perfect day for a long swim.

It wasn't even eight in the morning yet, but she was sure the guys would be awake by now; they were always up in the morning causing a ruckus on their front lawn.

The idiots knew what they were doing by throwing around the pigskin and laughing and yelling right outside her window. They were trying to be as obnoxious as possible to wake her up. Not to play with her—they weren't little kids anymore—mostly to just be douchebags and wake her up at the ass crack of dawn.

And now it would be her time to turn the tables on them.

With a chuckle under her breath, she dressed in a simple, all-black two-piece bikini, and blue jean shorts. Then jogging downstairs, she grabbed a glass of orange juice, downing it in five quick gulps before jotting off a quick note to her parents to let them know where she was going. Walking across the lawn to the Wrights' bright yellow Cape Cod home, she whistled under her breath and knocked on the door.

Julian answered a moment later.

He was shirtless and wearing only a pair of checkered sleeping pants. For the first time she noticed that his tattoos sleeved up the entirety of his arms, but also partially covered his scrawny chest.

She snorted when he ran his fingers through his bed head, causing the feather-like tips to lift up in many different directions.

Frowning, he glanced over her shoulder and began to sign.

"What are you doing here?"

"I want to swim. It's beautiful out. You guys need to come too."

He curled his nose. "Nah. Too cold."

"Jules," she said and palmed his chest. "Stop being such a baby, it's perfect. Go get Chris and Roman."

Shaking his head, he gestured furiously. "Passed out upstairs. Mom doesn't know, but they were out drinking at the Korbit barn last night."

"Oh, jeez." She rolled her eyes. "Those dorks."

He gave a soft chuckle.

"Then you come."

"I don't know." He wrinkled his nose.

"Please," she said and then clasped her hands together before vocally saying, "Pretty please. I'm leaving soon. Please. Please. Please."

Rolling his eyes, he held up a finger and turning on his heel, quickly trotted upstairs.

Fidgeting with her fingernails she peered inside the familiar door, preferring to stand on the stoop instead of going inside. When the Wrights had left after the death of Mr. Wright, rather than sell the house off, they'd locked it up. Tossing blankets over the furniture and only sending cleaners out twice a year to make sure it remained in good condition.

The Wrights, Elisa had learned in later years, were fairly wealthy thanks to oil stock Mr. Wright had bought into long before the boys were born.

Elisa still couldn't walk into the house without getting a lump in her throat at how familiar everything was inside. From the wooden coffee and dining room tables, to the navy colored overstuffed couch and loveseat Mr. Wright used to favor.

Mrs. Wright had more of a country flare to her decorating, thanks to Mr. Wright. She'd actually been born and raised in New York, but Mr. Wright had been a country boy from Tennessee and she'd adopted his style; she didn't decorate like most coastal locals did with pale blues and sea-foam greens and brilliant whites. It was woodsy and more Americana.

Julian returned less than a minute later wearing gray swim trunks and a white tank top. The black swirls of his tattoos looked so striking against the plain shirt and for just a second her heart thumped in her chest.

Snatching the car key off the hook hanging just inside the door, she jingled it in his face.

"I'm going to make you pay for this," he signed to her after he closed the front door and pocketed the house key.

Grinning from ear to ear, she tossed him his key. "No, you're not. You like me too much for that."

For a brief moment she saw something that looked like a flicker of heat glimmer through the depths of his sea-green eyes. And it was like a deer being caught in the headlights of an approaching vehicle. Her hands were shaking when he finally turned away.

What the eff was that? She hadn't had another one of those weird Julian moments since the night of the homecoming dance. She'd thought whatever that'd been had passed, but apparently not.

She shook her head, hating how jittery she still felt.

Then he was starting the car and she got in beside him and for the first time Elisa wondered what she'd been thinking when she'd invited just him along.

But her worries vanished the moment they got to her favorite swimming spot. It was an abandoned quarry tucked away in the woods that had a rickety old pier jutting out toward calm waters.

Julian impressed her. He wasn't as strong as she was, but he was good. Threading the water seamlessly with sure strokes. They swam back and forth along for a few hours. Laughing and splashing, until finally exhaustion made them both climb out. They laid out on a floating dock shaded by the large branch of an old oak tree.

The water had been frigid when they'd first jumped in, but now the day was getting warmer, and it was nice to close her eyes and sway up and down on the gentle tide as she inhaled the briny breeze.

Julian grabbed her hand and began to talk. "Do you remember the fireworks on the beach?"

She leaned up on her elbow, glancing down at him. His wet hair was plastered to his forehead and his breathing was smooth and even. Skinny as he was, Elisa could see that in a few more years Julian would be chiseled, and with his striking cheekbones and full lips there was a modelesque quality to his looks.

She frowned, uncomfortable with where her thoughts kept straying.

She'd just turned nineteen in May. This was really the very last thing she needed to be thinking about.

He shook his head and jerked his chin, indicating that he wanted her to lie back down. Nodding, she scooted over a little, needing to get some space between them. But he wouldn't release her hand. It was the only way they could talk without looking at each other.

Ignoring the strange dips and rolls of her stomach, she closed her eyes. She was just nervous. Less and less, Julian, or even Roman and Christian for that matter, looked like the boys of her dreams. They were becoming men before her eyes and it was weird for her.

"Do you remember?" he asked again.

"Yes. Why?"

"Because we did this then, too."

She smiled. "Did what?"

"We sat on the beach and we held hands and watched the fireworks."

A huge grin cut a swath across her face. "I can't believe you remember that."

"I remember a lot of things, Smile Girl."

It was the name he used for her. In sign there wasn't always an exact way to replicate a name, so sometimes a name would become words that were associated with a person. Julian had told her that anytime he saw her she was smiling. Hence, she'd become Smile Girl.

She still hadn't given him a name yet. She just called him Jules, which he never seemed to mind.

Not sure what to say to that statement she decided to confess something that'd been nagging at her for the past few weeks.

"I don't know what to do."

His fingers moved furiously as he asked, "About what?"

"School. Life. Plans."

"What?"

Rolling to the side, she saw the confusion that scrawled across his forehead.

"I thought you wanted to be a doctor."

"No." She sighed. "That's not me. That's my dad. He's the one that wants me to go into sports medicine. But that's not really my passion."

"Then what is?"

She plucked at his thumbnail with her fingers for a second. Why had she never noticed how calloused his thumbs were? There was still a lot about Julian she didn't know. Like his time in New York and what he'd done there. Why the Wrights had packed it all up to come back to Sunny Cove. That was still a total mystery to her.

"I don't know," she finally admitted.

He gave a soft throaty chuckle, which tugged a smile to her lips. It was always so easy to talk with Jules. He just seemed to get her.

"That's not good. Isn't there anything you love?"

She paused. "Not really. I mean, I love swimming. But that's not a career."

"It can be."

She shook her head. "Yeah, but I'm not sure I want it to be. I don't want to be my dad and chase one race after another."

Opening her palm, because now she was getting frustrated and didn't know what else to say that wouldn't come off as sounding bad, Elisa gazed up at the sky. She hadn't told that to anyone. Not her mom, her dad, not even Chastity. Everyone thought she had everything so together. Elisa the goody two shoes, the champion swimmer, the perfect daughter, perfect friend... She was terrified of what was coming. Terrified of the unknown, of moving on.

"Smile Girl." Julian's fingers danced across her palm a minute later.

Not wanting to sign anymore, she slipped her hand out of his and stuck it between her thighs. His pretty eyes studied her face for several breathless seconds. His eyes had always drawn her.

The way they were so blue around the outer edge but how right by the pupil they turned a dark shade of green. Like he'd captured the best parts of the ocean and sealed them inside himself.

Her lips tingled as she was bathed in a sense of déjà vu. As the world seemed to take a collective pause, suspending her and Julian inside a bubble where it was only the two of them and nothing else.

His throat worked hard and she couldn't help but wonder what he would have said if he could hear his words.

He scooted close to her and her stomach dropped to her knees because she knew what he was going to do.

She should move away.

But she didn't. She was frozen, almost paralyzed by her conflicting desires.

Her lashes fluttered when his large, warm hand framed the side of her face and his touch wasn't just friendly. It wasn't the kind of touch she was used to from him. This one was a slow, gentle stroke. Her pulse thundered in her ears as the calloused tips of his fingers traced the soft lines of her face.

Elisa had every intention of making him stop. This wasn't right. They shouldn't be doing this. Julian was her friend. Her brother.

She was too old for him. She knew better, knew how wrong this was. He was only sixteen, but his touch didn't feel unsure or hesitant. His body heat brushed against hers.

Stop, Jules, please stop.

But the words never left her tongue. Her brain and her heart were in utter chaos from the sensations wreaking havoc within her.

His fingers tapped out her name on her cheek.

"What?" she huffed, wishing she hadn't come out here with him by herself. Wishing she hadn't admitted what she had. Wishing so many things that she'd never confess to herself even within the privacy of her own thoughts.

He tried to grab her hand, but she refused to let him. "Don't, Julian." Somehow she managed to pull the words out from the depths of her soul.

His lips turned down into a deep frown and she hated that she'd hurt him, but she didn't like how she was feeling right now.

"Are you mad at me?" he signed quickly.

She squeezed her eyes shut. "No. I'm just. I'm..."

Rolling onto her back, she flung her arm over her eyes. She needed to get away from here, from him, from Sunny Cove. She was terrified of the future, but Elisa was also terrified of the things that Julian sometimes made her feel.

She was a woman now. What the hell was wrong with her?

His touch was gentle as he swept his fingers up her arms.

Stroking her bicep and causing her flesh to break out in a heady wash of goosebumps.

Wanting to jerk away from him, even while she wanted to lie still so that he could continue to glide his fingers over her skin, she growled.

"Julian, stop." She glared at him and jerked away. "This is wrong, okay?"

"What is?" He asked, and she noted his heavy breathing. The way his dark pupils were now dilated.

All she would have to do was move in just a little bit closer, wet her lips, any sort of a hint on her part and he'd be all over her. She could sense it, feel it in the way his body was so tight and tense beside her.

"You're my brother." She tried one more time to let him know they couldn't do this.

He shook his head. "I'm not your brother."

"Julian, please."

"Smile Girl, I—"

"No!" She jumped to her feet and, with a graceful swan dive, slipped into the waters, working her muscles furiously as she swam as fast as she could away from him and the things he made her feel.

Elisa wouldn't allow herself to be alone with him anymore after that. When they came to dinners, she'd smile and play nice, but she always made sure to sit as far away from Julian as possible.

And even when she'd be sunbathing in her back yard and could feel his stare on her from across the way, she wouldn't look up, she wouldn't encourage him. Whatever this thing was, it was wrong. And she was suddenly so grateful to be going away.

The night before her parents were to take her to campus, a knock sounded on the door. It was past eleven at night, way too late for a casual visitor.

Mum looked up with a frown dappling her brows.

"You expecting someone, Elisa Jane?" Dad had asked.

Muting the silly reality show she was watching to help waste time before bed, she shook her head.

Chastity had already come over earlier in the day. They were both headed off to the same campus, which was great. Even better was that Mom and Dad had surprised her by saying they would help rent her an apartment off campus so that she and Chas could room together. Chas had squealed like a little girl when Elisa had told her the good news.

But apart from that, Elisa hadn't been expecting anyone else.

"Not really."

A knock sounded again.

"Hm." Getting up, Dad went to the door and Elisa heard his surprised, "Loribelle? What's wrong? Are the boys okay?"

And just the thought of it caused her gut to wrench almost violently.

"They're fine, Dean. I'm...um...well, I'm actually here because I wanted to talk with Lisa if I could."

She frowned and glanced at her mother who only shrugged. Apparently she had no idea what this was about, either.

Clicking off the TV, Elisa glanced up just as Mrs. Wright came in. Her tiny form was swallowed up by the long, amber-hued turtleneck she wore, which, coupled with the dark gray stretchy pants, made it obvious to Elisa Mrs. Wright hadn't planned on dropping by at all.

"Mrs. Wright?" Elisa made to stand, but she held up a hand and shook her head.

"I told you, hun, call me Lori."

"Oh...okay, Lori. What's wrong?"

Turning on her slippered foot, Lori glanced down at Elisa's mother. "Bethy, could I have about five minutes with your daughter?"

Mum glanced up at Elisa with a soft little frown.

"I promise it's nothing bad, it's just sort of private is all."

Feeling as though she might puke, Elisa waited until her mother and father had walked out of the room before turning back to Loribelle.

She was now sitting on the section of the loveseat her mom had just vacated and was staring at her mother's glass-sculpted collection of seahorses hanging on the wall.

"What's wrong? Is Julian okay?" Elisa cringed the moment she said his name. The problem could just have easily involved either Roman or Christian, but deep down she suspected Mrs. Wright wouldn't have come over for either one of them.

Picking up a wrapped mint from the candy bowl her mother always had set out on the coffee table, Loribelle flicked at the plastic tip. The room was pregnant with unspoken words.

Elisa had no clue why Lori was here, but she really, really hoped it wasn't about the other day. She and Julian hadn't done anything.

"I don't know what—" she started to say, but Lori held up her hand.

"I'm just going to come out and say it, because I trust that if there is anyone in this world who might love my boy as much as I do, it's you."

It was like she'd swallowed a bag of stones. Her eyes flicked toward the kitchen where she suspected her mother and father listened in.

"What are you talking about?" she asked as she dug her nails into the recliner armrests.

"Elisa, when you go away, don't forget him. Please."

Thundering heart slowing just slightly, she cocked her head. "What?" That hadn't been at all where she'd thought this conversation might lead.

Crossing her legs, Lori pinched the bridge of her nose. "Julian has no idea I've come over—in fact, he'd probably kill me if he knew. But I had to, I had to get this out to you before you left."

Her blue eyes were rimmed with dark circles. Loribelle didn't work. The Wrights lived off of her husband's stocks and insurance, which was substantial to say the least. Elisa didn't know exact amounts exactly, but she'd heard it whispered that it had to be close to five million.

They didn't live like they were uber wealthy, so she wasn't sure whether to believe it or not, but then again the East Coast wasn't the cheapest place in the world to live.

The obvious stress Lori was under didn't come from bills, but more than likely stemmed from the fact that she was a young widow with three teenage triplets, one of who had health issues.

Lori's nervous finger tapping was starting to make Elisa anxious. She wiggled on her seat.

"I don't want to put pressure on you, Elisa. But you have no idea what you've done for my boys. Most especially Julian."

A hard lump wedged itself in her throat, making it hard to swallow.

"You know his problems. That's obvious. But when Carter died, Julian took it harder than the rest of them. Carter was his world. His dad made Julian feel alive." She smiled, her eyes distant and remembering a memory. "He'd always tell Julian that no matter how he was born, he could be whoever he wanted. Carter was so proud of our boys, but I think he secretly favored Julian most. I mean"—she shrugged, blinking back to the present—"he needed a lot of help in the first few years of his life. Deaf and colorblind, it was so overwhelming. I just thought it would be impossible, that Julian would never have the kind of life like his brothers would."

"But it hasn't stopped him at all."

"I know." She nodded and gave her a gentle smile. "He's perfect. And Lord if that boy ain't handsome."

Elisa's grin wobbled. That was a statement she'd like to stay far away from.

Lori sighed and the sound of it was so full of sadness that it squeezed Elisa's heart. "Kids were so cruel to him, even his own brothers at one point." She shook her head. "New York was no good to Julian. He suffered. He will probably never admit it, but the loss of his father has left a lasting impact on him. Where Roman and Christian threw themselves into sports and the validation of their peers, Julian withdrew into himself."

That much was fairly obvious to her. Julian had always been quieter than his brothers. "Julian's always been different."

"Yes." She looked at Elisa. "Quiet and shy. But in New York he grew wild and angry. Started hanging out with the wrong crowds. My parents tried to help the best they could, but"—she took a deep breath—"he was just too much for all of us. He started dealing drugs—"

"What?" That didn't sound at all like Julian. "Was he using too?"

"No, thank God." The relief in her voice was short-lived. "But he was getting into fights, and, well, you've seen the tattoos."

Elisa wouldn't admit to his mother that those tattoos were part of what intrigued her so much about him. She nibbled on the corner of her lip.

"My last hope was to come back here. But I was afraid you know. Would Carter's memory haunt those halls and make it harder for our boys?"

"And did it?"

"At first, a little. But"—her smile grew wide—"then they saw little Elisa Jane Adrian, and it was like my boys were five all over again. Bit by bit they came out of their shells. Roman grew less sarcastic, Christian, well..." She shrugged and laughed. "He'll always be Christian. But Julian," she said, nodding proudly, "Julian became my Julian again. It took a while, but soon I began to notice that you made him laugh, you brought him out of that shell and..." Her eyes began to swim with tears, and yanking a tissue out of the box from beside the candy bowl, she dabbed at them.

Elisa knew exactly what Lori was talking about. She'd witnessed the transformation herself. Just thinking about it brought a smile to her face, but reality came crashing down hard.

"He'll be fine. He has to be, I'm leaving."

Lori's brows gathered into a tight vee. "Elisa, I don't know what happened the other day when you guys went swimming."

Squirming, she plucked at her nightgown. "No...nothing happened."

But Lori didn't seem entirely convinced by her weak words.

Waving a hand, she said, "I'm not here to talk about that. Because like I said, I don't know. All I do know is he came back that day devastated. I suspect my boy has developed a serious crush on you."

Cringing, Elisa shook her head.

But Lori only nodded harder. "Not only do I believe that, but I think you know that. Which is probably why he returned to me as he did. I understand there's a fairly significant age gap—"

"Mrs. Wright—"

"Lori." She raised her brows.

Huffing, Elisa corrected herself. Habits were hard to break. "Lori. I'm nineteen. Yes, there is a huge age gap, and I'm sorry for how he feels about me." She squelched the little voice reminding her that he'd not been the only one affected that day. "But I would never cross that line."

"Oh dear Lord." She grabbed her chest. "I hope you don't think I'm asking you to. I would never."

Elisa flicked her wrist. "Then what are you doing?"

"I'm only asking for you to understand that it's a phase, and he'll get over you. He's got two more years before college, he'll understand it could never be, what I don't want though is for you to ignore him. You're good for him, Elisa."

Why had the thought of him getting over her made her feel such a heavy flash of sadness? It shouldn't, because the fact was that was exactly what she wanted. What she needed. Elisa was going to college and she was going to flirt, she was going to date, and, hopefully, she'd find the man of her dreams, graduate with honors, and forget all about that stolen moment on the pier that'd made her heart beat faster than it ever had before in her life.

"Write to him. Email him. Text him. Just every once in a while. Just let him down easy, Lisa, that's all I'm asking. I'm afraid what will happen if you shut him out. Once he realizes you two could never be anything, he'll move on, and he'll be happy again, but I'm begging you, please, don't lock him out."

She knew Jules. And the fact was, she knew Lori was right. What Julian felt for her was puppy dog worship, an infatuation that would end. But when it did the one thing Elisa wanted was to know that they would always remain friends.

"I really do love them all."

Lori dabbed at her eyes again. "I know you do, sweetheart. And I'm so grateful for that."

Then she got up and Elisa assumed their conversation was over, but Lori stood there fidgeting, glancing between the door and her, before with a loud sigh she reached under her shirt and yanked out a sheet of paper that looked as though it'd been crumpled at one point and tossed away.

She stared at the paper. "I wasn't going to give this to you. I figured you wouldn't want it anyway. But..." She glanced up and started to walk over to Elisa. "Julian is an amazing artist. One of the best I've ever seen, but this drawing..." She sighed and smoothed her fingers over the sheet lovingly. "It has his soul stamped on it. You can keep it or you can toss it, like he did, but..."

Then, with a twitch of her lips, she thrust the paper at Elisa. She took it without glancing down.

"Good luck in college, Elisa Jane. I'll always be pulling for you."

And without so much as a wave, she turned and walked away. Elisa waited for a good minute after Lori had left to finally glance down and when she did her vision began to shimmer.

Staring back at her was an image of her face. It was a charcoal sketch. Nothing but black and grays, and yet life had been breathed into the picture. Her eyes were wide and luminescent, her button nose tilted up just slightly at the tip. A smattering of freckles lined the bridge of it. Her lips were wide, but not too wide. Slightly thinner on the top than the bottom, and he'd even managed to capture the tiny dimple that sometimes dotted her left cheek when she smiled wide. Long strands of hair billowed off like wispy clouds in a strong breeze behind her.

And she knew there was no way she really looked like that—because the girl staring back at her was breathtakingly soft and lovely, a graceful picture of femininity. Elisa was none of those things. She was an athlete who almost always wore her hair in a sloppy bun, and acted stupid whenever a camera was placed in front of her.

Her fingers shook as she traced the line of her jaw. He'd drawn this, Julian had drawn this, and then he'd crumpled it up and tossed it away.

The next morning she was just getting into the car when the Wrights' door opened and Julian came running out with an anguished look burning in his sea-green eyes. He'd not been careful with what he'd picked.

His shirt was red, his shorts a glaring shade of neon blue. She recognized the clothes as actually belonging to Roman.

Neither one of them said anything as he rushed up to her and dragged her into his arms, hugging her as though he meant never to let her go. He smelled like Julian, like clean soap and mint.

Elisa had clung to his back, wishing for just a moment that things had been different. That either she was only sixteen or he nineteen, that life hadn't dealt them the cards it had.

The kiss he'd planted on her cheek had felt full of meaning. Pain. Misery. And love, all of it rolled up in that touch and it made her tremble. Made her want to say words she knew she could never say again.

His cheeks were wet when he pulled away.

And when she got into the back seat of her parents' SUV, she realized hers were, too.

Chapter 6

College was going smoother than she'd hoped and that summer spent with Julian and the boys was slowly becoming nothing more than a happy but weird memory.

It was hard sometimes to believe how much had changed in the few months she'd been away from home. She had a boyfriend who she was crazy about, she still hadn't really decided on a major yet, but there was still time for that.

All her fears and worries now seemed so silly in retrospect. And her momentary strange attraction to Julian was absolutely gone. Distance had been the best thing for them.

She did as she'd promised Loribelle and wrote to Julian once a week, updating him on her life, sending him pictures of whatever stupid thing she sometimes did. And while it was hard to judge emotions from words on a screen, she was pretty sure Julian was also over whatever crush he'd had on her. His emails were friendly, and most of the time short. Just a sentence or two. He'd sometimes ask for more pictures, but that was it.

The day she realized he was over it, she finally told him about Thomas. And just as she'd suspected, he hadn't seemed all that fazed by it. He'd simply written back a quick, "That's good. Glad you're happy," email and that'd been that.

Shutting her economics book with a weary sigh, she glanced up at Tom. He still had his nose buried in his anatomy books. He was studying to become a nurse. Something his parents didn't approve of. They still had the notion that if you were a boy and going into medicine, it was doctorate or nothing. But Thomas was adamantly sticking to his guns and Elisa admired him for it.

Thomas was a sophomore. They were actually teammates—it was how they'd met. Elisa's heart had nearly flopped out of her chest the first time she'd seen him come out of the pool. With his shocking red hair and slickly muscled swimmer's body, she'd almost drooled on herself the first time he'd smiled at her. That'd been almost five months ago now, and they'd been inseparable ever since.

His keen blue eyes looked up. "You ready to go home?" His deep voice always made her shiver.

They'd been dating for a while now, and Elisa was trying to decide if she was ready to go all the way. Some days she was sure she was ready, and other times, she wasn't. She didn't know why she kept holding back, he was hot, smart, and could swim his ass off.

They got along great.

She smiled.

Maybe tonight would be that night.

"Yes." She grinned wider when his blue eyes twinkled.

"What are you thinking, little fish?"

His pet name for her was probably the most unattractive thing about him. She rolled her eyes. "Seriously, Tom, call me something else."

He tapped his pencil on his books. "Like what?"

"I don't know." She kicked out her foot, tracing the length of his calf with her sneakered foot. Not nearly as sexy as it would have been had she been wearing sandals, but it was the second week of December and there was no way in hell she'd be walking around a snow-covered campus in sexy sandals just for her boyfriend. No matter how much she adored him. "Dolphin, or mermaid, or—"

"Barracuda!" He chuckled.

"Ssh." The librarian glanced up at their loud laughs.

Giving him a long eye roll, she got up. "Let's go before the ogre throws us out, and if you call me a barracuda, I'll—"

Running around to her side of the table, he wrapped his arm around her waist and planted a kiss on her lips.

Thomas kissed like he swam. With passion and intensity.

Heart racing out of control, she broke off the kiss before she made a fool of herself, like going into full-on porn mode in the library. Not cool.

Tonight would be the night, she was decided.

She was nineteen, it was time to pop the cherry at some point, and preferably before she hit twenty. She hadn't been hanging on to her virginity because she was scared, or because morally she felt it was wrong; mostly she'd hung on because she'd wanted to make sure that whomever she did it with for the first time would still respect her in the morning.

"Come home with me," she whispered, tapping her finger on his chest.

Chastity was already home for Christmas break. Elisa would have joined her, too, if it wasn't for the fact that her econ professor, Mr. Richards, had postponed the final for two days after Chas's last class because of some sort of filing mix-up.

The campus was pretty much cleared out and there really wouldn't be a better time than now.

"Fuck me." He groaned, closing his eyes.

"What?" She wrinkled her nose, because that had definitely *not* sounded like a yes.

Elisa took a step back and hugged her books to her chest. But Thomas latched on to her elbow and moaned.

"Baby, if you're inviting me over for what I think you are, I think I might cry. Any other night and I would, but I have that stupid meeting to—"

"Oh dammit," she groaned, only now remembering that as Treasurer of the Phi Sigma Kappas it was his job to allocate funds for the back to school social scheduled the second week of January. This was his last day to do it before campus officially broke for break. "I did forget."

Tugging her into his side, he tickled her ribs and she smiled. "Later tonight? I'll come over right after—"

It was already almost ten. Her exam was scheduled for seven tomorrow morning. He wouldn't get to her apartment until closer to midnight. She sighed. "No. My test is too early in the morning."

He grimaced. "Are you still going to be here tomorrow?"

It was at least nice to see that he actually did want to. "Yes. I'm not leaving until Sunday morning. I have too much to pack up still."

"Okay." He grabbed her wrist and placed an enthusiastic kiss against it. "Tomorrow then. My test is over by noon, we can spend the rest of the afternoon together."

"Bring *lots* of condoms." She giggled when they exited the library, inhaling the frosty winter air deep into her lungs.

Her words made him groan even harder and this time when he pressed her to him for a goodbye kiss something hot, hard, and long pushed into the lower part of her belly, making her stomach twist and dive to her feet.

It wasn't that she didn't know what a penis looked like, or for that matter that she hadn't held one before. She had, with him. Their make out sessions had become pretty X-rated at this point, they just hadn't gone all the way yet.

Planting her hand between his legs, she gave it a gentle squeeze.

"You're a wicked woman, little fish." His blue eyes gleamed with heat.

Snorting, she rearranged his brown crocheted scarf around his neck so that it would cover him all the way up to his chin; it was cold out tonight. "Yeah, but you love it."

"I do." He waved at her, heading off toward the frat house. "You know I do."

With a swift shake of her head and a smile still firmly latched on to her face, she turned on her heel and walked the quarter-mile to her apartment.

The place her parents had chosen was pretty amazing. Almost centrally located on campus, she was surrounded by the nightlife and pubs that all college students craved. There was nothing super fancy about hers and Chas's place, but for two freshman it was pretty damned good.

Walking up the stoop to her red brick-faced apartment, she wiggled her key into the blue-painted door. This side of town was fairly safe, because of its nearness to the campus; police cruised up and down its streets on a regular basis.

And even though it was practically Christmas time and the campus was almost entirely deserted, there were still enough locals milling around to make her feel like she wasn't really alone.

Turning on her light, she shut and locked the door.

Walking into her kitchen for a drink of water. Their place was barely a thousand square feet. Not very big, but because it was more of a loft style, it felt wide and open. The floors were an engineered blond wood, and the walls were painted a cherry red.

That'd been Chas's doing. She loved color. From black to color. The goth phase was officially over for her quirky friend. Now it was embracing her island roots, and Elisa was glad for it.

She grabbed a cup and filled it with water, sitting down at her kitchen table.

They'd managed to scrape enough money together between the two of them to sparsely decorate the place. There was a couch they'd found at a salvation store, a large geometric-patterned rug Chas's parents had brought over during a visit, and a kitchen table her parents had donated. Neither girl really had a decorating style, so it was mostly just a mash-up of things they saw in stores and wanted, like a coffee mug wall clock, and jellyfish-shaped standing lamp in the living room.

But it worked for them.

Even though the loft was small, both girls did have their own rooms. They weren't big enough to fit more than a full-sized bed and a small dresser, but that was all they needed anyway.

Moving her laptop from the couch to the table, Elisa opened it up. She'd not checked her messages all week because of last-minute crash studying for finals. In hindsight, it was probably good Thomas hadn't come over tonight. Now that she was home she realized just how exhausted she actually was.

But she had a few minutes left before bed and figured she should probably make sure her parents hadn't written with any sort of new instructions to her.

Last month Elisa had purchased her first car from the campus lemon lot. It wasn't much to look at. A cream-colored Beetle that Dad had driven all the way up to campus to check out first before she'd taken out a loan from the bank—with the help of her parents, of course.

It was the first car she'd ever owned and it wouldn't be her parents but her making the payments. It made her feel proud.

Mom and Dad had been freaking out for the past two weeks telling her to go get the oil checked, the tires checked, the heater checked. Which she'd done, or rather made Thomas do. She was pretty sure there'd be some more instructions waiting for her.

But when she opened her Gmail account, she didn't find any emails from them. She did however see an old email from Julian.

She clicked on it.

"When are you coming home?"

She grimaced. The letter was dated six nights ago. Feeling kind of bad, she jotted off a quick note, letting him know it wouldn't be until Sunday and clicked send.

Just about to close it down for the night and go to bed finally, an instant message popped up.

It was from Julian's address—JulesWrightDreams. Sure she was about to get her ass handed to her, she groaned. Elisa was ready to type off a quick "I'm sorry" when the words registered in her brain.

"Lisa, this is Lori, are you there?"

Cocking her head, she nodded even though she knew Lori couldn't see her.

"Yeah, I'm here. What's up?"

"Are you home yet?"

"Not for another two days. Why?"

"Julian got into a bike accident."

It was like someone had suddenly dropped a ton of ice into her veins. The tips of her fingers became chilled and her skin broke out in a wash of goosebumps.

"Is he okay? What kind of bike?"

Her pulse grew fluttery and her skin flushed as the need to jump into her car and drive home immediately gripped her by the throat.

The cursor blinked for so long that Elisa was about to pick up the phone and call, needing to know right away what was going on.

"Race bike. He got really hurt."

"Oh God. I'll come home now."

She didn't know what she was going to do about the test. But she'd have to figure something out. Elisa was ready to dash into her room and just dump whatever clean clothes she could find into her suitcase when Lori responded.

"No. Do what you need to do. He's alive. He's just hurt."

Feeling like an enormous weight had lifted from her shoulders, she quickly scribbled back.

"I have a final exam in the morning. I'll come right after. Tell him I'll be there. Okay?"

"Thanks, Lisa. Sorry to ruin your night."

"God no! You didn't ruin it. I'll be there as soon as I can. Which hospital?"

"Mid-Coast. In Brunswick."

It was almost impossible to fall asleep that night, and the next day when she took the exam, she was pretty sure she'd missed almost all the questions. Her thoughts had centered almost entirely on getting back to Sunny Cove. She'd packed up her car last night and was just about to go when she remembered Thomas. He'd be expecting to find her at the apartment after noon.

Cringing, she pulled out her phone and called him. But he didn't answer. So she left a message instead.

"Tom, I'm sorry, honey. But I just found out last night that my good friend got into a very serious motorcycle accident last night, so I have to go home. I really, really, really am sorry. But we'll have to um..."—her stomach flopped—"do our thing after Christmas break. Sorry. Love you. Hope you have fun skiing the slopes in Utah, okay?" Blowing him an air kiss, she hung up.

The drive to Brunswick took far longer than the normal two and a half hours; thanks to the gray skies and sleeting snow, she knew it wouldn't be safe to go faster than fifty miles per hour on the road. If that.

Suddenly grateful that her parents had forced her to get the car up to peak performance, because even with new tires on, she still slid on the icy roads. One time she'd fishtailed so hard she'd had to pull off the road just to give her jittery heartbeat a chance to calm down.

By the time she'd pulled into the Mid-Coast Hospital parking lot, she was driving at a very grandmotherly speed of thirty-five.

It'd taken her close to six hours to get home. It was almost three in the afternoon. When she'd stopped to top off her tank and grab a hot coffee two hours ago, she'd called Lori for an update.

Julian had been moved out of the ICU that morning, and aside from being in extreme pain, was well on his way toward recovering.

Jogging as quickly, but safely as she could across the frozen blacktop, she sailed into the elevator, punching the third-floor button. Wringing her hands as she watched each floor tick past, she wondered what she'd see when she got to his room.

Let his hands be okay...

The moment the doors opened, she spied Christian, Roman, her mother, and her father in the waiting room.

She almost couldn't believe her eyes when she saw the guys. They were huge. It shouldn't be possible that in just a short five months they could have grown so much, but they towered over her.

Not only that, but there was definitely more meat on their bones.

Which only made sense, in three days it would be their birthday. Seventeen now, they were practically men.

She smiled when Roman hugged her. "My God, Rome, is that a beard?" She scratched at the hard scruff on his square jaw.

Giving her a bashful grin, he rubbed the back of his neck.

Christian hugged her next. "Glad you're back, Lisa."

Turning to her parents, she gave them each a hug.

"How was your trip?" her father asked almost immediately.

"Fine. Fine," she said, wanting to talk about what was really on her mind. "How's Jules?"

Suddenly the temperature in the room cooled. Christian and Roman blew out deep breaths.

"He's okay. Thank God." Roman rolled his eyes, sounding both relieved and disgusted.

She shook her head. "What happened? How did he get into a bike accident in December?"

Christian glowered. "Right! That di—" He glanced at her parents and gave them a weak grin at their turned-down lips. "Dip weed." He cleared his throat.

Roman said, "Don't know what happened, honestly. Past few weeks have been tough for him, he hasn't told us much. And then yesterday he took off on his bike, barely got down the road when we heard a loud crash."

"By the time we got out there," Christian took over, "he was on his ass and all we saw was the tail end of a van turning down the street, peeling rubber. God." He shook his head and picked at his thumbnail.

He look was so haunted that Elisa knew Christian had probably been the one to find Julian. The mere fact that Julian had been in ICU yesterday meant he must have looked half-dead. Bile rose up the back of her throat at the thought of it.

She grimaced.

"Where is he? I want to go see him."

Her father gestured for all of them to take a seat. Once they did, he said, "Lori's in there with him now. He's sedated. On some pretty heavy pain meds. Only one of us can go in there at a time."

No sooner had he finished saying that then Elisa spotted Lori walking out of the room closest to the waiting room. Shooting up to her feet, she rushed to Lori's side and gave her a big hug.

Their mother seemed so frail, almost nothing but skin and bones. The garish purple sweater made her already pale skin seem more washed out than normal.

"Thank God you're here. He was asking for you all morning," she said.

"Can I go see him?" Elisa glanced at the door, the tension of waiting to go see him was almost too much to handle. She nibbled on her lower lip as her nerves chewed her up from the inside out.

"Yeah. I'll walk you in. He's still asleep, but I know if he were awake he'd tell me to bring you in. Just don't freak out when you see him, okay?"

Stomach sinking to her feet, she nodded and wiped her sweaty palms down the front of her snow-white sweater.

"Just tell me one thing first." She tapped Lori's hand before she could walk away. "How are his hands?"

Lori smiled softly. "He was wearing riding gloves and a helmet, all things considered, it could have been much worse."

First thing Elisa noticed when they entered Julian's room was the gentle hum and swishing sound of medical equipment.

Steeling her nerves, she finally looked at him.

Julian didn't look as bad as she'd feared. Which immediately helped to ease the worst of the adrenaline rush. She'd seen pictures of victims in car accidents and had expected to see his face swollen to twice its size and crusted over with blood.

His face wasn't swollen, and apart from a vertical scratch that went from the bottom of his left eye to his mouth, there wasn't a mark on him. His injuries were obvious, though.

His right leg was propped up in a black brace and looked like it belonged on Frankenstein's monster and not him. There were bolts and wires everywhere. His toes were a hideous shade of mottled purple, almost black in some spots. The brace extended from his foot all the way up to his thigh.

She covered her mouth. "Oh my God."

Lori shook her head. "That asshole almost ripped his leg off. From what the medic said, Julian was dragged under the back of the van for about a minute before being released."

Just the thought of it brought tears to her eyes. That he wouldn't have been able to scream, to tell the person to stop. That he'd been trapped and caught like a freakin' caged animal enraged her. "What kind of monster would do something like this?"

A laugh that sounded more like a sob escaped Loribelle before she shuddered and knuckled a tear from her eye. "That boy is gonna be the death of me."

Placing a hand on Lori's shoulder, Elisa patted her gently. "Go get some coffee or something, I'll stay here with him."

She nodded and then opened her mouth and Elisa could have sworn there was something she wanted to say, but instead she simply turned on her heel and walked back out.

With a heavy heart, Elisa studied Julian.

They had placed a cannula in his nose, and apart from a few

minor scratches, his face was pretty much as it'd always been. His skin tone was a little paler than she remembered, but that could just be because of the fact that it was now winter.

"Oh, Jules, what's happening to you?" Walking over, she sat on the chair beside his bed and grabbed onto his hand, tracing the thick veins that extended down from his knuckles.

His right thumb had an angry red burn on it, and there were rashes on both palms, but the wounds were superficial and would definitely heal in time. She shuddered in relief. These hands were his only means of communication. What if it had been his hands and not his leg that'd been chewed up?

What then? What would he have done?

Jaw trembling as she fought back the tears, she brought his hand to her lips and kissed it with all her heart. Then turned it over, opened it up, and brought his palm to her cheek.

Quivering under his touch, even though she was the one forcing him to touch her.

She'd been so happy to be at college, so happy to get away from the things Julian made her feel, if she'd lost him she would never have forgiven herself.

"Julian, if I lost you again. I don't know—" Her nostrils flared and the words died on her tongue as the sobs came harder.

He was her family, would always be her family, and it was stupid to think that a little time and distance could ever dull that. She was just so relieved that he was going to be okay.

Moving the chair even closer, she lowered the side panel on Julian's bed and pressed the pedal to bring the motorized bed low enough that she could lay her head on his lap. Just for a minute.

She only meant to close her eyes for a second, just long enough to gather herself, but the sleepless night coupled with the anxious drive suddenly overwhelmed her and before she knew it she'd fallen asleep.

She moaned when the soft glide of fingers moving through her hair woke her up. Confused about where she was, she was slow to blink her eyes open, only to realize that it wasn't Thomas rubbing her head, but Jules.

His familiar sea-green gaze hypnotized her. Now, with his eyes open and alert, she could see what she hadn't seen before.

Julian was becoming a man.

He'd lost a lot of the softness in his face. His lower lip was pierced, and, just like Roman, he had whiskers. His hair still hung longer than normal in that familiar skater style that she'd always secretly adored.

Feeling suddenly hot, she cleared her throat and wiped her mouth with the back of her hand, hoping she hadn't drooled on him.

"How long have you been here?" Julian signed.

"Umm." She turned to glance over her shoulder at the clock mounted on the wall. Elisa rubbed at her stiff neck. "About an hour," she said, and then remembered that she'd neither signed it nor looked at him while saying it.

Turning back around she signed it quickly. "Jules, what happened? Why were you on your bike in December?"

His jaw clenched then, and he glanced down at his leg. She noted the lines shading the corners of his eyes and mouth and the faint sheen of sweat dotting his forehead.

He was obviously still in a lot of pain.

She tapped him, only talking once he looked up. "More medicine?"

Shaking his head, he said, "No."

But she refused to give up. Anytime he'd so much as move, he'd wince. "You're in pain. You need medicine."

"Can't." His teeth clenched.

"Why not?"

"Because then I'll fall asleep."

She sighed. "That's good. You need sleep. You'll get better quicker."

Brushing her fingers away, he shook his head harder. "No, because then I won't be able to talk to you."

Oh.

She sat back on her chair as her heart beat a galloping rhythm in her chest.

He looked away after he said it, glaring down at his leg and then signed, "Not my fault. Dumbass came out of nowhere. I looked three times before I crossed that intersection. Cops said he was speeding."

She grabbed his fingers and brought them to her lips, wanting to touch him even though she knew she had no right to do so. His mouth opened just slightly and his breathing hitched when she kissed him.

Then trying something she'd seen done in a movie a few weeks ago, she placed his open palm against her throat and said, "You scared me."

"El…e." He didn't sign that, he spoke it.

And she cried to hear that broken sound because she knew it'd come from the very bottom of his heart.

For just a moment she allowed herself to forget that she was nineteen going on twenty in another five months and he basically seventeen, or that she had a boyfriend that she was wild about, because this was her Julian and he was safe and the world was a better place because of it.

Placing a knee on the side of the bed, she tried to be as careful as possible when she wrapped her arms around him and pressed her ear to his heart.

The steady beat soothed her frazzled nerves. But his grunt of pain made her pull quickly away.

His face was shiny with sweat as he signed, "Don't pull back."

"God, what am I doing?" She didn't sign it or speak it to him, because she needed to remember that she did have a boyfriend and Julian was like a brother to her. Not to mention how much younger he was. "What the hell am I doing?"

But she must not have been careful the second time around, because he signed furiously at her. "Don't leave me, Smile Girl."

Tears shimmered in her eyes. "I'm here for Christmas break, Jules, and then I have to go back."

His lower jaw jutted out.

And it was so bizarre to see him, looking so much like a man, but acting so much like his age. She wanted to cry and laugh and run away all at the same time.

"Don't pretend like I don't exist."

She frowned. "What are you talking about? I've never pretended—" She stopped what she was saying when the door opened.

It was Lori, she glanced between the two of them before signing, "I'm calling a nurse, Julian, you look like hell."

His grunt of dissent landed on her ears only as Lori had already turned and walked back out.

Realizing that so long as she remained in the room Julian would refuse the medication that could help him get better, she held up her hands. "I'll be back."

"Smile Girl?"

The hurt was evident in his gaze, and it was everything she could do to steel her heart against it.

She walked out of that room feeling as though she'd been sliced right down the middle. Like she was walking away from something that was vital and crucial to her well-being. Her heart.

Glancing at her parents, she motioned toward the elevators. "Let's go home, Julian needs to rest."

She didn't return again that night. Or even the next one. Her thoughts and emotions were so confused that she didn't know what to do and when Thomas called her the next night, she knew she'd blown it big time.

It was obvious that her one-word answers weren't going over very well with him, that he could sense the last thing in the world she wanted to do was be on the phone with him.

Because even while she was holed up in her room, her mind was constantly in that hospital.

She hated herself, knowing that her absence was hurting Julian, but she didn't know what else to do.

Only when her mother hugged her later that night and told her she needed to stop ignoring Julian and remember that no matter what her personal problems were they weren't bigger than his did she realize that hiding out was definitely not the right answer.

Still completely confused but determined to put it behind her, she drove back to the hospital. Today they'd be releasing Julian, and it also happened to be the triplets' birthday.

She felt like an idiot picking up a rose from the flower shop for him; as far as birthday gifts went, it was pretty awful. Not to mention she'd gone in with the high hopes of finding white, but there'd only been reds available.

By the time she'd finally made it up to his room, Julian was already in a wheel chair and surrounded by not only his family, but a nurse ready to wheel him out. His black brace stuck straight out in front of him, he didn't look comfortable at all and she suffered another pang of remorse for not coming to visit him more often.

Everyone stopped what they were doing and saying when she walked in. Julian didn't look happy to see her at all. His eyes were narrowed into thin slits and his lips pressed tight.

She cleared her throat. "I thought I'd come and see you home, Jules."

He turned his face to the right.

Christian and Roman pretended like they weren't embarrassed for her by clearing their throats and glancing down at their feet, which only made the humiliation worse.

Lori tried as best she could to save the day. "Oh, Elisa, thank you for coming. And look at that rose, isn't it lovely, Julian?" She signed it in such a way that he had no choice but to see it.

Then with a fake but cheery smile on her face, Lori turned to the nurse. "Can she push?"

"What?" Elisa frowned.

Lori nodded. "Mmhmm. You push. It's his birthday—"

"Hey!" Roman and Christian piped up. "It's ours too, butt turd seems to have forgotten that."

Julian's glower grew deeper.

"Oh shush." Lori waved her hand. "You guys are seventeen now, stop acting like such babies. Elisa, come." She gestured her forward.

Feeling more than stupid, and with cheeks flaming a heated crimson, she marched over to Julian's side. He still wouldn't look at her.

The male nurse dressed in Scooby-Doo scrubs stepped back. "If you guys are ready to go, I'll show you the way down."

She felt like an ass. And that was only putting it mildly. Of course she deserved the silent treatment. But why did things have to get so complicated between her and Julian? Why couldn't it have stayed the way it had with Roman and Christian?

By the time they got to the handicap minivan Lori had rented for the duration of Julian's rehab, Elisa was in a crappy mood.

It wasn't his fault he was mad at her, she deserved it, but that also didn't mean that she liked it. She hated it.

Hated. It.

It took about twenty minutes before Lori figured out how to lower the lift so that Julian could be wheeled on it. Those twenty minutes had been some of the most awkward of Elisa's life. Her thoughts had vacillated between an obligation to stay mingled with the need to run away and hide from him like a chicken.

Only through sheer force of will did she stay put.

She heaved a mighty sigh of relief when Lori finally lowered the lift. Once Julian was settled in, Elisa saw her chance to make a break for it.

Running away wasn't the answer, and yet that was exactly what she meant to do.

"And just where do you think you're going, young miss?" Lori asked with an arch to her thin brow.

Elisa hooked her thumb over her shoulder. "I brought my car, I probably should—"

"Yeah, good try. That boy is driving me crazy. He's in a horribly pissy mood and now, seeing you, I'm pretty sure you both have some talking to do."

"But my car."

"Can be driven home by Roman or Christian, we are neighbors, remember? And you guys need to talk. I'm serious. Do not throw years of friendship away over nothing."

Nothing?

Couldn't she realize what was happening? Didn't she realize that the way Elisa viewed Julian was beyond inappropriate? Why did she continue to insist on pushing them together?

Elisa had been fine back at college. Things had been normal and getting great. She was going to have sex for the first time with a boyfriend she loved. A guy that was just about perfect in every way but one.

He wasn't Julian Wright.

Roman stuck out his hand. "Give me the keys, Lisa. You know you can't win when she gets like this."

Giving him a hard side-eyed glare, she yanked her keys out of her pocket and thrust them at him. "Take care of it."

"Oh, whatever. I'm stopping by the Grease Burner to pick up some food. I'm starving."

"Yeah, right." Christian laughed. "You just want to go flirt with Diane."

Roman snorted and gave a carefree shrug.

And then heaving a dramatic sigh, Christian said, "Diane Thorn, goddess of Bay High. Hey." He jerked, trotting after Roman, who'd already started walking off. "Wait up, I'm coming with you."

"Take care of it—I'm serious you, guys!" Elisa cupped her hands around her mouth.

They never even acknowledged her.

Lori was already sitting behind the wheel of the car when Elisa reluctantly climbed in. Sitting beside an entirely too broody Julian wasn't going to be fun at all.

"You guys fix this," Lori commanded, and then, turning on the radio, proceeded to ignore them the rest of the trip home.

The first few minutes that ticked by were agony for her. With a frustrated growl, she smacked Julian on the shoulder.

Which caused him to groan and immediately she was horrified because she'd completely forgotten about his injury.

"Oh, Jules, God, I'm such an ass. I'm—"

His lips stretched into a wide smile.

Balling her hands into fists, she realized he'd just played her for a fool. "You're a jerk, Julian Wright," she signed at him furiously.

Finally, finally he looked at her. And even though the ice had been broken, she could see that he was still irritated by what she'd done.

"I'm sorry, okay. I'm sorry." It was hard not saying the words aloud as she signed them, but this conversation was just for her and Jules.

"You said you'd come back."

"Julian, you don't understand."

"What, Smile Girl? What don't I understand?"

This was getting way too deep. Moving into places that she really didn't want to go. What was going on between them, it had a lot more to do with the heart than just an annoying miscommunication.

"You set me aside." He signed it.

She frowned. "What the hell are you talking about? I wrote you every week. I sent you pictures."

"Yeah." He snarled. "Pictures of you with that dickhead."

Crossing her arms, she gave him a mutinous glare.

"Why would you do that to me?"

She shook her head. If she said anything, hell, if she signed anything right now, she knew she would regret it.

"Answer me!" He grunted.

Her gestures were full of fury. "He's my boyfriend and I love him. I wanted to share that with you because I love you too, you're my brother, we share things."

That was clearly the wrong thing to say. He didn't get angry, but he stopped talking. And no matter that Lori wanted them to fix it, Elisa knew things had only gotten a million times worse.

By the time they pulled up to the house it was with so much relief that Elisa jumped out of the van. But she wouldn't run away this time. She was a grown up and it was time to start acting like it. Turning back to him she laid it all out there.

"Friends, Jules. That's what we are. Please, understand that."

He didn't sign back, and his beautiful sea-green eyes grew heavy with shadows, but he did nod his head.

Every night after that the Wrights came over. Dad had built a temporary handicap ramp to go up their stoop so that Julian could be wheeled in for nightly dinner.

It was with shock that Elisa saw him laughing with her family, with his brothers. Sometimes even making noises as he did it.

In fact, it was as though what'd happened in that hospital had never happened at all.

And every day that passed that Julian would gave her a quick hello before acting like she didn't exist at all only made her feel worse and worse.

It wasn't even the same guy. Yes, he was still dressed in his monochromatic shades of black and white, with his long skater hair and his mesmerizing tattoos, but he didn't seem nearly as...well, broken.

It was like Julian, but without all the drama.

And what sucked more than anything was just how badly that made Elisa feel. She wanted him to stop looking at her like he did, like he saw beyond her skin, into her very soul. Wanted him to stop touching her like he did, wanted him to be just like Roman and Christian... she'd wanted all that, and now that he was, she hated it.

Flat out wanted-to-murder-something hated it.

Every night she'd talk to Thomas on the phone and could hardly concentrate on what he'd be asking her because she'd be wondering what Julian was doing now. Who was he smiling at? And now she suddenly couldn't seem to get the idea out of her head that if she had a boyfriend it only stood to reason that he must have a girlfriend.

The thought made her so intensely jealous, and then filled her with guilt, because she had a boyfriend. A great one. He'd be devastated if he knew where her thoughts were now, but no matter how many times she mentally chastised herself, nothing helped.

Julian Wright was becoming her obsession all over again.

The worst of it was, she had nobody she could talk to about it. On the surface they were just nineteen and seventeen and maybe if she'd been the seventeen year old and he the nineteen year old it wouldn't have mattered to her, but that wasn't the case. She'd been raised to view Julian, as well as Chris and Rome, as brothers. But here she was viewing him as so much more.

She should be obsessing about the men in college, not a boy back home still in high school. She shouldn't be wondering how his lip ring would feel, or groaning when a memory would flash through her head of them on that pier the summer before she'd left. How he'd touched her, how his callused palms had made her skin sizzle and her thighs ache.

She counted down the days until she could return to campus with the desperation of a woman drowning.

Today was Christmas, technically campus opened back up on the eighth. But since she didn't live on campus, she could theoretically go back tomorrow. Her parents might be a little upset, and they wouldn't understand why she was leaving so quickly, but if she told them it was because Thomas was returning early, they might at least understand that.

When she thought it, she wondered if she could actually convince Thomas to come back early. All she needed to do was see him again, be around him, and away from Julian and things would go back to normal.

The meal was jovial that night. The presents exchanged. It'd been a secret Santa kind of deal, so that there weren't a ton of gifts being passed around. She'd pulled her father's name out of the hat, and Christian had pulled hers.

Her father had pretended to love the map of the campus she'd gotten him. Considering it was his alma mater, she'd figured he'd love it and hang it up in his study somewhere, but he'd actually become more animated when she'd shown him her bronze medal from her last meet.

Christian had bought her tiny diamond studs, which had made her eyes open wide. "Oh wow, Chris, you really shouldn't have. These must have been so—"

"Cubic zirconia," he snorted. "You know I'm broke as a joke."

Laughing as she slipped them on, she said, "I love you. They're awesome. Thanks."

Julian hadn't looked at her as he'd handed his gift to her mother. It was a rolled sheet of paper and Elisa knew without even seeing it that he'd sketched her something.

"Oh my goodness, Julian." Her mother had covered her mouth. "This is so...I'm just so..." She shook her head and then stood to hug his neck.

He accepted her touch with an awkward pat to her back. And when her mother finally flipped the sheet around Elisa could see why her mother had reacted as she had.

Julian had taken the time to painstakingly draw a photorealistic replica of her beloved rose garden. From the tiny gnomes that hid amongst the bushes, to the "I love my garden" placard her father had built for her mother four anniversaries ago.

And this time when she glanced up, Julian was looking right back at her.

Pretending like she needed to go to the bathroom, Elisa excused herself and instead locked the door, splashing cold water in her face.

"Get it together, Elisa," she muttered, staring at her crimson reflection in the mirror.

She'd put on makeup tonight. She never put on makeup. The mascara was now streaking down her cheeks. Snatching up some tissue she scrubbed it off her face.

Everything he did was perfect. Everything.

"Why couldn't he at least have one freaking flaw? Just one." With a disgusted roll of her eyes, she walked back into the living room.

But apart from Julian, everyone else was gone. Stopping short in the doorway, feeling a lot like being in there alone with him would be like walking through a mine field, she gripped the wall.

"Where is everybody?"

"The den."

She was just about to head that way when she caught him signing. It would have been beyond rude for her to pretend like she hadn't seen it.

"Come here, Smile Girl."

"Julian." She frowned. "I don't know."

"Please."

And if it had been anyone else, she could have just said no. She could have just walked away, but she was bound to Julian in a way she'd never been bound to another soul in her life.

Each step she took closer to him made her body tremble harder and harder.

He patted the sofa beside his wheelchair.

She was stiff as a board as she took a seat, placing her hands primly in her lap.

"I made you a present, too."

He looked shy when he said, and she wondered what he would think if he ever found out that the picture he'd drawn of her was even now framed and resting on her dresser. That it was the first thing she saw every morning when she woke up and the last thing she saw every night.

Reaching into a black cylinder by his side she hadn't seen earlier, he pulled out another sheet of drawing paper.

Even rolled up she could tell this one was different from her mother's. The weight of the paper was heavier. Her hands shook.

"Open it."

"But I didn't get you anything."

He shook his head and when his finger traced the length of her jaw she didn't even try to pull away. In fact, she swayed just a little toward him.

Julian was the magnet to her iron shavings. It was almost terrifying how much she wanted to kiss him right now.

It took her two tries to unroll the drawing, thanks to her fingertips being so numb, and when she did all she could do was gasp.

This drawing was different from any of the other ones he'd ever shown her, because this one was done in color.

The drawing was of her. And him.

They were in the hospital room. He was in the bed, and she was lying with her face on his lap. Her hair spilled over his thighs and her lips were slightly parted. He'd captured her likeness completely.

But the colors were a frightening clash of hues. Her skin was yellow. Her hair brown where it was a rich blonde in real life. Her white sweater was painted a pale pink.

But she was the only part of the drawing done in color. He, and the room, were merely shades of black and gray.

"When I look at you, it's like I can see the colors," he signed. "I love you, Smile Girl."

Words lodged in her throat and all she could do was shake her head. "You're too young, Jules. You're a kid."

He swatted her hand away. "No."

"I'm almost twenty. You're a kid."

"I won't be forever."

"You don't know what you want."

"I want you. I always have."

"You're seventeen."

"And when I'm eighteen? What then? Will that make a difference?"

She wanted to cry. Bawl like a baby. Because the words he was saying...she wanted it too.

"I love you like a bro—" she began to sign, but he grabbed her hands and brought them to his chest and in his eyes she knew that he knew the truth.

And with an inarticulate sound of pain and longing she did what she'd wanted to do from the moment she'd stepped into his hospital room.

Elisa kissed him.

At first he was stunned, his lips didn't move. And just as she was about to pull back, just as she was about to run away, a growl of such fierce need tore from his throat and his hand cupped the back of her head.

Smashing her lips down even harder on his. His tongue traced the seam of her mouth, soft and gentle, but still hungry.

She was helpless to resist. Opening on a hungry moan, she glided her tongue along his. Tasting the sweetness of mint and coffee.

The painting fell from her lap as she hopped to her knees, twisting around without breaking contact so that she could kiss him deeper. Explore him better.

The hunger she felt, it was new and vast, and so breathtakingly terrifying that she knew if she pulled away she'd jump in her car right now and go.

Leave.

Leave him.

Leave Sunny Cove.

Just go.

But she didn't pull away. Instead she shoved her cold hands underneath his sweater and mewled when her nails scraped nipple piercings.

When had he done that?

But the words fled as his mouth devoured hers. The lip ring she'd fantasized about for nights was on her, touching her, and she couldn't stop herself from sucking it into her mouth. Swiping her tongue over it once, twice, three times.

His breathy whimpers only enflamed her more. And when his hands landed on her breasts and he squeezed, nothing else mattered.

"Jules," she whispered his name.

There was more, so much more she might have said, if she didn't suddenly hear the clearing of a throat.

Shocked, she snapped back.

Julian looked confused for a moment, until he glanced over his shoulder and spotted her very startled-looking father.

"Oh. My. Oh no." She shook her head. "I'm, I didn't…" And without looking at Julian, she swiped up her drawing and ran out of there.

Elisa left early the next morning, never getting a chance to say goodbye to him.

When she got back to campus, she stopped writing Julian.

It was over.

It had to be.

Forever.

She didn't go back home for spring break. And when summer rolled around she signed up to go abroad in Italy. That was where she turned twenty. And that was also where she gave Thomas her virginity.

And though she never really forgot that kiss or Julian Wright, it was finally easier to breathe.

Chapter 7

"**M**om, no, I'm not coming home for Christmas break. I'm really busy." Elisa kicked her feet up on the sofa and leaned her head back, as Missy—Chastity's fat tabby—tried to make herself comfortable on top of her head.

Giving her a gentle shove off, she sighed.

"Elisa Jane. You haven't come home all year. Now your father and I have been very patient, coming up to see you whenever we can, but honey, I think you know this isn't fair. It's your turn, you owe us."

Closing her eyes, she wondered why her father had never told her mother about what he'd caught her doing with Julian that night in the living room.

It would almost have been easier, because she didn't know, and now the thought of bringing it up broke Elisa out in a cold sweat.

Julian turned eighteen tomorrow.

She'd been thinking about it all day. Which was ridiculous. They hadn't spoken in nearly a year. At this point he was probably so over her it wasn't even funny.

She should have been entirely over him too.

She thought she was.

Until today.

Until the only thought she kept having was that after today he was legal. What a sad, sad person she was.

"I don't know, Mom. Thomas has asked me to go skiing with him this year, but I'm also watching Chastity's cat."

"Bring that filthy animal here, and like hell you'll go to a ski lodge. You make time for your family, young lady."

A hard knock sounding on the door spared her from having to answer. "Mom, that's my door."

"It's eleven o'clock at night, who in the world could possibly be—"

"Mum, you do realize I'm almost twenty-one, right?"

She sighed. "Don't remind me. We're setting a place for you at our table, Elisa Jane. You'd better show up."

"Goodbye," she said as the pounding increased.

Hanging up, she grumbled under her breath. She wasn't expecting anyone, so it had to be Thomas. Chastity was already home. He was probably showing up for a late night booty call.

Not that she minded, but she minded.

"Thomas, what?" she groused as she swung the door wide and then yipped when not Thomas, but Julian Wright stared back at her.

"Holy shit!" She covered her mouth and peered over his shoulder to see if any of the other Wrights had shown up. Parked out in front of her apartment was the beat-up Corolla.

How in the hell had he found her apartment? He'd never been here before.

Sucking her bottom lip into her mouth, she looked slowly back at him. A strange flash of memory came to her then. In tenth grade science class she'd been forced to watch a nature documentary about deer. Beautiful, graceful, stupid deer. There'd been one scene in particular that had imprinted itself on her mind. A speckled doe had been minding her own business, munching on sweet blades of saw grass, and then suddenly its head had snapped up, and, standing very still, it'd scented the air. And all the fine hairs on Elisa's arms had gone up when the camera had zoomed right to show the shadowy image of a gray wolf hiding in brush. The deer had tried to run away, but it had only managed to take two steps before the wolf brought it down by its throat.

That's what she felt like.

Like she was that deer and Julian Wright was the big bad wolf.

Dressed entirely in black, his gaze was intense.

Julian was a man.

Her pulse thundered.

No longer was he hinting at manhood, or just a scrawny, skinny boy.

He'd filled out nicely.

Even under the layers of clothes she could see the fine definition of muscle. Not only did he have the lip ring still, the one that would sometimes wake her up in a cold sweat in the middle of the night when she'd dream about that thing moving across places it never had before, but he also had gauges in both ears. They weren't stretched wide, but they were definitely stretched, and he was looking at her with the kind of force she'd only ever witnessed in that documentary.

He shivered and that's when she noticed that fat flakes of snow drifted outside her door. She couldn't leave him out there, but she wasn't sure she should bring him in either.

Throwing caution to the wind, she grabbed his hand and pulled him in. "Jules, you must be freezing, come inside."

And even as she did it she couldn't help but glance down the street one final time, feeling entirely too guilty for her peace of mind. What if someone walked by who knew her, knew Thomas? What would they think, or say?

But the street was deserted.

He stepped in, and she closed the door quickly.

It wasn't until she turned around and looked at his back that she felt like her comfortable apartment was suddenly cramped and too small. With fingers that shook just a little, she helped him out of his jacket and hung it up on the coat rack Chastity had found at a garage sale last year.

"What are you doing here?" she asked when she finally walked back in front of him.

For the longest time he didn't say anything, not when he walked into her living room, not when he sat on her couch, and not even when she sat across from him on Chas's boyfriend's hideous taupe-colored recliner. Some piece of crap thing he'd found just lazing about outside of a dumpster a few weeks back.

Elisa hadn't wanted the flea-ridden thing in her house, but now she had to admit that ugly as it was, it was more comfortable than anything else they had in the apartment.

Leaning back on the couch, Julian seemed to be grappling with his words. His fingers kept twitching on his thighs.

Trying to break the ice, because she was still totally shocked that he was here, she signed, "You walk good."

"Thanks."

She nodded and tried to hide the sigh when he didn't take a lead off her cue to say something.

Elisa had to admit, though, it was good to see him walking with barely a trace of a limp. Even though she'd stopped writing to Julian personally, she'd never stopped asking about him.

In fact, she'd taken to calling Lori every so often to find out how physical therapy was going. It was how she knew that he'd flown through therapy much faster than his doctors had anticipated. Instead of a year, he'd learned to walk on his own after only five months.

He was also going to be graduating with honors and was even now trying to figure out where to apply to go to college.

But as much as she tried to occupy her thoughts with something other than the fact that Julian was in her apartment, her brain just kept circling around to the big question.

Why was he here?

"How have you been?" he finally asked.

The question was so awkward and strange that it only served to ratchet up her nerves.

She wiggled her hand to indicate so-so. Then decided that if all he wanted to do was shoot the breeze, she needed to relax. He'd eventually get around to his real purpose for being here.

"Finished my final exam today. It sucked hard. I'm hoping I made a B at least."

He nodded, but didn't actually seem to be paying attention. By the way his knee kept bopping up and down she could tell he was anxious.

"So where are you planning to go to college?" she asked.

His shoulders slumped and his stare was a mile long. "Smile Girl, has it really come down to this?"

She dropped her hands, sensing that he was finally going to get to the reason for his coming.

"A year. You called my mom. Why?"

Was he upset that she'd kept tabs? "Because I wanted to know how you were doing."

"Then you should have texted me. Called me."

She swallowed hard. For the past three nights Thomas had been showing up at random, odd times. What if he came over tonight? The last thing she wanted was for Thomas to see Julian and get strange ideas.

"I didn't call you, Jules, because I didn't know what to say."

"We're friends! That's what you told me."

"Yes." She nodded. "Just like I am with Chris and—"

"Stop. Stop lying to me. Stop lying to yourself. It's not like Chris and Rome, because you still talked to them. But you locked me out. You stopped writing. I have a girlfriend."

Why that should feel like a blow to the gut she didn't know. But it made her feel cold and sick to her stomach.

"I kiss her. She kisses me back."

She frowned. "Jules, why are you telling me this?"

"Because she loves me, Elisa. Me." He patted his chest. "She didn't keep pushing me away, telling me she didn't care."

"I did care. I do. But too much. You're in high school."

His brow rose and his nostrils flared. "So what? I'm eighteen."

"You're seventeen. Not eighteen until tomorrow."

He rolled his eyes.

"Jules, why did you come out here? Why did you find me? If you have a girlfriend, that's good." No, it wasn't, it really wasn't. Not to her. But it needed to be and he needed to see that.

"Because she's not you! Because I kiss her and I hold her and she's not fucking you!"

Elisa couldn't catch her breath. Fire skated through her veins, rushed through her blood, made her feel hot and dizzy.

"You said I didn't know what I wanted. I want you, I've always wanted you. And it seemed like the more I wanted you the more you pushed me away. I know you felt it that night, Smile Girl. Because I felt it too."

She shook her head. Mostly because she didn't know what to say to him. She had felt it, still did. The second she'd seen him standing in her door all the old feelings, everything, it'd all come crashing back with a ferocity and intensity that had terrified her.

He closed his eyes and tears sprang to hers. She had a boyfriend. A good one. She loved him...

God, she was liar. Even to herself, Julian was right. He always had been right about her. She'd never felt a tenth for Thomas what she'd always felt for Jules.

But it just couldn't work. He was still in high school. What would it look like to everyone if she dumped Thomas for some freaking senior in high school?

But Julian wasn't just anybody either.

"Can I sleep here tonight?"

Could she tell him no? If he wanted in her bed, was she really capable of pushing him away again? It was why she hadn't gone home, because she'd known the truth of it when her father had broken them up that night.

Julian was her kryptonite.

She nodded, sucking her bottom lip between her teeth as her stomach danced with drunken butterflies.

"Don't worry, I'll go home tomorrow."

Then, shucking off his shoes, he sprawled out on her couch. It was almost midnight, but she was far from sleepy. Now that he was here she was wide awake, nervous, and excited all at the same time.

She should call Thomas, let him know what was going on, just in case he decided to try and come over. But she didn't want to talk to him.

Not about Jules.

Getting up slowly, she walked into her room, pulled down one of the spare blankets from her closet, and brought it out.

When he wouldn't take it, she opened it up and laid it over him. He didn't say thank you, but when she turned to go she caught him dragging her blanket up to his nose and taking a deep breath.

Turning off all the lights, she locked the door and went to her room, texting to Thomas that she was going to sleep early tonight and she might see him tomorrow.

Stripping down to her bra and panties, she crawled into bed and tried to sleep. But she couldn't. Because every creak and groan in the apartment made her terrified that Julian would try to sneak out without saying goodbye.

She tossed and turned for a long time, staring up at the ceiling and feeling like the world's worst girlfriend because all she wanted to do was go back into that living room and kiss him.

Touch him.

Make sure that he was really real. That he was really here.

Why had he come?

Rolling over she stared at her bedside clock. The glowing red numbers read eleven fifty-five.

It was so bizarre, him just showing up this way. After so long not talking, after so long of pretending that she didn't really care anymore that she'd actually begun to believe it. And then he showed up and every lie, everything she'd told herself for the past year just came crashing down around her feet.

Elisa cared too much.

Eleven fifty-eight.

"Why did you come?" she whispered to the shadows on the walls.

And why did it hurt her so much to think of him letting some girl touch his body, trace the lines of his tattoos? How far had they gone? All the way? Like her and Thomas?

It made her sick how angry the thought of that made her feel. She'd done the right thing by leaving him alone. She had.

Eleven fifty-nine.

He was a kid. There was no way that at age fifteen he could see her and think she'd be it for him. No way. It was a phase. Just a crush.

But that kiss last year. And now him here.

What if she'd been wrong? What if it hadn't been crush? And if it hadn't been a crush then how perverted was she for wanting him in the same way? When she should have been looking at guys her age, Elisa had been falling madly in love with Julian Wright.

Little Julian Wright.

She squeezed her eyes shut as midnight rolled over.

"Happy birthday, Julian."

Sniffing, she closed her eyes, wrapped the blanket tightly around her, and kept telling herself that she'd done the right thing.

Ten minutes later, she heard the distinctive sound of a creaking floorboard.

He was up. He was leaving.

Heart trapped in her throat, she sat up just as her door opened.

His dark shadow filled the door, and she realized she was practically naked. She felt his gaze raking over her flesh like a caress and she shivered, clutching the blanket to her chest like her life depended on it.

Utter silence could sometimes be louder than words. In that silence she could feel the throb of her beating heart bang against her ribcage as he made his way unerringly to her side.

A sliver of moonlight sliced across his body from the tiny crack in her bedroom window. He was still fully dressed.

Sitting down beside her, his body heat so warm, and his smell of soap and mint so strong, he turned her hand over and danced his fingers across her palm.

"Tell me now."

She grabbed his other hand. "What? What do you want to know?"

He hesitated a second. "Is it just me?"

She could lie. Tell him it was just him and she knew, knew with every fiber of her being that he'd leave. He'd walk away and she'd lose Julian Wright forever. Or she could finally open up and be honest with him, with herself.

There was Thomas. There was his girlfriend. People would get hurt.

Heaven help her...

"No, Jules, it's not just you."

With a moan that tugged at her heartstrings, he placed his forehead to hers, his fingers still trapped inside her palm.

"I tried to move on, Smile Girl. For you, I tried."

"Jules." His name came out a broken whisper.

And even though she knew he couldn't hear her, he seemed to understand exactly what she wanted. His hands were so gentle as they glided up her bare arms and where she'd been warm just a second ago, now her body broke out in a wash of goosebumps.

He was slow and methodical, trailing his nose down the side of her face, and along her neck, taking his sweet time to get to her lips. When he finally got there he didn't devour her like last time, he flirted. Moving against them so softly it felt like the brush of a rose petal.

The simmer in her stomach turned into liquid flame. There'd never been anyone like Julian.

She framed his face as tears squeezed from the corners of her eyes, because she knew what would happen tonight and there was no way in hell she would stop it.

When he finally took her lips, he claimed them like a brand. Tugging her bottom one between his teeth and suckling. She moaned, needing to get as close to him as possible. Wanting to feel him all over her.

Reaching for his shirt, she wasn't gentle as she tugged it off, forcing them to separate so that she could toss it to the floor. With a growl he pushed off her, getting to his feet and for a second she panicked when she thought he meant to leave.

But he didn't. His fingers fumbled on the buttons of his jeans as he slid them down and kicked them off.

Elisa placed a hand over her heart.

He wore no underwear. He was long and thick, and even in the darkness she could see that the very tip of him was pierced too.

She'd almost expected to see him covered in more tattoos, but he hadn't added to the collection.

She looked up at him. Shadows danced through the room. But there was just enough streetlight that she knew he could see. Moving to her knees, she brushed her hair over her shoulders and taking a deep breath, undid her bra, and tossed it to the floor.

Elisa wouldn't look at him when she reached for her underwear.

She was shy about her body. Not that she wasn't toned or athletic, but she didn't have the kind of large breasts men liked. They were small and perky, and what if he was disappointed?

His hand stopped her when she went to pull her panties down.

And gently pushing her back down onto the bed, he sat on his knees beside her and pulled them down her legs himself.

Her center ached, her breasts tingled, every inch of her felt like an exposed nerve. Like if he even breathed on her she'd combust.

His fingers danced over her stomach.

"So beautiful."

And the breath she hadn't realized she'd been holding suddenly expelled from her lungs in a slow whoosh, and she smiled.

He was too; he was so beautiful. But Julian wasn't waiting around to hear her response.

Draping a heavy leg across hers, he rested his weight on his elbow, almost as though pinning her in, and proceeded to lick and nibble along her bellybutton for a while, so long that she began to giggle.

"Julian, I'm ticklish." She smacked his shoulder.

Which made him smile in return. But then he went from teasing to serious, and his kisses began to trail languorously upward, moving right up the center of her until he got to the valley between her breasts.

And as he kissed her, she began to writhe and moan. Her body filling with heat and need, with desire she'd denied them for so long.

His mouth captured her left breast and she hissed, arching into his touch and raking her nails through his hair.

Julian was tender, taking his time. Increasing her desire with every touch, every kiss, moving his tongue along her flesh until she felt that she would die from the pleasure. He was masterful in his worship of her and she sang from his touch.

"Please," she mumbled incoherently, undulating her hips until the center of her touched the hardness of him. "Please, Jules."

He stopped moving, his gaze going to hers, and his beautifully callused fingers fluttered along her bicep as he rested the weight of his other hand against her throat.

"Say my name," he signed.

"Julian," she smiled as her vocal chords rubbed against his palm.

A visible shudder rippled through him. He kissed her deeply, and though he'd never be able to verbally talk with her, she heard his words.

Felt what neither of them seemed to be willing to say. Because this moment was so fragile, and yet too full. It was like birth, like opening her eyes and seeing Julian for the first time. Really seeing him.

"Condom?" he asked.

And she thought it was exceedingly adorable and totally clueless on his part not to have brought one himself, she shook her head.

"Pill," she wrote the letters on his back.

With a happy sigh he slid deep into her and they moved together as one, and Elisa saw the truth for what it was.

Julian had been made for her from the very beginning. Crafted just for her. And though their paths didn't always align as they should, they always intersected. Lying there in his arms, Elisa was sure of one thing.

Julian was her partner in every way, but there were still problems. He was still in school, and she in college. There'd be distance, but she believed deeply they could weather it because this was more than just lust. More than chemistry.

It was destiny.

And right before they shattered in each other's arms, he asked her to say his name one more time.

"Julian. Julian Wright."

Chapter 8

She blinked her eyes open and then proceeded to do a long cat stretch. She was facing the window, Elisa vaguely remembered rolling over at some point during the night and him scooping her into his body so that every inch of her lay flush against every inch of him.

They'd made love.

For the first time in her life she really felt like she understood the definition of that word. And the little girl who grew up dreaming what her Prince Charming would someday look like and imagining what kind of wedding she'd someday have suddenly saw all the pieces click into place.

Not that she'd ever tell him so, but deep down, it felt right to think it.

Yawning loudly and wanting to talk about what'd happened, what this meant for their relationship, she realized he must have scooted back at some point. Patting his side of the bed, her heart leapt to her throat the moment it dawned on her that he hadn't scooted back, Julian just wasn't there.

Wide-awake now, she sat up and blinked, staring at his empty side of the bed for a solid ten seconds. Where had he gone? Was he in the house? What'd happened?

That final question finally kicked her numb brain into gear.

Kicking off the sheets, she called his name. "Julian!"

She knew he wouldn't hear her, but she padded out into the open living room, uncaring that she was still naked as a jaybird. The sheet she'd laid over him last night was on the floor. But his shoes were gone.

Where in the hell was he? "Jules?" she asked with a thread of despair, even while she clung to hope that he was just out of sight somewhere.

She peeked into the bathroom. He wasn't there. Her hands were shaking now.

Elisa even went so far as to open Chastity's door.

A sinking, bottomless pit that felt a lot like the beginnings of heartache took hold of her when all she saw was an empty room and a made-up bed. There was one last place to check.

Opening the front door, she gazed out at the empty parking spot. A fresh blanket of snow had covered the asphalt where he'd parked, which could only mean he'd left hours ago.

Julian was gone.

Racing back to her room to grab her cell, she stopped dead in her tracks when she saw a white envelope resting on the framed drawing he'd done for her of her and him in the hospital room what seemed like a lifetime ago.

No way had he left her a Dear John letter.

Just no way.

Not Julian.

He'd never do something like that to her.

Each step she took felt like a lead weight had wrapped itself around her feet. Her breathing was short and choppy when she finally tore it open.

His familiar, artistic scrawl greeted her eyes.

"Elisa,"

The first tear fell.

"I had to know. Had to know if what I've been chasing for so many years was real. You told me once that I didn't know, couldn't understand what I was feeling. And maybe you were right."

A strangled sound spilled from her lips. Her head grew suddenly dizzy as she stutter-stepped back onto the bed, clutching the letter like her life depended on it.

"For an entire year you kept me away, and I think a part of me began to understand why. I even started to feel human again, feel okay with it. It wasn't easy at first, it was like you'd ripped my heart out and had taken it away with you. I might see in only in shades of gray, but whenever I was with you it was like my world exploded with life. So maybe I clung to you because I needed that. I don't know. All I do know is I'm sorry."

It was like someone had shoved their fist down her throat, it was so swollen and thick and full of heat. All she could do was shake her head. Reading the letter with the vain hope that there'd be a silver lining even while intrinsically knowing there wouldn't be a happy ending for her.

"Smile Girl, sometimes I think I've loved you all my life. Like I've stopped living my life because of how much I needed you. But this year apart helped me to see that I could survive without you.

"And then last night, I don't know. I felt something I hadn't felt in months. Desperation. Need. I wanted you to see me for who I was now. And last night when I held you in my arms and you said my name and I felt your laughter move through me, God, Smile Girl, it brought it all back.

"I'm so sorry for leaving you this way, but I can't do this again. I can't sit and wonder and hope. I'm still in high school, you're in college. This could never work, no matter how much I might wish it were otherwise. I know that now.

"I came to you last night, Elisa, because it had to be you. I'm no Saint, but I held myself back from everyone, because it had to be you.

"And if you don't understand what that means I don't think I have the strength to explain it further. I'm sorry that I could never let you go. I'm sorry that I barged back into your life the way I have, and I'm sorry for what I'm doing to you now. More than you can ever know.

"But part of loving something sometimes means you have to let it go. I learned that lesson with my dad, I clung to his ghost to the point that I thought I would die from the pain. I can't make that mistake with you. I won't do that to you.

"I love you. I think I will always love you, but I'm finally ready to say good-bye.

Julian."

A violent wave of nausea had her shoving off the bed and racing to the bathroom. She gripped the toilet bowl, gasping and dry heaving, feeling as though her soul was trying to forcefully expel itself from her body.

Nothing came up, but all she could do was curl against the wall and sob until there were no more tears left to be shed.

But gradually misery began to turn to rage.

He would not do this to her. Not like this, she deserved better than this.

Getting up, she brushed her teeth, took a comb to her ratty hair, and marched back to her room. It was past noon—she'd spent three hours in that bathroom like an idiot.

Yanking on whatever clothes she could find that smelled halfway decent, she snatched up her phone and called Lori.

She answered on the first ring.

"Elisa, hello. How are you, honey?" Her words sounded entirely too chipper and happy for how Elisa currently felt.

She frowned. "I'm fine." *Not really*. "Is Julian there?"

"Oh," she sighed, "well, you just missed him, sweetie. He's out with Mandy."

She squeezed her eyes shut as her insides grew cold. Telling herself not to ask. "Who's Mandy?"

"Um. Well..." She drew out the words. "That's his girlfriend, hun."

Shaking her head as tears she'd thought she no longer had began to drip down her cheeks.

"Lisa?" Lori's voice sounded strained and worried. "What's wrong? Are you okay?"

She sniffed. "Lori, what time did Julian get back home?"

"Back home?" she asked and suddenly Elisa understood.

Julian had snuck out and returned home before anyone in his house had realized it. Making her feel like she'd been nothing more than a dirty, little secret.

Anger spent, and feeling like all she wanted to do now was curl under her sheets and pretend like the rest of the world didn't exist, she said, "I've got to go."

"Are you coming home for Christmas?"

"No. Tell the boys I said hi."

"Aw, I'm sorry to hear that. I'm sure Christian and Roman are going to miss you. They talk about you all the time."

And the only name that mattered to her hadn't even been mentioned. Julian had written her off. It was what she deserved really. She'd pushed him to it. But only because she'd had to. Because she'd had no choice. It'd never been because she'd actually wanted it to be though.

"Sorry, Lori. I'm..." She hung up.

It was rude. But if she'd had to stay on that phone for another second, Lori would have heard her tears. Heard her heartache.

Julian had shattered her, but how could she hate someone whom she'd shattered first?

Two hours later a knock sounded on her door and for the briefest moment her heart had twisted with joy. Until she'd opened it to see Thomas smiling back at her.

"Hey, baby," he said, rubbing his hands together and giving a shudder. "Cold out here, can I come inside?"

The day had gone from bad to worse.

She was still dressed in her canary-yellow sweatpants and pink Juicy tank top. Her hair was a rat's nest on her top of her head, her nose was a bright red from crying and screaming for the past two hours, and in all that time she'd not thought of Thomas once.

He cocked his head as he glanced quickly over her shoulder. "What's the matter?"

A good guy. That's what he was. An honorable and good guy and she was about to do to him what Julian had just done to her.

She blinked.

Why couldn't Julian have stayed out of her life forever?

"Elisa?" he asked, gripping her elbow and stepping inside, dragging snow in with him.

Extricating herself from his hand she wrapped her arms around her chest.

"Oh shit," he drawled and drew his hand down his jaw. "Are you doing what I think you're about to do?"

He'd grown his hair out longer, because she'd mentioned once how much she liked longer hair. But it'd never quite feathered out the way Julian's would. Never seemed as natural on him as it had on Jules.

"Thomas, I—"

His blue eyes grew stormy. "What the fuck happened last night?"

She was sick to her stomach. Because last night, before Julian had shown up, everything had been right between them. Happy. Comfortable.

And now she couldn't stand for him to touch her.

She shook her head. "I'm sorry."

"Elisa, what the hell did you do?"

Sobbing, she stuck a hand in her mouth. "I can't. We can't anymore."

His chest heaved like a bellow. "We're going to Aspen, you said you were going with me. What changed?"

She shook her head harder. "Things just change."

"Not that fast. Not this quick. Who'd you sleep with?"

That he'd jump to that conclusion—even though it was entirely accurate—hurt her deeply. Never in her life had she cheated. She wasn't that kind of girl. Never had been.

And yet...she was that kind of girl.

Julian Wright had ruined her.

She blinked through her tears. "Tom, I'm so...I'm just so sor—"

"Save it," he said through clenched teeth, swiping a hand through the air. "We're over. Don't—" He held up a finger, and the way his throat worked, she knew there were words on his tongue.

Probably terribly, hurtful, shameful words. Words she deserved to hear. But Thomas Mason was a good guy. Would always be a good guy.

Snapping his mouth shut, he turned on his heel and walked out the door.

Elisa stood numb as she watched him go, swallowed up by the gentle snowflakes of winter's embrace.

He'd been safe. Warm. She'd loved him. In her own way. Not in a fireworks and destiny kind of way, but she'd cared for him deeply. He was the kind of man any woman could be proud of, she'd had him and she'd lost him.

Thomas Mason walked out of her life not with a bang, but a whimper.

Knowing there was no way she could go home now, she pulled herself together as best she could and called her mother.

"Mum?" She said it like she used to when she was little.

"Baby girl?" she asked, and Elisa heard the anxiousness. Even though Elizabeth Adrian would never learn of what'd happened to her daughter that day, mother's intuition told her everything she needed to understand.

"Mum, I can't come home."

Elisa had expected an argument from her mother. But she heard none of that. "Don't worry, honey. Daddy and I will go up there this Christmas."

When they hung up five minutes later Elisa didn't know what to do with herself. She was stuck in the apartment for the winter. There was no boyfriend to whisk her off to Aspen. No Chastity to make her laugh. And most especially there were no Wrights she wanted to go home and see.

She was too raw, too hurt to even consider going home and sucking it up. But if she didn't tell someone soon, she felt like she might do something stupid she'd regret later.

If only she could have talked to her parents. But they didn't know.

And after that one time her dad had caught her, and the way he'd kept silent about the incident, she was pretty sure he *wouldn't* want to know, and if her mother found out she'd go to Lori and then Julian would find out and that was the last thing in the world she wanted.

Sinking into the ratty recliner, Elisa called the one person she could trust not to tell a soul.

"Yello?" Chastity's chuckle filtered through the line. She sounded happy, and Elisa didn't want to dump this kind of baggage on her. But there was literally no one else she could talk to.

"Chas, oh my God."

"Hey, hold on, Luke."

Elisa could hear Chastity whispering something to her boyfriend before quickly getting back on the phone. "Girl, what's wrong? You sound like death."

She snort-chuckled. An ugly sound, but a comment like that deserved a snort-chuckle. "I feel like I am dying." Her words trembled and she had to take three deep breaths before she trusted herself to speak again. "I broke up with Thomas."

"Oh no. Why, Lisa?"

Chastity must think all of this blubbering was because of Thomas—God, if she only knew. For so long Elisa had ignored her true feelings for Julian. Buried it so far deep down that not even Chas would have a clue.

"Did that asshole cheat?" she growled, "because I will stick a fist up his—"

"Not him." She shook her head, rocking hard. "Me. I did."

"You what!" she shrieked. "No, wait a second, hold on. Say that again?"

Cringing, because it sounded worse when she actually said it out loud, she sighed. "I cheated on him, Chas."

"With who?" Her voice sounded incredulous.

"Julian. I slept with Julian." It was the most bizarre thing, but she literally felt like she couldn't feel her tongue anymore. Her insides were cold and her stomach rioted as she waited for that to sink in.

"Wright? The boy who made you those drawings?"

Elisa's eyes snapped open. "How did you know that?"

"Lisa, did you really think I wouldn't notice the way my best friend mentally undressed the weird emo kid in school?"

"I did not!"

"You most certainly did. And I never said anything about it because I could tell how much it freaked you out. But I saw. Hell, I bet the whole school saw."

She shook her head. "Stop it. I didn't either."

Rather than try to pound the point home, Chastity asked another question. "How old is he?"

She plucked at a spot on her bright yellow pants. "Eighteen last night."

Chastity sighed loud and long. "So how exactly did this happen? Did you go home?"

"No, he showed up here, out of the blue. And my God, Chas, he was gorgeous. And my heart—" Voice quivering, she clutched at her chest, wishing she could just cut the thing out and throw it away into the icy river.

"He loves you too. I know he does."

"He dumped me with a Dear John letter. Just bailed. Ditched." She swiped at the hot tears. "Didn't say goodbye. Nothing. Told me he was letting me go."

"That asshole."

She laughed, but it really wasn't funny. Because she wanted to hate him, wanted it desperately with every fiber of her being, but she just couldn't. "It's not his fault. He's always tried to tell me how he felt and I was always the one pushing him away."

"So this was payback?" She sounded disgusted.

Sobbing, it took her a minute to say, "I hope not. I mean, I don't think so. The way he touched me last night. The words he said. I felt something I've never felt before. Not even with Thomas. And I think he felt it too, Chas, I swear he did."

Memories shoved through her brain. The way he'd moved on her, how he'd worshipped her with his mouth and hands, the attention he'd laved on her. It had to have been real. His letter even said it was.

"Why did he do that to me?"

Chastity sighed. "Because he's eighteen and an immature little prick."

She shook her head, but couldn't vocalize anything. Elisa was crying ugly now, the tears welling from the deepest depths of absolute pain.

"That boy has been a fool for you ever since I've known him, Lisa." Chastity's words were soft. "He's just confused. And he's still in school."

Elisa croaked out a choking, "I know. It's why this situation sucks so much. Because even though it's okay legally, it's still not okay. It's like were ships in the night, constantly passing by."

"It won't always be that way."

She clenched her jaw. "I can't allow myself to think like that, it has to be over. I can't go through this again. It hurts so bad, Chas."

"Are you going home?"

"No." She rolled her eyes. "I can't. I just can't see him. Not like this. He has a girlfriend."

She growled. "Forget him, Elisa. You're beautiful, you're smart. I'm sorry about Thomas. He was a good guy."

He was a good guy, but Elisa wasn't as sorry as she knew she should be. What if down the road he'd ever asked her to marry him? And what if she'd said yes? Was it fair to marry someone who she couldn't even cry about breaking up with now? That wasn't fair to him or to her. Maybe sometimes comfortable was good enough, but maybe sometimes comfortable was just cruel.

"I'm going to get off now. I hear Missy scratching at the back door."

She didn't really, but she didn't want to stay on the phone anymore, either.

"I wish I could be there for you right now."

"It's okay. I'm a big girl." Elisa gave a watery grin then, saying a quick goodbye, she hung up the phone.

Talking with Chastity hadn't helped much at all. Her heart still felt like it'd been shredded and tossed into a meat grinder. For the next two weeks the most that Elisa could do was get up, nuke a Lean Cuisine, and crawl back under her sheets.

By the time school was ready to start back up she'd gotten over the worst of the pain. Showering, she took her time getting dressed and decided that as much as it hurt, she was done crying over Julian Wright.

The rest of the term went by in a blur. So fast that it was like Elisa had barely blinked and now it was time to pack up and head home for summer break.

She'd barely eked out a C in advanced chem. Elisa was starting to get to a point in her college career where she really needed to decide on a major. She still didn't really have a clue, but at least she had the summer to mull it over.

Chastity slammed the trunk closed and waved to Luke as he walked back into their apartment.

Dressed in a powder blue kimono robe with flower print, she walked around toward where Elisa stood by the driver's side door of her Beetle.

"You sure you wouldn't rather just stay with us this summer?"

Luke would be temporarily renting out her portion of the apartment while Elisa was home.

It wasn't that Elisa hadn't looked to go abroad this summer. But she was tired and she was so over Julian. Staying away seemed ridiculous at this point. Plus, she was still paying off her time spent in Italy; the last thing she wanted to do was add anything else to her credit card bill.

"Nah." She shook her head and tucked a thick strand of Chastity's ropey hair behind her ear. "The way you and Luke go at it like rabbits, yeah, count me out."

She punched Elisa on the arm. "Hey! Need I remind you that I was definitely *not* the only one."

Elisa snorted. "I brought two guys over, and one time it wasn't what you thought it was anyway."

Chastity laughed and gave an exaggerated wink. "If you say so."

Both girls seemed to realize at the same time that it was time to go.

"Well," they said in unison, and then Elisa chuckled.

"Yeah, it's...yeah. It's that time."

Drawing Elisa in so that she could give her a big hug, Chastity squeezed tight. "Take care of yourself, babe. And don't let Julian get to you, okay?"

"Oh please." She turned and opened the door, sliding into the seat and shaking her head. "I'm over him. One hundred percent."

Leaning forward, Chas placed her hands on the open window. "If you were over him, you would have taken those pictures down, just saying." Her pretty brown eyes looked sad. "Be real with yourself at least, Lisa."

Then pressing a hard kiss onto Elisa's forehead, she stepped back and waved.

Elisa didn't bother waving back.

She was over Julian. And whether she'd taken the pictures down or not really meant nothing. She'd simply been too busy and had forgotten.

By the time she pulled up into her parents driveway two hours later she was in a pissy mood. The first thing she'd do when she got back to campus would be to take those pictures down.

Why she hadn't already was totally beyond her.

Getting out of the car, she pocketed her key, noting the absence of her father's red Ford pick-up.

Likely her parents were out doing some last minute grocery shopping. Mom had a thing about keeping a well-stocked pantry when Elisa came home.

Thankfully she knew where her parents hid the spare key. She was just about to walk to her trunk to pull out some boxes when she heard the loud banging of drums.

Snorting, because either Christian or Roman had obviously decided to learn something new while she'd been gone, she thought it might be fun to surprise them.

She'd told her parents not to tell the Wrights she was coming home today. Mainly because she didn't want to see Julian.

Biting her lower lip, she brushed her hand down her slightly wrinkled crop top, and jogged toward the Wrights half-open garage door.

Whichever one of the boys was playing, was actually not too bad. She didn't play an instrument, and didn't know the proper terminology for things, but the banging of the cymbals and the steady beating on the drums reflected some sort of skill. There'd be an occasional cringe-inducing sound that came out, but overall, not too bad.

Skipping under the half-opened door, she smiled. "Guess who's back?"

Her smile died when not Roman or Christian glanced up at her, but Julian.

He had his shirt off and there were definitely more tattoos on him now, highlighting the sculpted planes of his muscled stomach.

Her pulse went from zero to sixty and her mouth watered the moment her eyes landed on the dark hint of hair that trailed beneath his jeans.

His longer hair had been cut too. But it still wasn't a pretty boy look. His head was shoved close on the sides and longer on top, which should have made him look stupid, but, because of the thickness of his hair and the way that it naturally feathered out, looked amazing on him.

Julian seemed stunned to see her there, the whites of his eyes large as he yanked ear buds out of his ears.

The sudden lack of silence was the only reason why she finally noticed they weren't alone.

A loudly clearing throat caused her to jerk and yelp in surprise, twirling around to look into the very hostile face of a glaring brunette with electric purple eyes that could only come from wearing contacts.

The girl was slim, and dressed almost exclusively in black. Her lips were painted a dark, rich red, and her hair was caught up in a sweeping ponytail that highlighted her razor-sharp cheekbones.

"You must be Elisa Adrian," the girl snarled and from the way she said it, with such venom behind it, Elisa knew exactly who she was too.

This was clearly Mandy.

Humiliated, Elisa didn't look back at Julian as she did a sharp about-face and ran away from there like the hounds of Hell were nipping at her feet.

She was halfway to her car when a pair of strong hands landed on her shoulders and turned her roughly around.

Julian was panting heavily, and his throat working furiously, and she didn't think. She slapped him.

Hard.

Hard enough to leave an angry red mark on his cheek.

His nostrils flared and he gazed at her with a look that she couldn't possibly decipher.

"Smile—"

He started to sign, but she couldn't. She couldn't look at him another second. Forgetting all about unpacking her car, or even hiding out in her parents' house, she yanked the key out of her pocket and, jumping into her car, took off in a squeal of rubber.

Elisa didn't return again until much later that night.

She'd gone swimming at the quarry, knowing she needed to call her mom and dad and at least let them know where she was. They'd have no idea why she'd run away the way she had. They had no clue about her and Julian. No one did.

But she was weak and ashamed, because as much as she'd told herself it wasn't true, the second she'd seen Julian her soul had crumbled.

Her mother stood up from where she'd been sitting on the

bottom step when she finally returned home.

"Where have you been?"

In twenty years Elisa knew she'd look just like her mother. They were pretty much the spitting image of one another. Blonde hair and light brown eyes. Her mother had a few extra wrinkles, wrinkles Elisa had probably added to tonight, but her look wasn't hard or angry. Merely worried and confused.

"The quarry for a swim."

Her mother held out her arms, and Elisa fell into them with a heavy, shuddery, sigh. Squeezing her eyes shut when her mom brushed her fingers through Elisa's long blonde hair.

"Julian told us you were home."

Just then a light flickered on in the Wright house. As if just the mere mention of his name had beckoned him to his window. Julian stood silhouetted in his room, and she knew because of the absolute stillness of him that he was looking out at her.

"I'm sorry, Mom," she whispered. "I really am."

Elisa didn't come out of her house for the next two days.

By the time she finally did, she'd come to one unmistakable conclusion. She was just as much in love with Julian Wright now as she had ever been, and she hated him for it.

Chapter 9

"Roman." Elisa rolled her eyes when he snapped her with his beach towel. "C'mon, you know you want to." He grinned a supermodel smile down at her.

Julian wasn't the only Wright to have grown into his looks.

Roman and Christian by any definition were the epitome of male sex gods. They'd been swimming a lot judging by the lighter tone of their hair, which now had an almost burnished look to it, their skin was nice and tanned, and their muscles...well, they pretty much dripped muscled yumminess.

Both boys had their shirts off, they were sitting on her large bedroom window sill, and flexing their pecs with raised brows, being as absolutely goofy as possible as they wheedled and tried to get her to agree to go hang out with them at Chris's girlfriend's pool house.

"Why, do you want me along?" She sighed, placing a bookmark on her Kindle page before powering it down. "I'm an old, uncool college nerd."

"Hells yeah, you are," Roman nodded, giving her big wide eyes, as if to say, *Duh*. "Can you imagine how much game I'll get if I stroll in with a sexy co-ed on my arm?"

"Oh Lord have mercy. You do know that the world isn't actually one giant porn movie, right?"

One thing she knew about her boys, they were horndogs. Sexy as hell, but they were typical eighteen-year-old horny bastards.

"C'mon, Lisa." Roman sat next to her on her day bed and squeezed her kneecap. "You've been hiding yourself away in this musty room half the summer already. You need to get out, act like a person, and like you're, you know, twenty-one instead of sixty."

She stuck her tongue out at him as he rolled his white tank top on. She knew what this was. Neither of the boys was really coming here to ask her because they were just that desperate to hang out with her. Lori had most definitely put them up to it.

Which almost made her feel worse.

"You guys don't really want me there."

"Well..." Christian rubbed the back of his neck. "Thought maybe if you came you could buy us some beers."

She scoffed. "Get bent, losers. I'm not contributing to the delinquency of minors."

Roman growled. "Fine. Whatever. But you really should come. It's gonna be fun, and I heard that Joshua got a kegger anyway." He said the last part to Chris.

"No way, bro. His dad's gonna shit a brick if he finds out." Christian grinned and then fist-bumped his brother.

She gave them both a droll look. "You're not going to leave until I say yes, are you?"

Rome shrugged. "Nope."

"Fine." She jumped to her feet. "Get out of my room so I can change."

"Well if it's all the same to you"—Christian waggled his brows and leaned against her dresser—"I think I'll just stay and watch."

"Freak." She shoved him out of her room. "No, you will not, you want me to go, you act like good boys."

Christian panted like a dog in heat. "I'm good. I can be real good."

"Lord help me," she said with a roll of her eyes and slammed the door in their faces. Those boys were ridiculous.

But they were right. She really did need to get out of the house. Apart from her morning swims she'd been pretty much locked away in her room for the past month. Trying as best she could to avoid Julian, which hadn't even been possible because her room and his were right across the lawn from each other.

Every once in a while she'd see him walk past his window and even though she'd been hidden, she could swear that he knew exactly where she was.

Did it make her a chicken?

Hell yes.

Did she really care?

Hell no.

But she was bored out of her mind. And if she had to brave seeing him in the flesh, than that was just what she would do. She was tired of feeling like a prisoner in her own home.

Ignoring the small voice that kept asking her why she was pulling out her sexiest two-piece she owned—a white thong bikini bottom with a lacy off-the-shoulder top that had a little frill flowing down to her navel—instead of the black one-piece she swam in for her meets, she fluffed out her hair, deciding to leave it down for a change, and even applied a hint of nude lip gloss.

She was a woman. Not a hermit. Not a nun. Julian didn't want her. So what? She didn't want him either. She might be older than all the boys that would be there today, but she was going to at least make them drool when they saw her, dammit.

Yanking out the shortest pair of blue jean shorts she had, she threw on some slinky leather and beaded flip-flops and opened the door.

"Well, boys, how do I look?"

She tossed her arm out to the side and modeled for them. Christian blinked several times, and Roman's mouth dropped.

Smirking, she grabbed her gold aviators off her nightstand and slipped them on. "You can look boys, but you cannot touch."

And when they finally laughed, she did too. It felt good to feel alive again.

She was still smiling, until she got to their truck. They'd traded in their beat-up Corolla for a shiny silver Hemi V-8. A boy's toy for sure.

Sitting in the bed of the truck was not only Julian, but Mandy. Julian was dressed in black and white board shorts and a white shirt that made his tattoos pop. Mandy was dressed in a cherry-red bikini top and shorts. Her pale skin was almost entirely exposed.

If she wasn't wearing sunscreen, that girl would burn in minutes. And quite frankly, Elisa almost hoped it did, which was probably totally evil, but true.

"Get in the back seat, hot stuff." Christian winked at her and then glanced at Rome. "Hey you, think if I tell Melissa that I found me a real woman she'd get too upset?"

"You guys do know riding in the bed is totally illegal, right?"

Rome and Chris rolled their eyes. "Oh God, who invited the mom?"

"Hey!" She slapped Chris's chest and snorted. "I'm just saying, don't cry if you get pulled over by a cop."

Sighing, Roman gave her a cross-eyed look. "Okay, Mom. But

just so you know, if we see a cop, we'll pound on the door, and that means lay down and stay out of sight. Got it?"

Giving him a jaunty salute, she said, "Whatever. But don't expect me to pay the fine if you get ticketed."

"Get in the truck," Christian grumped good-naturedly and Elisa laughed when he pinched her side, but Julian glowered. He had his arm draped across Mandy's shoulder. There were words written on the bottom side of his arm, she couldn't make out what it was, since the script was so elegant and swirly, but it made her curious because it was clearly a new tattoo.

Even though her palms were slick and her heart raced a little harder than it had when she'd been up in her room, Elisa was determined to make it through this day.

She'd already allowed Julian to ruin too much of her summer.

Averting her gaze from both of them, she scooted as far away as she possibly could and to make it even more obvious that she wasn't in the mood to talk, pulled out her cell and popped in her ear buds, playing whatever she had on her phone. Which just so happened to be a blues record.

The country road zoomed past her periphery.

She could do this.

She could.

Squeezing her eyes shut, she swayed from side to side as the truck bounced along the paved road, imagining that she was seven again, the boys were five, and they were just headed to the beach to have a little fun.

Gradually her heart rate slowed and her shoulders relaxed. How many times had she done stuff like this with them in the past? Countless.

And regardless that she and Julian were no longer what they

once were, it didn't mean she had to shut all of them out.

When the truck finally rolled to a stop, she took a deep breath and opened her eyes.

Julian and Mandy were already climbing out of the bed.

Getting up, she scooted down, ready to hop off. Julian turned and held up his hand to her.

Just that simple gesture was enough to make all the nerves she'd worked so hard to squash in the truck ride over come screeching back to life. Averting her gaze, she ignored his hand and got down herself.

Mandy slapped Julian's arm, jerking him furiously back toward her. She couldn't be sure, but Elisa didn't think Mandy knew any—or very little—sign. The few times she'd seen them interact it was with gestures that weren't actually words so much as motions.

If you were going to date a deaf guy, you ought to at least take the time to learn how to talk to him. Just saying.

Roman came and stood beside her just as Christian jogged off, picking up a slim, somewhat attractive blonde and twirling her around with a loud whoop.

That was either Melissa or Christian was seriously about to get dumped today.

"I don't like her."

"Who?" She frowned, turning to Roman.

"Mandy." His lip curled.

Her heart thumped. Not that it should matter to her what Roman thought of Julian's girlfriend, but she'd be a liar if she said that it didn't feel like a small victory to know he at least was on her side.

"I don't like her either." She shook her head. "Can she even freaking sign?"

"Not a damn lick." He growled. "Anyway." He flicked his wrist.

"Let's go have fun."

Already she regretted her rash decision. The pool house wasn't just a tiny little bungalow tucked away behind a larger home.

The pool house was massive, and because all of its glass doors were opened, it had a sort of inside/outside kind of vibe. The lawn was perfectly manicured and so green it would have made a leprechaun envious. There were also gardens.

Not the kind her mother had either. Like this was a garden-garden. With hedgerows and wildflowers, topiaries cut into the shapes of animals. There was also what looked to be an actual maze of vines.

The pool itself was as wide and large as an Olympic sized one, tiled a deep, rich blue, it shimmered like the deepest part of an ocean. The whole place had a kind of Wonderland vibe to it, whimsical and almost fairytale-like.

There were white tables laid out on the lawn, and just like Christian had said, there was a keggerator. Well, actually two of them—and judging by the way the males attacked them, they wouldn't last long.

Elisa recognized a few of the faces as kids who'd been on the boy's soccer team back when she'd gone to school with them.

A few girls waved hi as they passed by on their way to the snack and drinks table, but on the whole, she was pretty much ignored.

She blew out a heavy breath, forgetting for a second that Roman stood right next to her.

"You okay?"

"No. Not really. Rome, I don't know anyone here."

"C'mon, you know me." His blue eyes twinkled. "And Chris. And Jules. Who else do you need to know, really?"

She snorted. Wrapping his arm around her shoulder, he led her toward a row of white wicker lounge chairs.

"Let's go swim, okay?" He gave her one of his swoon-worthy grins, and yeah, she was helpless to resist him.

"It's no fair, how you use that thing. You're so dirty, Roman Wright."

He chuckled and then immediately stopped once she'd pulled her shorts down. She'd completely spaced on the skimpiness of her bottom. In fact, when she glanced up, it was to note quite a number of heads turned her way.

To include Julian's.

He sat in a chair across the pool and she felt his eagle gaze like a hot brand, breaking her out in a wash of goosebumps.

"Dayum, girl." Roman laughed, tossed his shirt on the chair, and then without even so much as a bit of warning, grabbed her by the waist, hauled her into his body, and laid a hard kiss on her.

The shock of it made her go limp in his arms. And she had to ignore her immediate impulse to glance up and see if Julian had noticed.

Whether he had or hadn't, she didn't care.

It was a lie she'd continue to chant to herself until she believed it.

"When did you get so hot?" Roman chuckled less than a second later, and then he scooped her up with a wicked gleam in his eyes and she knew immediately what he was planning to do.

Squirming, she tried to kick out of his arms. But he was much stronger than her.

"Roman! Don't you dare!" she screamed just a second before he jumped feet-first into the pool.

The cold water was an immediate shock to her system and she kicked to the surface with a spluttering laugh.

Roman was already waiting for her when she surfaced.

Her skin broke out in a rush of goosebumps.

With a grin he flicked water at her face and shrugged. "See, have fun, Elisa Jane. We won't bite, though I can't promise that I won't try to kiss you again. You are so hot!" He wiggled his brows and, with a wink, turned and swam away, moving toward a group of guys who were whistling and catcalling as he neared.

With her cheeks stained crimson, she couldn't fight the silly grin that seemed firmly embedded on her face. He was right, have fun. That's all this was, all it was supposed to be.

She didn't look over to where she knew Julian still watched her. She didn't look for Mandy to see if she'd seen her in her bikini. Because it didn't matter. Being petty and silly and mopey wasn't going to solve anything.

Just like her father said, sometimes you couldn't change things. But the key to living was just to do it, even when it hurt and it sucked, because eventually things would get better.

No longer worried about impressing anybody, she sank into the coolness of the water, remembering that she had other passions in life. Like swimming.

Like feeling the waves wash over her skin. Feeling as the water parted beneath the flex and pull of her body. Kicking into a clean stroke, she swerved around the bodies, swimming the length of the pool three times before deciding she couldn't really enjoy the swim as much as she would have liked with the press of people all over the place.

Lifting herself up the wall, instead of using the ladder, she climbed out of the pool and walked to her chair.

She'd forgotten to bring a towel, but the sun was out and there was a nice breeze. Putting her sandals back on and grabbing her phone and ear buds, she looked around for Christian or Roman, but both of the guys were doing their own things and she didn't want to seem like a clingy crybaby.

She didn't see Julian at all.

Which was fine.

Really.

She'd seen him and she'd not become a blubbering mess; she'd passed her first test admirably and was rather proud of herself when she decided to go take a stroll through the maze.

Nobody seemed to care as she left, no one called her name to tell her to come back, and even though she was surrounded by countless people, she no longer craved attention.

Elisa just wanted to be alone for a little while. Tucking her wet hair behind her ear, she walked over to the white wooden garden door and pushed it open. It really was a maze. A massive, green wall of ivy, like the kind you'd see in a romantic drama movie.

Glad she'd decided to come out after all, she walked inside and put her music in her ears, humming "House of the Rising Sun" softly beneath her breath.

How had Julian figured out how to play?

Silly, random, nonsensical question, and yet she hadn't been able to stop thinking about it since the day she'd seen him banging his drum kit in his garage. He wasn't like Tommy Lee good, but he was good.

Elisa shook her head. Why was she thinking about Julian? Why couldn't she just stop thinking about him for like a second? Just one freaking second of her life, was that too much to ask?

Purposefully making her thoughts go blank, she shoved everything out of there except the rhythm of the music. This was her time, and by God she was going to enjoy it, even if it killed her.

She took twist after twist, getting hopelessly turned around, but eventually she'd find her way out. If not, the boys would just have to send search and rescue to find her.

Hopefully they were hot.

She snorted and took another turn before stopping dead in her tracks. The music had helped to mask the sounds of a fight.

Julian was gesturing furiously at Mandy, who was screeching and stomping her foot.

Pretty sure that whatever kind of issues they were having should be private, she made to turn around, and it was just at that moment that Mandy noticed her.

"You little shit!" she yelled, and it wasn't at Julian.

Taking her buds out of her ears, she shook her head. "What? Are you talking to me?"

Planting her hands on her hips, she snarled. She might have said something else, but Julian grabbed her and shook his head hard, his glare hot on her face.

Her already pale face seemed to drain of color, and giving him a violent shove to his shoulder, she turned and ran past Elisa. Forcing her to plaster herself against the wall of ivy so that Mandy didn't bump into her.

For such a little thing, the girl was fast, and she was gone in a blink.

Snapping her mouth shut, heart banging so hard in her chest Elisa didn't know what to do. They stared at one another for an awkward silent minute.

"Sorry," she signed. "I'll go."

"No." He held out his hand and his brows furrowed. "Stay."

She wanted to go. Desperately. Her legs felt shaky, her toes tingly to move, to run away as fast as Mandy had, and yet she might as well have been a chunk of concrete for how fast she moved.

"What do you want?" she asked him vocally, dropping her hands to her sides. Signing just felt too intimate with him now.

He walked up to her, his steps measured and slow, as though he were approaching a wild animal caught in a snare.

And she did feel like one.

She was a riot of emotions. Anger. Desperation. Desire. Fury. Want.

Elisa flexed her fingers.

"We should talk," he signed to her.

She snorted, and suddenly everything she'd bottled away just came pouring out of her. "We should talk? Yeah, let's talk, Julian. Let's talk about the way you bailed on me. How about that? Or how about that letter, because yeah"—she hated that her eyes were getting hot and that soon he'd see her crying; it was the last thing in the world she'd ever wanted him to see—"that was awesome."

She clenched her jaw, turning her face to the side.

Elisa wanted to bite his fingers off when he touched the side of her jaw, nudging her to turn her eyes back his way, she batted his hand away. But Julian was persistent.

"What?" she snapped, tossing her hands up in surrender. "What do you want from me?"

"You, Smile Girl. I screwed up. I thought I knew what I was doing—"

Knowing he'd understand her better if she signed, she moved her fingers with purpose. "Have you told her? Did you tell her what happened that night between us, huh? Because you owe her that much. I told Tom. I broke it off with him. Did you know that?" She didn't give him a chance to respond. Everything came pouring out of her, everything she'd sworn she'd never share with him, never tell him, she told him now. "And not for you either, Julian. But because he deserved better than what I did to him. He loved me and I—"

He grabbed her hands and brought them to his chest. And even through the thin layer of cotton she felt his heat, felt the electricity of his body. When she inhaled, she smelled his soap and mint. This was her Julian. Her passion and her anguish, it was all rolled up into this one man.

Elisa wanted to shove him away, wanted to kick him, wanted to scream at him, even while her body ached for his. No one had ever made her feel the way he did.

She was breathless and terrified, like standing on the edge of a tall cliff, knowing the fall would kill her but excited by the thrill of adrenaline that would come before it.

Those sea-green eyes of his shaded by long black lashes stared down at her with the same type of longing and intensity that raged inside of her.

Finally, it was Julian who let her go.

"I thought I could do it, Smile Girl. I thought I could, but I can't. I just can't. I came home and I told Mandy that day."

She frowned. "You told her?"

He nodded. "I tried to dump her. Because she wasn't you. It just didn't feel right anymore. But she wouldn't let me. She said that if she wasn't willing to let me go, then I couldn't just leave her that way. So I stayed, I tried, because you're right, she deserved better than what I'd done, but it's been fake and she knows it."

Where before the beating of the sun had felt inviting, now she felt scalded by it. Too hot. She wanted to get away from here, from him. From this.

"I love you," he signed.

"No."

"Es," he croaked, and stepped in closer to her, so close that his chest brushed hers, breathing in her air, and making her feel like she was a fish on dry land, gasping for breath.

His hands slid down her waist, his touch gentle but firm. Possessive and wonderful and she couldn't stop the tears from flowing. She felt his fingers speak to her.

"Love you." He whispered it over and over. "Love you so much. Only you, only you."

And then he claimed her lips, taking her with a fierceness that only Julian could. She was so lost to his touch, crying into him even as she wrapped her leg around his, as she plastered herself to him. Every fracture, every tear that she'd worked for months to mend ripped open. As his tongue slipped along side hers, she remembered the days in her bed after the note.

When his legs spread and she felt the thickness of him brush against her aching center, she remembered the weeks she'd spent talking late into the night with Chastity about how she was sure she'd never be able to forget him, that no could ever compare. That it was all her fault because if she'd only been honest from the beginning...

And when his hands massaged her breasts, she remembered herself bent over that toilet and heaving, gasping for breath as the reality of just how much she actually did love him had seized her by the throat. She'd given Julian all of herself and he'd left without a word, and even though she'd done it once too, she'd had valid reasons, but when he'd done it, it hadn't felt so valid. She hadn't felt okay with it. Her soul had been devastated and the truth of it was, she still wasn't okay.

"No," she snapped, shoving him back. "No. I can't do this again, Julian, I don't think I'll survive it."

He reached for her, but she was done. They were over. So over.

Elisa ran.

It took her over an hour to find her way out of that damned maze, by the time she did the worst of the tears were over. She didn't say a word to either Christian or Roman, and she was so grateful that even though her nose was red and her eyes puffy, neither one of them had asked.

And when Julian and her had climbed into the bed of the truck and Mandy was nowhere to be found, neither one of acted like anything was wrong.

When she got home and didn't say goodbye, neither of them made her feel bad about it, either.

And when she refused to come out of her room for the next three weeks, even her parents had seemed to understand.

No matter what she had to do, or how long it took, Elisa would get over him. There was simply no choice in the matter.

Chapter 10

"Elisa, you have a week left before you go back to school, would you please get out of the house?"

Her mother's tone was more than exasperated—it was worried. Which bothered her. She didn't want to make her parents worry.

"Mom, please, just tell them I don't want to go to the movies."

Crossing her slippered feet and leaning against the doorframe, Elizabeth Adrian gave Elisa the look.

The one that'd always made her squirm when she was a little girl. The pinched lips, raised brow, and the one pointer finger that tapped, tapped, tapped across her freckled bicep.

Elisa squirmed on her bed, hugging a pillow to her middle.

"We've been patient, Elisa Jane. More than patient, really. We've not asked you what's going on, but I know that it has something to do with those Wright boys and if you don't tell me right now what it is I'm going to march my butt over to that house and ask Lori what's going on."

Intelligent brown eyes glared at Elisa.

"Mom, please," she moaned. "It's nothing, okay."

She scoffed. "Yeah, and I've got ocean-front property in Arizona.

You think I don't know my own daughter by now? You've been moping from the moment you got here. And, oddly enough, Lori tells me that Julian has been too. In fact, he refuses to come out of his house."

Her eyes widened.

"Yes, now I think you see where this is going. How long?"

"What?" She gave a stuttery, nervous chuckle. "Are you talking about?"

Impossible as it was, her mother's lips pinched even tighter. "Do not play me for a fool, young lady. Now I want to know what's happened between the two of you."

She opened her mouth and then promptly snapped it shut. Her mother knew. There was no way she didn't know. She might not know the particulars, but her asking was merely her method of getting Elisa to confess what she already suspected.

Elizabeth sighed, pushed off the doorjamb, and made her way over to the edge of Elisa's bed, before sitting down. "Baby, what happened?"

What hadn't happened, really? That was probably the more appropriate question. She doubted her mother wanted to know about her sex life, and besides, that was private anyway.

She shook her head.

"He told you he loves you."

She frowned.

"Oh, come on, Elisa. I'm no fool. I've seen the way that boy has looked at you, well, worshipped you really." She snickered. "Ever since he was just a baby in diapers. So what happened? You turned him down?"

Obviously her mother didn't know everything.

"No, I didn't turn him down."

Her pencil thin brow shot into her forehead. "Oh. And did you..." She cleared her throat, and then did something with her fingers that Elisa was pretty sure was a horrible pantomime of them having sex.

"Mom!" She tossed a pillow at her as her face heated crimson.

It took Elizabeth a second to gather herself, by the time she did, she was shaking her head and chuckling beneath her breath. "My baby has finally turned into a woman."

"Mom, oh my God, please, I'll leave this room if you keep it up."

"I'm sorry. I'm sorry." She held up her hands and tried very hard to wipe the smile off her face, but she did a poor job of it.

"You don't seem disgusted by it." Elisa picked at a loose thread on another pillow. A heart-shaped one—well, really more of a blob—she'd been forced to sew at her grandma's house one summer, and this lumpy monstrosity was the end result.

"Disgusted? By love? Are you insane?"

"Who said anything about love?" She wrinkled her nose even as her heart pounded from the truth of those words.

"Oh, baby girl, only love could make someone as depressed as you are right now. That boy is crazy for you—"

She snorted. "Crazy for me. Yeah. He left me, Mom. Wrote me a Dear John letter and stuck it on my dresser. Told me that it could never happen."

"Hm." She placed a hand to her chin. "I mean, I'm super curious when in the hell this could have happened, since as far as I know you two haven't been alone since you've gotten home. You haven't been sneaking that boy into your room at night, have you?"

"Mom, please get serious. No, I haven't done that. And it happened while I was at college."

"Ahh." She nodded. "Well, that certainly explains a lot."

"Like what?"

She shrugged one shoulder. "Like why you were so adamant about not coming home this past Christmas."

Cringing, Elisa glanced down at her socked, pinstriped foot.

Elizabeth tipped her chin up. "Elisa, I don't know why he said what he did. But I know that boy, almost as well as I know you. And the advice I'm giving you now, I wouldn't give you with anybody else. Not even Rome or Chris, God bless 'em but those two are trouble with a capital T."

She clenched her jaw, feeling as though she might cry. Which, how that was even possible anymore was beyond her—it seemed like the past year she could have filled the Saint John River with her tears alone.

"Baby, he loves you. He's just young. And sometimes when you're young, you're stupid. But in his case, I really feel that he was trying to put you first."

She scoffed. "How in the world is breaking my heart putting me first?"

"Honey." Her look turned serious. "I don't know how long you two have been, well, you know." She shook her head. "And the truth is, I don't want to know. It doesn't matter anymore anyway, but you're two years and five months older than him. He only turned eighteen in December. He was still in high school. You in college. What do you honestly think he could have done?"

That had been almost verbatim her reasoning for staying away from him all those years. It was like her mother was throwing her words back in her face and she didn't like it at all.

"Two and a half years is nothing when you're thirty and twenty-eight, but it's an enormous divide when you're fifteen and eighteen."

Dropping her right leg to the floor, she bopped it up and down nervously. "I see him now, Mom, and it's like I don't know who I am.

Like I'm two different people. I love him so much, and yet I hate him."

"You don't hate him." She touched Elisa's chin.

"Then what do I feel?" she snapped, knuckling her left eye and sniffing. "Because it sure feels like hate."

"Love. The same kind of frustrating love I've felt for your father over twenty years now. Love isn't perfect, it isn't always beautiful, and most times it just flat out hurts like hell. But if you're lucky enough to find someone to share in that level of pain with you, then you should count yourself a lucky girl."

She laughed, even as a tear spilled out of her eye. "Only you would equate love with pain."

Giving her daughter a warm hug, Elizabeth patted her knee. "You have to face this, Elisa, and just be open to whatever happens. Julian might be Mr. Right, or he might only be Mr. Right Now, or Mr. Not At All. But either way, locking yourself away in your room like this, it's not healthy. Live your life, baby girl, and let time do its thing."

Wrapping her arms around her knees, she gave her mother a weak smile as she made her way to the bedroom door.

"What movie did they want to see?"

"Oh, I don't know." Elizabeth shrugged airily. "Knowing them, probably some cheesy action flick."

"Oh yay." She rolled her eyes.

"So can I let them know that you're in?"

Why had she avoided telling her mother for so long? The pain was still there, but now with it in perspective, she could see what she needed to do.

"Yeah, I'm in."

It was Julian who came and knocked at her door later that evening. He was actually wearing some color tonight. Instead of the usual blacks and grays he typically wore, he was dressed in dark blue jeans and a hunter-green ringer tee that made his sea-green eyes seem almost electric.

It took everything she had just to swallow.

His hands were in his pocket as he jerked his chin toward the truck, where Christian and Roman already sat waiting.

Waving goodbye to her parents, she grabbed her shell-pink cardigan off the wall hook and was just about to slip it on when Julian took it from her and helped get her into it.

Then very gently, he lifted the hair that'd gotten caught beneath her collar and freed it loose. Just that simple touch made her skin tingle and warm with a rush of blood.

"Thank you," she whispered it to him.

He nodded, as if he'd heard her, then turned and headed for the truck.

"C'mon, then, girl," Roman called out, slapping his hand on the truck door. "We're already gonna be late for the previews thanks to you."

She stuck her tongue out at him and when Julian extended his hand for her to take it, she took it.

Reveling in the feel of his firm hands, so different from her soft ones. His touch lasted just a second longer than it should have, but she wasn't in a rush to free herself of him either. And when he squeezed the tip of her thumb, she squeezed his back.

She wasn't sure what they were saying, but they were definitely saying something.

The truck took off and she was glad she'd clipped her hair back and decided to wear the white capri pants instead the floral skirt. With how windy it was tonight, Julian would have caught several flashes of underwear. Which he probably wouldn't have minded, come to think of it.

Neither one of them spoke, mostly because of how dark it was. But she felt his stare all over her.

She couldn't help but wonder where Mandy was. Was it just going to be three of them tonight?

Deciding she needed to know, she asked him when they stopped at a red light. "Where's Mandy?"

He made the sign of breaking up and her eyes widened.

Had he broken up with her? For real this time?

She would have asked him more, except the light had turned green and it was once again too dark to have a conversation. They could talk into each other's palms, but she wasn't sure she was ready for that level of intimacy just yet.

The drive to the theater was probably one of the most intense fifteen-minute rides of her life. So much so that by the time they pulled into the parking lot, her thigh muscles were popping and snapping like Mexican jumping beans.

Let things happen as they would. That was her new running mantra. If it was meant to be, then it was. And if it wasn't, then it wasn't.

She went back to school in a week, and Julian's life was completely up in the air. She knew nothing about his plans, where he was going, what he was doing. For all she knew he'd be staying in Sunny Cove and bagging groceries. She really just had no clue.

That stupid "ships in the night" analogy came back to her then, but she was determined to have a good night and to take her mother's advice and stop worrying about things that couldn't be changed.

"Thank you," she said to Julian as he helped her from the truck, and she might have kept her hand in his forever if she hadn't spotted Mandy glowering at them from beneath the neon marquee sign.

He must have spotted her at the same time, because a growl slipped from his throat. Dropping her hand, he marched over to Mandy just as Christian moved to join her.

"That psycho bitch needs to learn what 'over' means," Chris snapped.

Feeling as though she'd just swallowed a ten-pound bag of rocks, she shrugged. "Let's just go get our tickets, okay?"

Elisa tried not to stare at them, tried to respect their privacy, but when she saw Julian gesture, "We broke up," her brain suddenly seemed to stop sending signals to her feet to keep walking.

Mandy may not have been able to sign, but judging by the way her eyes drilled holes into him, Elisa knew she'd understood the meaning.

As if aware that Elisa was there, Mandy twirled on her. "Dirty whore!" she spat, causing several couples to stop and stare at them wide-eyed.

Roman tossed his arms out wide and stepped in front of Elisa. "Go away, Mandy, he dumped your ass. Get a fucking clue, how about that?"

Julian was trying to get a grip on Mandy's shirt, but the girl was beating a warpath that headed directly for Elisa.

Elisa dug her fingers into Rome's teal polo shirt.

"You perverted freak," Mandy rushed her, but again Roman blocked her.

This time, Christian also came to his brother's aid and helped tug Mandy back.

Elisa's nostrils flared, aware of the scene they were making. Aware of all the eyes and faces staring at them. Her cheeks flamed scarlet as her blood pressure rose.

She could defend herself, but really, what could she say that wouldn't make it worse? Julian's eyes were dark and heavy as they gazed on her. It was easy enough to read his anguish of the situation, which only made everything about a million times worse.

"Yeah, I don't care if they hear," Mandy yelled, trying to jerk herself free of Julian and Christian's hands. The boys were tugging her away from the main entrance of the theater, around toward the side where the crowd was thinnest.

But Mandy was far from done. "You just couldn't take it, could you? Had to come back for more, you nasty ho. What, men your age just don't do it for ya? You into kiddie porn, too?"

"Enough," Christian roared and gave her a rough shove back. "You're a girl, so I won't punch you for saying that shit, but—"

"But what?" she spat as she adjusted her black corset top.

"You keep it up"—he got in her space—"and I'll conveniently forget that my mother raised me to have manners."

Her snarl was full of piss and vinegar as she shook her head. "She's the fucking pedophile and you guys come at me. Nice. Just wait till I tell everyone."

"Oh, fuck off, Mandy," Roman snapped. "We've already graduated, that schoolyard crap doesn't mean shit to us anymore. Get the hell away from here and don't come back. Ever."

Mandy twirled on Julian, and as much as Elisa hated to admit it, she saw the hurt and pain mingled inside the rage. It was why she kept her mouth shut, not because she was scared, and not even because she didn't deserve it—because whether Mandy believed it or not, Elisa had never meant to hurt her—but because Mandy was hurting as bad as she was.

Elisa knew what it was to feel that kind of pain. So she swallowed her words and allowed herself to look like a coward hiding behind Roman's back when the truth of it was that she was angry too.

Furious, not just at Mandy for saying what she'd said, and not even because of what Julian had done. She was angry because if life had dealt them different cards, this would never have happened in the first place, she'd have been with Julian from the beginning and Mandy never would have been at all.

Raising her hand, Mandy struck Julian's cheek and Elisa winced as the sharp *crack* of it reverberated down the alley, and then, turning on her heel, Mandy walked away.

Elisa had done the same thing to Julian just a few weeks ago, but seeing someone else do it to him, it made her livid, made her see red, made her want to forget the fact that Mandy was in pain and just squash that bitch for hurting him that way.

For a second no one said anything. Elisa could only watch as Julian tipped his head skyward, and his look was so shattered that her soul ached.

"Guess we shouldn't go to the movie now," Christian murmured and signed it at the same time, even though Julian still wouldn't look at him.

But Elisa surprised Chris when she said, "We only missed the previews."

Elisa was tired of hiding, of running away from her problems.

Roman looked shocked. "Are you sure? I don't think there's a person inside there who didn't see that, or at least hear it."

Was she humiliated? Yes. Absolutely.

Did she really want to face the crowd? No.

But who where they to her?

Nobody.

She didn't know them. And they didn't know her.

She wasn't a freak. She wasn't a pedophile, what she and Julian had done, it'd been pure and beautiful and perfect. Did she regret how things had gone down? Of course. But it was nobody's business but hers and Julian's, and she was so over giving a damn what people thought about her.

"Roman, I came here to see some rippling muscles with guns and I'm not leaving here until I do."

She turned when she sensed Julian's eyes on hers. Giving him a brief nod, she turned and led them back to the theater. And even though her hands shook when she handed the cashier her card, she plastered on a brave smile and walked inside.

The theater was crowded, but they were able to find four seats on the very front row. It was uncomfortable as all get out being forced to crane her neck the entire time, not to mention the movie had to be in the list of the top ten worst films she'd ever seen.

But at least it was easy to pretend like she was okay, because she didn't need to talk. She didn't need to smile, or try to be witty, or silly. She could sit there, beside Roman, and feel like it was okay to just be sad for a while and trust that he'd give her the privacy to do it in.

They drove home in silence. Julian had sat three seats away from her at the movie, and now in the bed of the truck, he was leaning against the frame of the bed, gazing off to his left with a pensive, mile-long stare.

She waved goodbye to the Wrights a short while later and when she walked back into her house, she got about halfway up the stairs before it dawned on her that she wasn't sleepy at all.

Her parents were asleep, and she wasn't really in the mood to veg out in front of the TV.

Last thing she wanted was to be trapped in another building, even if it was her home. So she walked back outside and headed toward her mother's sitting area in the garden.

The moon was full and golden. The sky a deep navy blue with fluffy streaks of white dotted upon it.

Crickets chirped and bullfrogs sang. It was slightly chilly for being so late in the summer, but that sometimes happened living so close to the coastline.

Elisa wasn't sure how long she'd been outside when she became aware of a presence standing behind her.

With a gasp she twirled around and grabbed her chest. It was just Julian.

His hair was messy, as though he'd been running his fingers through it. He hadn't changed out of the shirt and jeans he'd been in earlier.

"You scared me," she gestured and then frowned. "How did you know I was out here?"

He was quiet as he joined her on the bench, his palms ran along his jeans a couple of times before he finally said, "I saw you walk outside. I figured it out."

The wind picked up his clean, soapy scent, and she couldn't seem to help swaying toward him.

He grabbed her hand, and it was like all the nerves that led to her heart connected from his fingertips to hers. Every glide of his callused fingers over her skin made her tremble.

She swallowed hard when he finally began to talk into her palm.

"I'm sorry."

She shook her head and he looked at her lips, waiting for her to speak to him. The moon was so full and bright that it was more than enough light for him to see her by.

Her gaze devoured him. Julian was just one of those guys who commanded attention wherever he went. And not just because of his piercings and his tattoos, but because of his quiet intensity, the way he moved through life with purpose and intent.

"It's okay. I deserved it."

He frowned. "No, you didn't. She should never have said that to you. Roman told me what she said." His jaw clenched and she couldn't stop herself from using her free hand to palm his whiskered cheek.

A visible tremor coursed through him when she did.

"She loved you, Jules. We do stupid things when our hearts break."

Hanging his head, he said, "Yes. We do. Like me leaving you."

She took in a shuddery breath.

"We could never really have worked, could we, Jules?" She enunciated each word slowly so that he'd have no problem understanding her.

"We could work."

"I don't see how." She sniffed as a single tear slid down the corner of her left cheek. "I'm going back to college in a week."

Leaning forward he pressed a kiss to her wet cheek, and there wasn't a power strong enough on Earth to have forced her to move from that spot.

"Elisa, I got accepted to two colleges."

Lips tugging downward, she gave him a wimpy smile. "That's good, Julian. I'm so proud of you."

"I didn't know where I wanted to go, so I toured both."

Biting onto a corner of her lip, she asked him, "And where did you decide?"

"I hadn't decided until about fifteen minutes ago."

She cocked her head. Confused why he'd switched the subject the way he had. What did colleges have anything to do with—

She gasped. "Are you saying that—"

He nodded. "I'm going to go to Ashe College."

She'd read that wrong, she had to have. "Say that again."

His lips tugged into an indulgent smile. "Smile Girl, I tried and I failed, and now I've come to one unavoidable conclusion."

"What's that?"

"That home is wherever you are."

The silence of the night didn't tremble with tension, but instead with hope and possibility. Another tear slipped from her eye, he groaned as he swiped it away with the pad of his thumb. Then his beautiful, long-fingered hands framed her face and she knew he was going to kiss her, but there was something she needed to tell him first.

Grabbing one of his hands, she rested his palm against her throat and said, "Look at my lips, real good."

He nodded and she shivered under the weight of his gaze.

"I. Love. You."

He closed his eyes and this time it was his turn to shed a tear. But just to make sure that she drove the point home, she whispered it to him one more time.

"I love you, Julian Wright. I think I always have."

And whether he understood all of what she'd said, didn't seem to matter to him. Tugging her into his arms he did what she'd been dying for him to do since the morning she'd discovered him missing.

He kissed her with reckless, wild abandon.

Neither of them went to sleep that night, they stayed on that bench, kissing, and touching, and learning not only each other's bodies, but each other's souls.

As much as Elisa wanted to take him to her bed and make love until the sun came up, that was impossible right now. For either of them.

So they remained where they were until the sky turned a soft shade of peach and pink.

"Julian, I'm going back two whole weeks before you get there." She frowned as she spoke the words on his palm.

Tracing the line of her cheek with his thumb, he smiled. "Then we wait. Because that's all we can do. We've waited eighteen in a half years, Smile Girl, what's two weeks?"

For their last few days together the two of them were inseparable. They'd find any open moment they could to sneak away and kiss and touch and dream about the day they'd finally get to come together again without the threat of parents or siblings getting in the way.

No one acted surprised by their relationship. In fact, everyone gave them looks that almost seemed to imply, *Well duh, what in the hell took you so long?*

When the day came that she packed up her Beetle and drove back to campus and she watched as his silhouette became smaller and smaller in her rearview mirror, those two weeks suddenly seemed like a lifetime away.

Chapter 11

"**W**ill you stop fidgeting? You're making me have to keep redoing your eyeliner," Chastity growled and gave Elisa a stern look.

"I can't help it," she cried, grabbing hold of her stomach. "He's going to be here today."

Chas sighed and then chuckled, setting the black eyeliner down. Her bold magenta silk top and black slacks attested to the fact that Chastity hadn't even bothered to change out of her work clothes before cornering Elisa and telling her in no uncertain terms that she would be in charge of her beautification for the evening.

"Lisa, if you're worried that the kid's changed his mind, I really doubt it. You guys have only been Skyping every night, and making goo-goo eyes, it's really enough to make a girl nauseous."

She swatted Chastity's thigh.

Chas had dragged her into the bathroom almost an hour ago, plopped her down on the toilet seat, and taken out all manner of torture devices. Flat irons, foundation, mascara, eye shadow, everything Elisa never did to herself.

Julian was going to be here any minute now, and the thought of it made Elisa feel almost sick.

Dropping her head to her hands she groaned, which caused Chastity to shriek and slap her hands away.

"You're ruining your makeup. You have got to stop."

"Easy for you to say," she snapped. "You and Luke have been together almost two years, it's so easy for you guys."

"Yeah, easy." She rolled her eyes. "I don't think so. You know he wants me to move in with him. Me." She thumped her chest and sounded like the idea was absurd. "I mean, really, we'd kill each other. We almost did that summer he stayed here."

Elisa's jaw dropped. "You didn't tell me he'd asked you that."

"Yeah." She smiled, and then, picking up a jar of blush, dusted a little on Elisa's cheeks. "Asked me over the summer."

She laughed. "He got used to your yummy cooking."

Snorting, Chastity rolled her eyes. "He probably did, the jerk."

But she said it fondly. Elisa knew how much Chas loved Luke, and vice versa. Luke was Chastity's Julian. It was easy to see how sprung Chas was whenever she looked at him. Even when they fought, Elisa never worried that they wouldn't work things out.

What they had was what Elisa wanted too. And there was only one guy in the world that she wanted that with.

Julian Wright.

"You should move in with him," Elisa said.

Chastity shook her head. "I couldn't do that to you, Lis, the monthly payments would be way too expensive to just bail on you that way."

But Elisa could hear that even though Chastity was saying no, she actually really wanted to say yes.

It would have been perfect if she could have convinced Julian to move in with her, especially since he hadn't settled into his dorm yet, it would be unbelievably convenient, but they were only just starting out and moving in together was a big deal. Huge, really. There was only one more step after that, and that was a walk down the aisle.

As much as the thought of having him here every day and every morning appealed to her now, she also knew that that level of intimacy could ruin such a fresh relationship by putting too much stress and expectation on it right out of the gates. It was why she'd never tried approaching Thomas with it.

"Look, I'm a big girl. I can figure something out, but if you want to go, Chas, then don't worry about me."

The beatific smile that broke across her friend's face told Elisa that she'd said the right words.

Just then a heavy knock sounded on the front door.

Elisa leapt to her feet, nearly knocking Chastity down in her excitement.

"Whoa!" Her friend held up her hand as she clutched the bathroom sink. "Try not to kill me."

"How do I look?" she asked and twirled.

Chas had even gone as far as picking out her outfit for the day. A hunter-green thigh-length summer dress that showed off the toned muscles of her body beautifully.

She'd secretly been thrilled at the selection since the color green always tended to remind her of Julian.

"You look stunning," Chas said without a hint of sarcasm.

The knock sounded harder, more impatient. Stomach swarming with a nest of butterflies, Elisa glowered. "Do not come back home tonight, Chastity. I'm warning you."

With a laugh and a finger wave, her friend walked out of the bathroom first. "I wouldn't dare. Now you knock 'em dead and make that boy remember that there is only one Elisa Jane Adrian."

Rolling her eyes, she swung the door open and both girls stood there stunned. But for entirely different reasons.

Elisa's heart raced as she gazed at Julian. Dressed in a black leather riding jacket that highlighted his wide strong shoulders and dark blue jeans that hugged his body, she was glad that she'd planned to keep things home tonight.

His eyes were only for her as he stared right back, biting onto the corner of his lip piercing and sucking it into his mouth.

Tucked under his arm was a motorcycle helmet. And if she wasn't desperate to get her hands all over him, Elisa might have considered asking him to give her a ride.

"Wow," Chastity sighed, and then cleared her throat with a sharp jerk of her head. "Holy wow, batman, you never told me how hot he got, Lisa."

Julian's lips twitched, he'd obviously understood her.

Even though Chas dressed femininely now, deep inside she still had that dark streak. Luke was about as sweet a guy as they came, but Julian was definitely the stuff bad boy fantasies were made of.

Tattoos, piercings, leather, and a motorcycle. It didn't get much more sexy than Julian Wright.

She grabbed his hand and yanked him in the door, even while she none too gently shoved her friend out.

"Yeah, and he's all mine. So go away."

Chastity snickered. "Just answer me this." She placed her hand against the door as Elisa tried to close it. "Are the brothers this hot too?"

Elisa rolled her eyes. "Goodbye, Chas."

She pouted.

"You have a boyfriend, Chas."

"I know, but a girl can have a fantasies too. Are they coming to this school too?"

"Go away, Chas."

"Just a yes or no, come on, Julian, put me out of my misery." She turned and pleaded with him.

His eyes sparkled as he nodded once quickly.

"Yes." She rubbed her hands together. "At least your boy still loves me," she said with a twist of her lips and then, with a melodramatic glower, she stomped down the steps and headed toward campus, where she'd be spending the night with Luke.

Elisa had just barely closed the door when Julian was on her.

Lifting her off the floor, until she was forced to wrap her legs around his waist, he slammed his mouth to hers. His kiss wasn't gentle, or tender, but she didn't want it to be.

They banged into walls as he slowly made his way toward her room, groping her with one hand, while groping the wall with the other. His excited, frenzied movements made her groan deep into his throat as she clawed at the back of his skull.

All the nerves were gone. Replaced by a fire that made her burn and ache down low, made her feel as though she might combust if he didn't slack it now.

If it'd been possible to climb inside his skin just then, she was pretty sure she would have.

Clothes dropped at the speed of thought.

Shirt.

Pants.

Underwear.

Her dress.

Her bra.

Her panties.

All of Chastity's hard work was gone in less than three minutes.

Then he was shoving her down onto the mattress and she laughed as he crawled on top of her. But she stopped laughing when his strong hands parted her thighs and his head dipped straight toward the center of her.

Julian had clearly come with one purpose in mind and he was making no bones about what it was.

Good, because she felt exactly the same way.

"Oh my God," she moaned at the first touch of his tongue, grunting as he stroked her masterfully.

And she didn't care at all that her makeup was now hopelessly ruined, or that he'd never even complimented her dress, because she felt his need for her in every touch and caress of her sensitive flesh.

She came so unbelievably quick that she hadn't even been prepared for it. The sweeping tide of her orgasm frightened her with its ferocity, making her thighs twitch as he wrenched every last drop of pleasure from her.

But just because she'd come, Julian was far from done. He kissed his way back up to her lips, making a short detour between each breast, planting a wet kiss on each nipple, and stoking the fire deep inside her to a raging inferno all over again.

She'd just had the best orgasm of her life, she should have been sated, but her hunger had only grown.

When his lips finally founds hers, she tasted her scent on him, but it didn't freak her out or make her ashamed. She felt like she'd branded him as surely as he'd branded her.

His fingers danced along her forearm as he said, "Can't wait, Smile Girl. Slow later."

She nodded, because she didn't want him to wait either.

Then he was slipping hot and hard deep inside her and all she could do was sigh and close her eyes with relief that he was finally where she'd needed him to be all along. Elisa met his flexing hips thrust for thrust, crying out as his mewls of pleasure spurred her own desire to incendiary levels.

His eyes squeezed shut, and now it was her turn to dance her fingers on him. "Close?" she asked.

He nodded.

She was about to tell him to just come, that she could wait, he'd already given her one orgasm, but his fingers reached down between them, until he found her hardened nub and just that touch of his deft, callused fingers against her sensitive core made her cry out his name as pleasure washed through her.

Julian hugged her tight as his own spasms made him jerk and flex on top of her. It took a second for her beating heart to get under control.

They finally blinked their eyes open a moment later, both of them sweaty, and wearing huge grins.

"Welcome home," she said, and he gave a soft snuffling laugh before burying his head in her neck and breathing her in.

Just as he'd promised, Julian was slow afterward. He cleaned them up, and then stretched out beside her. The sensual glide of his fingers up and down her skin had her panting almost immediately.

They'd never had time before to just sit and trace each other, learn the little nuances of one another.

She sucked in her stomach when his fingers danced along her pubis line, laughing because it tickled so much.

"Stop," she laughed, and swatted at his hand, but now he knew where she was ticklish, and he was merciless in his attack.

Tossing his muscled leg over hers, he pinned her down and played his fingers along her skin like a master violinist. Making her sigh and laugh and gasp as the pleasure spiraled tighter and tighter inside her.

He talked with her as he worshipped her. Every once in a while signing, "So beautiful," or, "Smile Girl. My Smile Girl."

And she came alive for him, whimpering when he'd suckle her nipples into jagged little peaks. Running her fingers through his hair when he'd nuzzle the hollow of her throat.

There wasn't a part on her body that he didn't take his time learning. She gasped, she sighed, and when he leaned in to kiss her, she reversed their position, so that now she could be on top of him.

Straddling his thighs, she gazed down at him. He was a marvel of lines and swirls and raw masculinity.

Wearing a small smile on his face, he nodded. Signing at her that she could touch him anywhere she wanted to.

Biting her lip, heart pounding so hard—not because she was nervous, or timid, or even shy, but because Julian was a feast to her senses—she decided to start slow. Using just one finger she traced the word tattooed on his collar.

"Spirit," she read it out loud.

His fingers moved, anticipating her question without her even having to ask. "Because I am only as strong as I believe I can be."

She smiled and continued her exploration of his body. Julian was covered in tribal swirls, but also words. Words like 'will', 'determination', 'knowledge', and 'faith'.

Grabbing his left arm, she traced the letters she'd noticed a few weeks ago when he'd had his arm draped over Mandy.

"Reality?" She said it like a question and cocked her head.

He ran his fingers through the tips of her hair that danced along her right breast.

"What does that mean, 'reality'?"

She got lost in his sea-green eyes. And when he smiled, so did she.

"I got it after I left you."

Elisa tried to glance down, but he wouldn't let her. Tipping her chin up, he sighed and traced his tattoo.

"This was my reminder."

"Of what?"

"That life isn't a fairytale. I lost my muse, Mandy was my reality."

She glanced at his other arm. There was an empty space beneath his tribal swirl. "What will you put there?"

His grin grew wide. "Destiny."

She laughed. "Then that's the only arm you can ever put across my shoulder."

Wrapping his arms around her, he forced her to lie down on him. Julian captured her lips and there was no more talking after that. Only kissing. Only tongues dueling.

She moaned, undulating slowly along his rigid length until she almost came from the friction.

But Julian wouldn't allow that. He shifted, so that he now rested against her heated core and neither of them broke their kiss as he slowly slid his way home.

It was several more hours before either of them came up for air.

Elisa was now kissing her way up and down his body. They'd made love, for hours. Not just sex, but love. Caressing, fondling, kissing, kneading, groaning, nipping, and nibbling their way all around each other. Her body was sated and so was his. In fact, she was even a little bit sore, but her need to continue touching him hadn't abated in the slightest.

She traced the rigid scar on his right leg from his calf all the way to his upper thigh. She shuddered remembering that day. He tipped her chin up, and his smile was small but satisfied.

"It's okay," he said.

The memory of it was still so strong, that she shivered, and planted a row of tender kisses along his leg. "I don't know what I'd do without you, Jules."

"You'll never have to know that again, Smile Girl."

And this time when she shivered, it wasn't from excitement, or pain, but from the memory of something her grandmother had once said to her the day of her grandfather's funeral.

"Never speak in absolutes, Eli girl, because you just never know what tomorrow might bring..."

Chapter 12

Elisa hefted a stack of papers she'd gotten Xeroxed. It was a notice for a new roommate. Plans were well underway for Chas and Luke to move in together; classes had started last week, and now it was just simply a matter of them finding an apartment they could afford to rent.

In the meantime Chas had had her half of their apartment packed up and waiting in boxes. Rent would be due in another three weeks; she really needed to find a roommate soon. If she didn't get one within the week, she'd very likely have to ask her mom and dad to help float her, which she really didn't want to do. As it was, she'd have to pay a larger portion of the rent this month regardless, since she wouldn't expect anyone to pay a full share when they wouldn't have been living there the entire month.

Leaning against the red brick building, she waited for Julian to come out of his English class.

They'd not had a chance to spend more days together after that first one, well, not alone anyway. Chas had had to move, and Julian had been sweet enough to come by each night and help her pack, but Elisa was desperate for a little alone time with him.

If she hadn't been so desperate for the rent money she would have just opted to keep the place for herself, but there was no way she could swing the seven hundred dollar a month rent on her own. Not when her monthly paychecks totaled up to a princely sum of eight hundred bucks and some change.

She'd have just enough to pay rent, get some gas, and if she were really lucky pay her cell bill, and that would be it. Which, of course, was a slight problem, as she'd have to eat at some point.

Elisa sighed.

The campus was super green thanks to all the melt off from the snow last winter. The towering trees, and old colonial era architecture of the college was already beautiful on its own, but add to the fact that she now had Julian here, every day and every night, and suddenly the world felt just a little bit brighter.

The chiming of bells signaled the end of the hour and she shoved off the building, watching the doors open as the students came marching out.

Her heart flipped in her chest the moment she spotted him. Julian no longer just dressed in shades of black and gray, he was still really careful in the clothes that lined his closet, the jeans were all dark, and the shirts either very light colors, or dark colors with enough range to them that he could easily pair them together and not clash.

But even in a place like college where kids no longer felt the need to dress like everyone else because they were free to express themselves as they were, he still stuck out.

There was a potent magnetism to him, one that made anyone who looked at him—man or woman—take a double look. And then sometimes even a third.

She smiled when he glanced up, and even though she was across the street, she felt the strength of his stare move through her like a hot current.

A brunette dressed in a short blue jean skirt and a teal floral top came up to him and waved, her cheeks dimpling prettily when he smiled back at her. It was obvious she was flirting with him.

And why not? The last thing she felt was jealousy; she was secure in Julian's feelings for her, and it was even kind of a turn on to know that he was so wanted and all he wanted was her.

Elisa would be the first to admit that a girl would either have to be dead or a lesbian not to notice that Julian was in an entirely different stratosphere when it came to levels of hotness.

Chuckling to herself, she shoved the papers into her book bag, not bothering to zip it up before jogging across the street to catch up to him.

She tried to hide her smile when she took his hand and the girl's blue eyes dimmed just a little. Elisa didn't want to crush the girl, but she was also making no bones about the fact that he was very much taken.

Julian waved goodbye to the girl, and then, without missing a beat, wrapped his arm around her waist and pulled Elisa in for a short but sexually charged kiss.

"Mm," she moaned, breathless and slightly dizzy a moment later, then slid her hand underneath his hunter-green t-shirt and danced her fingers on his hot skin. "Who was that?"

Giving her one more hard kiss, he shook his head. "Not sure. She's in my English lit class."

"She likes you." Elisa verbalized it as she took his elbow and started to head toward the quad.

His soft chuckle made her lips twitch.

"I've only got eyes for you, doll face."

"Doll face." She stuck out her tongue, gesticulating rapidly. "You've been hanging around Chris too long."

He nodded, and then snatched one of the sheets from out of her book bag.

"Hey." She swatted his shoulder. "Give that back."

But he was looking down at the page with a frown and hadn't seen her speak. "What is this?" He glanced up, signing it a second later.

Thinning her lips, she took the sheet out of his hand and crumpled it back into her bag. "You know Chas is moving out."

His frown only grew larger. "You're asking a stranger to move in with you."

She rolled her eyes. "It's not like that, Jules. I'll be careful. It's not like I'm going to room with a guy anyway. So you don't need to worry."

He shook his head and stopped her, forcing the students walking the sidewalk behind them to pass around.

"I'm not comfortable with that."

She sighed. "Julian, I can't move into a dorm this late in the game. I have to stay in that apartment."

He grabbed her fingers, kissed their tips, and then pointed to his chest.

She frowned. Not that that wouldn't solve all her problems, or that a part of her didn't desperately want that, but...

Wiggling her hands free, she signed. "Jules, think about it. We're dating."

His eyes widened as if to say, *Yeah, and?*

"We're just starting out."

His brows lifted even higher.

Cocking her hip out, her lips tugged into an exasperated frown.

"What if we get on each other's nerves?"

"I can wake up every morning and make you happy."

Her stomach flopped.

"I read in bed late at night." She tried again.

He shrugged. "When I'm tired, I'll just give you an orgasm and make you fall asleep."

Snickering, she covered her mouth when a group of people glanced their way with perplexed frowns. She sometimes forgot how foreign it must look to others to see people speaking sign, it was just second nature to her.

"Jules, I'm serious. What if this doesn't work out?"

His face went serious as he said, "So am I. I love you, Elisa. And I know you. You know me. It's not like this is really that new. We've been preparing for this for years. You know I'm right."

She tucked an errant strand of his inky hair back into place. Elisa loved touching him. Loved being with him.

Would it really be so scary?

"Julian, what if you live with me and then find out you can't stand me?"

He shook his head rapidly. "Can't happen. We've already been through more stuff than most couples, Smile Girl, and we're still together. I could say the same to you, what if you wake up one day and realize you hate me?"

She might have laughed that off, except that she could see a hint of the unsure fifteen year old he'd been peeking out of his gaze. "No," she said, and then placed his palm to her chest. "I could never hate you." She finished her sentence vocally.

It was crazy how just one smile from him made her feel. Like there was nothing impossible, nothing she couldn't do. Nothing she wasn't capable of. Julian made her feel complete.

"But I still don't know, Jules. I'm terrified of messing this up. I love you too much to even think about—"

He kissed her. Swept her into his arms, and held her tight against him. So tight she could feel the tremors coursing through him.

How had she ever thought she could live the rest of her life without this? Without him? How had she managed to do it for the first twenty-one years of her life?

"We don't go into this blindly," he said. "We realize we'll have problems, and we prepare ourselves for it. But I want to be wherever you are, Smile Girl."

And she proved his nickname for her correct, as that smile stayed firmly in place for the first of the day.

Chastity and Luke finally found a place a week and a half later. Which was perfect, because Lori had scheduled a drop off of some of Julian's artwork around that same time.

He'd moved out of his dorm with very little fanfare. Christian and Roman had also stopped by to help Julian move a few pieces of his furniture into her apartment.

Well…their apartment now.

Since they now shared a bed, Lori had opted to leave his bed at home, and instead she'd brought down his art easel and a few other art supplies.

At least that's what she'd claimed.

But when the truck had rolled to a stop in front of her place, Elisa's eyes had almost bugged out of her head. There'd been rolls of tarp, and sheets and sheets of canvas, thick pads of sketching paper, watercolor paper (she'd never known before then that there were actually different kinds of paper for the style of art used) not to mention hundreds of bottles of ink, paint, and empty canisters full of sketching pencils.

She'd had no idea just how much of an artist Julian actually was. She should have known, considering he was majoring in art. But yeah, somehow she'd never really taken it into account.

By the time they were done, Chastity's room had been converted into an artist's paradise. And even though it was crowded it was also cozy. Lori had bought five giant metal racks to stack everything neatly on it. They'd laid down the tarp, set up the giant easel, and in a flurry of hugs and kisses, said their goodbyes and they were gone.

Elisa turned to look at Julian, who merely signed, "No going back now."

Turning into him, she wrapped her arms around his stomach and pressed her cheek to his chest, then tapped out a quick, "This is going to be a fun ride, Jules," on his bicep.

"Speaking of rides," he chuckled and then swept her up into his arms and walked them both into the bathroom. Laughing, she wrapped her arms around his neck.

"Where are you taking me?" she asked him.

"Shower. We're dirty."

She nibbled on her lower lip and then gave him a seductive little grin. "I'm super, super dirty."

They didn't leave that shower for a long, long time.

She ran out of the bedroom naked as the day she was born with a wild look on her face the next Saturday. "Jules." She stomped her foot to get his attention.

Julian was super sensitive to the vibrations of sound. He was sitting on their couch, sketching on his art pad, wearing nothing but a pair of lime-green boxers.

She'd bought him the underwear. Elisa was determined to see him in brighter colors. Even if it was only in underwear, she loved Julian's sense of style and didn't want him to change at all, but she also didn't want him to be afraid to try different things.

He glanced up and even though her heart was currently clipping in her chest at a furious pace, she couldn't help but grin. He was just so adorable.

His hair had always driven her wild. Just the way it feathered out whichever way it wanted to, she'd asked him to grow it back out again, which he was letting happen. Of course it also meant this his bed head was in that weird, funky stage as it grew out. But she didn't care.

"Where is my bathing suit?" she asked.

He sucked his lip ring into his mouth and his eyes got a wicked glint to them as they swept up and down her very naked body. "I think you look fine."

She clapped her hands and gave him a stern look to get him to focus. "I'm serious, Jules, I have to be at the meet in half an hour and I can't find it anywhere."

He frowned and jumped to his feet, suddenly aware that as much as she might want to, there was no time to flirt.

Her scholarship depended on her doing well not only in school, but in athletics too.

"Which one?" he asked a second later.

"The one for the trials today!" She tossed up her hands and ran back into their room, getting down on the floor and lifting the bed skirt. She hadn't worn that particular suit for months, so the odds of finding it crumpled under the bed wasn't good, but she'd literally looked everywhere. They had regulated suits they had to wear, and she hadn't yet washed the other ones.

It was stupid, she knew, to be freaking out about one suit when she had three others she could grab. But she was superstitious that way. She had meet suits, a heat suit, and she had her trial suit.

A grunt sounded behind her.

Twisting, she huffed at him.

Julian was leaning against the frame of the door, with her blue spandex swimsuit dangling from his finger. He was also doing a terrible job of hiding his laughter at her.

His blue-green eyes twinkled.

Shoving to her feet, she snatched the bathing suit out of his hand. "Jerk," she said, but there was no heat behind it.

Lips twitching he hauled her into his body, and gave her a kiss that left her breathless. When he pulled back, Elisa was clinging to him like a whimpering, baby kitten.

Framing her face, he touched the tip of his nose to hers and rubbed it gently as his fingers tapped out, "You're going to do great," on her cheek.

Lashes feathering her cheeks, she allowed herself just one more second in his strong arms before reluctantly pulling away.

"Today's the trial for the start of the year. This is when we find out who makes the team and who gets to ride bench. I'm just..." Her wrists fluttered. "I'm nervous."

"You're the fastest swimmer I know. You own this." Then he took her hands, gave them a quick kiss, and patted her bottom. "Now get dressed before I forget that we don't have time for me to go down on you."

With a hungry little groan, she spun on her heel, and raced to get dressed.

They made it to the pool with less than five minutes to spare.

Coach gave her a withering look. If there was one thing Coach Carl emphasized, it was timeliness being close to godliness. Cringing, because this was so not the way to start her junior year, she raced to the locker rooms.

Ava—a slim, raven-haired minnow of a swimmer with precision-like turns—glared at her as she skidded to a stop in front of the lockers. Ava was tucking all that hair into her neon blue skullcap.

Not only was Ava a good swimmer, Ava was also Elisa's main rival. The girl had been gunning for her ever since she dumped Thomas.

She'd had no idea why until the day she caught Thomas and Ava holding hands on the quad.

"You're late," she spat, yanking her goggles out of the locker and slipping them over her head. "Carl's gonna ride your ass this year, Adrian, mark my words."

Already frazzled, Elisa shoved her pants off, tossed them into the locker, and, grabbing her goggles and black skullcap, slammed the door shut in Ava's smirking face. "Like hell he will. I'm still the best fifty-meter swimmer he's got."

"You wish." Her upper lip turned into a snarl. "I'm gonna take that spot from you this year and it's gonna be so sweet when I do."

They had two minutes to get out there. But Elisa had to get some things off her chest.

"It's over, Ava. Thomas and I are over, I don't know why you still care. But you need to drop it. Let's just be teammates." Elisa roughly shoved her hair into her cap.

Rolling brown doe eyes, Ava shoulder bumped her hard enough to make her stumble back into the lockers.

"I feed off adrenaline, Adrian. You don't know it yet, but I'm about to eat you up."

Then, sauntering off, she exited the locker room.

Feeling more than just a little sick to her stomach, Elisa headed out too.

She was the last one out. Coach Carl's whistle was a loud, ear-splitting shrill when she walked out.

"Get your ass over here, Elisa!" He yelled.

Her face turned crimson under Ava's hard, triumphant glare.

Elisa wouldn't lose her scholarship if she didn't win the trial. But it set a bad precedent to everyone else. She'd been captain of the team last year, regardless that she'd only been a sophomore, and there was no way in hell she could let anyone take that title away, especially not Ava.

There'd only be four heats. Two for the females, and two for the males.

Because this was an upperclassman trial—meaning everyone here, to include Thomas Mason who was currently standing behind his evil girlfriend and rubbing her shoulders, were experienced swimmers—they were doing a sort of face off to establish captain, co-captain, etc. for the start of the season.

Coach Carl had a very unorthodox way of training. Two swims, one short and one long, that would set the pace for the rest of the year. Elisa normally thrived on challenges, but today she was already feeling out of sorts thanks to being so late, not to mention that little *chat* with Ava back there, had done nothing to settle her nerves.

"You know the drill," Coach Carl said to the six of them.

Three females and three guys. Her entire year depended on today. Elisa scanned the faces of the people she'd come to know fairly well in the past two years.

Sad to say, but she was friends with none of them.

At one point she'd been in, thanks to dating Thomas. But after that whole fiasco, sides had been chosen, and hers hadn't been it.

"I hope you ate your Wheaties today, kids." Carl's eyes fairly glowed with the thrill of adrenaline. "'Cause it's on. Ladies, get to your starting positions."

Thomas and Ava kissed and then did some sort of funny fist-bump thing before she walked over to lane one.

Elisa was right beside her on lane two. Getting to her starting position, she worked her muscles loose for a while. Swinging her arms around, rolling her neck from side to side, kicking out her legs, and smacking her quads hard so that the blood would get to pumping through them.

"On your marks!" Carl's voice echoed through the rafters.

Elisa blew out a deep breath and got into her stance. Her muscles quivered like a taut bowstring as she waited for the "Go."

This was her favorite part of an event. The adrenaline that pumped through her veins, making her tense and queasy all at the same time as she waited to hear the beep that would signal the start of the race.

"Get set."

There was a black box inside of her, one that she shoved all her worries, thoughts, emotions, anything that made her lose focus on the task of winning, that's where she went to right now.

There was no Ava.

No classes.

No bills.

Nothing.

Just her and the water.

This was a one-lap heat. Blazing, lightning quick.

No matter what Ava said, Elisa owned freestyle.

"I got this," she whispered.

The blast of the *beep* jerked her into a frenzy of motion. Vaguely she could hear the calls and screams of teammates rooting Ava on.

And though Elisa had no voice calling out to encouragement to her, she knew her man was right there with her, cheering her on the best way he could.

Releasing a breath as she dived beneath the water, she kicked and pumped her arms in a rhythmic motion. *Stroke. Stroke. Stroke. Breath. Stroke. Stroke. Stroke. Breath.*

Over and over.

It felt like no sooner had she dived into the water than the race was over. She shot up the instant her fingers touched the wall, gasping for breath, as she waited to see who'd won.

Short distance was her race. Her time to shine.

Coach Carl jogged across to their side of the pool and leaned down with the stopwatch in his hand.

Ava and Jenna—the other girl they'd been racing against—had their goggles shoved up. The room suddenly felt unnaturally quiet, as if everyone waited with bated breath for the results.

Elisa had felt Ava's wake pulling at her, she knew they were close, probably within half a second of one another. Races could be decided by as a little as a tenth of a second; this level of competition wasn't for the faint of heart.

"Ava, you clocked at a twenty-five point two four. Elisa." His smile widened. "You came in at twenty-four point eight nine. Your fastest time yet. Good job. You'll owe me laps later for being late."

Then he stood and snapped his fingers, ordering the guys to their starting points.

Ava smacked the water before swimming off in a huff toward the side of the pool.

Elated, Elisa got out too. She'd have to swim the four hundred meters once the guys were done, but she was relaxed—she'd won the heat that mattered. Elisa wasn't a long distance swimmer. Not for sport anyway. There was no way she could win that, which was fine—that swim she could just relax.

Smiling broadly, she glanced over to where Julian sat. He was standing and clapping his hands for her. Too overcome with happiness to just walk away from him, she jogged to his side and pulled him down by his shirt for a swift kiss.

Coach wouldn't like it, but she was already in trouble, so she might as well make it worth it.

He sighed into her lips as his fingers traced words across her back. "You won. I knew you would."

"Elisa!" Coach cried and she grimaced.

"I have to go. Love you, Jules." Then, patting his cheek, she jogged back to where Coach and Ava stood.

The raven-haired witch didn't seem at all impressed by Elisa's spontaneous show of affection. Ava rolled her eyes and turned aside, whispering something to Jenna.

"Now you owe me another ten minutes," Coach Carl said. "Get your asses back to the line. Time for the four hundred."

"Yes, Coach." Elisa saluted him smartly, too happy to be upset by the fact that she'd be forced to stay behind an extra twenty minutes after everyone else.

As expected, Elisa took the early lead; her short, powerful burst off the starting block helped her to maintain that long lead, at least until the first turn. By the second turn she was lagging, and by the third, she was so hopelessly behind the other three that there was no chance of her catching up.

She came in a whole ten seconds behind Jenna, which, in swimmer's time, was nothing short of pathetic.

Elisa clung to the edge of the pool, gasping for breath, chest heaving in and out as she blinked the chlorine out of her eyes. The moment she did she saw Thomas bending over to give Ava a hand up.

Needing to get out of the water so the guys could have their turn, Elisa slipped under the floats, intending to head to the ladder to get out. Her arms felt a lot like wet noodles now. She was just about to step up when something sharp and painful crashed into the side of her head.

Grunting underwater, she grabbed the side of her aching head, completely disoriented by what might have happened. Bobbing to the surface she looked around in a daze. Rubbing her aching temple, she watched as Julian rushed to her side. Ava and Thomas turned and walked off in the other direction.

Jules hand was warm as he gripped her wrist and hauled her out. Without a care to getting his clothes soaked, Julian pulled her tight into his arms.

"Are you hurt?" his fingers gestured rapidly.

Elisa was confused by how angry he seemed to be. She blinked. "What happened?"

"That bitch kicked you in the head," he said it quickly, nostrils flaring as he glanced over in their direction.

"What?" She said it out loud. That didn't make any sense. Ava might have been her rival, but she'd never been petty enough to stoop as low as that. "Jules, are you sure it wasn't something else?"

His sea-green eyes blazed. And even though she could sense the tension of his anger, he rubbed his hand gently up and down her arm. "I saw her do it myself. That guy saw it happen too. It was obvious."

Thomas had seen Ava do that?

Now that really didn't make any sense. Not that she didn't trust Julian, she did with her life, but it was hard to believe that that had really just happened. But there was no denying that her temple was still pounding, especially now that the shock was wearing off. She almost felt like she'd been kicked by a mule.

Unfortunately, no one else seemed to be aware of what'd happened. All the swimmers, to include Ava and Thomas were leaning around their kneeling coach and listening as he gave out his beginning of the season instructions.

They were the leaders. They were upperclassman. Strive to always excel, blah, blah, blah. She'd heard it before, and had no desire to walk over there now.

Elisa sat with Julian as she waited for Coach to wrap things up. Jules was still tense, still casting murderous glances at both Ava and Thomas whenever they'd walk past.

And Elisa might have been tempted to write the whole thing off as just a fluky misunderstanding, except that when Coach finally released them for the day, Ava turned back around and with a tiny smirk said, "Have fun swimming extra laps."

Thomas didn't say anything, but his jaw clenched when he glanced between her and Ava and there was a look in his eyes that Elisa vaguely recognized. She'd seen it the night they'd broken up: regret.

He stood there looking at her for a moment, his shock of red hair standing up around his head. Julian vibrated with tension so thick that Elisa had had to rub her hand up and down his arm in a soothing stroke to make sure he didn't do something stupid.

If Thomas meant to say something, she'd never know it. With a heavy sigh, he gripped Ava's left elbow and almost dragged her behind him toward the locker rooms.

"Elisa, laps!" Coach cried out, twirling his finger in the air as he'd walked off toward the men's locker room, confidant that even if didn't hang around she'd do exactly what he'd ordered her to do.

Julian squeezed his eyes shut.

"Baby," Elisa spoke into his palm. "I have extra laps I have to swim, can you just sit there and wait for me?"

His nostrils flared as he gave her a choppy dip of his head.

"Hey." She patted his chest until he looked at her.

When he did he still seemed angry. "I wanted to punch her." He said it slowly.

And though she'd generally frown at the thought of him wanting to do bodily harm to a lady, she didn't quite feel the same way when it came to Ava March.

But she didn't want to escalate the situation either. Whatever it was that Ava had done today, Elisa would make damn sure she never gave her the opportunity to do again.

"I love you, Jules. I'm okay though, I promise. I'm a big girl."

His knuckles grazed her cheek tenderly. That touch made her smile, it also made her anxious to hurry up and finish because there were a couple of things she wanted to do with him tonight.

One of which had to do with her, and him, their bed, and a big bottle of chocolate syrup.

Chapter 13

A month later Elisa sighed as Julian straddled her sore aching body and began to knead lavender oil onto her naked back. She'd stripped down just to her bikini thong.

Coach had been brutal today, two hours of almost nonstop swimming, her body was spent, but unfortunately she didn't have the luxury of getting to go to sleep just yet. It was past eight at night, however she still had to wrap up her English lit paper for Stringer's class in the morning.

They were studying John Milton's neoclassical epic poem *Paradise Lost*. The point of the paper wasn't to expound on the fall of Satan and the rise of man, but on what the movement itself was all about.

Neoclassicism was the concept of restrain and order. That given the flawed nature of mankind, putting limits on what one said or did was actually better than trying to reach for something beyond expectation. Elisa couldn't figure out how the movement had gotten to be so popular, in fact, she'd even been irritated by it, everything had had a "this is this and that is that and the world is flat and don't look to the stars" kind of feel to it. Maybe she was an anarchist, but she much rather preferred the freedom of romanticism to neoclassicism.

But maybe the real reason why she couldn't enjoy neoclassicism was because being with Julian wasn't reasonable and sensible. It was carnal chaos, combustion and fire, madness and an all-consuming passion for more. They were the very definition of romanticism.

It was like playing with fire. Beautiful to look at, but dance too close to the flame and you'd be consumed by the very fire that'd given you life.

She sighed, sinking her face deeper into his pillow.

Elisa wondered if Julian had any clue that on the mornings when he'd be the one to get up early for class, she'd roll over to his side of the bed and breathe in his scent. She loved the way he smelled, nothing in the world smelled quite like him—spicy and cool and clean and sweet all at the same time.

"What's the matter?" Julian tapped out on her lower spine, as if sensing the heaviness of her thoughts.

Grabbing her laptop, she powered up her voice recognition software before slipping the mouthpiece on. It'd been Julian's idea, so that when Elisa's hands weren't free she could still carry on a conversation with him.

"I don't know what to do, Jules," she said, tilting the screen so that he could read her words.

An instant later he asked, "About what?"

"About my major."

His hands were so firm and strong as he kneaded out sore muscles. She wiggled when he hit a particularly sensitive spot just above her hipbone. If he didn't watch it, she'd soon be nothing but a puddle of goo at his feet.

The man had the most amazing hands ever. Elisa couldn't decide what she liked more, his body or his hands. Most days, it was body. Definitely his body.

But then he'd touch her with his masterful hands and her opinion would flip on a dime.

She tugged her lip between her teeth at the feel of his hard thickness poking her bottom, causing her to squirm, and him to groan in response.

"Stop moving or I'll get off," he said and then gave her a gentle swat, which didn't bank her heat a single bit.

Elisa had told him before the massage that as much as she would love to fool around for hours, she just didn't have the time. So she'd made him promise to be good. With Julian it was a feast or famine type of thing for her. If they started, they'd go at it like bunnies for hours, so it was best in a case like tonight to not start at all.

Problem was, just getting a massage from him, smelling his familiar scent, and knowing that beneath the sleep pants he was commando, made her forget things like papers and responsibilities.

She buried her face in the comforter and forced herself to think about Ava, which helped kill the lust immediately.

"Sorry," she said, and then muttered, "Not sorry." Elisa thought she'd said it softly enough the mic wouldn't pick it up, but it had.

Feeling the tremors of his laughter coarse through her, she tossed him a flirty grin over her shoulder.

Sometimes, like now, when the reality of their situation impressed itself upon her, Elisa felt like her heart might burst from too much emotion. The past month with Julian had been amazing, feeling more like a dream than real life. Like it couldn't last. Like being this happy for this long was impossible, that right around the corner waited heartbreak and broken street.

That soon reality would come crashing down around them, they'd fight, or she'd wake up one morning and realize that the bond they'd developed growing up side by side had been nothing more than a temporary phase and now that they'd scratched the itch they were over it. Or she was over it, or he was over it.

His knuckles grazed her cheek; his sea-green gaze swallowed her up. "Roll over," he signed.

Yanking out the mouthpiece, she rolled onto her back. Julian set her laptop on the floor, and then lifted her palm up, sliding his fingers slowly through hers.

The air quivered between them like the delicate string of a spider web in a gentle spring rain. Elisa swallowed hard, unable to tear her gaze from his as his eyes grew soft and his heavy thigh moved between her own.

With their hands still joined, he traced the valley between her breasts. She gasped, rising up to meet his touch, stomach quivering at the trail of heat he left in his wake.

There was a type of intensity to utter silence that was hard to define. Julian made no moaning sounds as he caressed her. He only breathed, in and out. Filling his lungs with her scent as she filled her own with his.

Soon his lips joined in on the assault of her body. She bit her lip, swallowing the cry of his name when he took her nipple into his mouth. There was an inherent eroticism to silence she'd never understood before. Each kiss, each swipe of his tongue on hers, where only the sounds of their breathing could be heard painted everything in shades of the illicit.

They weren't in their apartment, in their room, safe from the prying eyes of the outside world. No, they were Romeo and Juliet stealing away into the night, hidden in shadow, quiet despite the racing of their hearts, knowing they had only this moment to come together. Being with Julian felt like eating from the forbidden fruit; that was the type of passion they shared.

The cool metal of his pierced tongue, coupled with the heat of her body, made her shudder and tremble beneath him. Releasing her hand, Julian slid his fingers up her throat, framing her slender neck in his callused grip.

She tipped her jaw, arching up beneath him as she clutched at his back, scoring his flesh with her nails.

His other hand moved down, down, down, sliding beneath the hem of her thong, until his questing fingers slipped between the slick folds of her sex.

The hand on her throat moved up just a little, just enough for his thumb to stroke her bottom lip as two of his other fingers slipped deep inside her.

Elisa sucked his thumb into the heat of her mouth as their eyes met.

Julian couldn't speak, but she heard him nonetheless.

She swallowed hard as his fingers pumped harder. Wanton, and desperate to get him closer, she clawed at him, wanting him all over her. Wanting not only his body, but his soul too.

When she tried to close her eyes, too overcome by the sensations coursing through her, he shook his head, refusing to allow her to look away.

Needing him to feel as crazed as she now did, she moved her hand from his back, to the piece of steel wrapped in velvet beneath his pants. A thrill of adrenaline pulsed through her when his body trembled. Julian yanked his thumb out of her mouth, planting his hand firmly on the mattress beside her hip for support.

The muscles of his arm flexed and trembled as she rubbed her thumb along the tip of him, her movements sure and strong as she stroked him. Playing with his piercing and watching as his pupils dilated. He pulled his lip into his mouth, and she found herself mimicking his movements.

His nostrils flared, so did hers.

He blinked, and she did too.

He thrust harder, she moved faster.

She was so close, so close. It was hard to focus, to concentrate on keeping her eyes open, wanting desperately to lose herself in the darkness of the little death, to shatter in her lover's arms as he splintered in hers.

Then he smiled, just a small twitch of his lips before he claimed hers, and the sweetness of that touch, mingled with the wicked play of his skilled fingers deep inside her channel, it was her undoing. With a final flick of her wrist, Julian came for her as she shattered beneath him.

Nuzzling her cheek, he said, "Now, let's talk."

Laughing, feeling suddenly much less sore, she gave him a peck before getting up to clean herself off. She was just turning off the sink when Julian padded in behind her.

Tossing on a pair of comfy sleep pants and top, she then leaned against the doorframe, and crossed her arms as she watched him. His eyes found hers in the mirror. Elisa could read him so well that she understood the question in his gaze and answered immediately.

"This is nice." She shrugged. "You and me. I like it."

Turning off the tap, he wiped his hands on a towel before pulling on his sweats. Julian wasn't as ripped as some of the guys on her team; he didn't have eight-pack abs. But his stomach was lean and chiseled, and he had that vee where abs met hips that always drove her absolutely crazy, made her weak in the knees.

His body was a masterful work of art and Elisa didn't think she'd ever get tired of looking at him.

Her smile grew wider when he came back to her side and took her in his arms, running his hand lightly up and down her spine, making her skin tingle.

"I like it too, Smile Girl." He kissed the top of her head.

Thinking it was probably safer to do her homework on the couch instead of the bed, she grabbed her books and laptop. Julian joined her just a minute later, bringing her a glass of water and a red apple.

Giving him a grateful nod, she took a bite and then handed it back to him. He took a bite right over the top of hers. They shared everything. Their lives, their bodies, even her apples.

Tossing his legs up on the coffee table, he asked, "So talk to me—what's wrong with your major?"

"Other than the fact that I still don't have one," she snorted, "nothing."

His lopsided grin caused her heart to stutter. "You're a junior. I'm sure by now you've found something that interests you."

Nibbling on her lip, she gave him a suggestive wink.

Planting a hand against his chest, he groaned and shifted in his seat as if adjusting himself. "As much as I don't think I'll ever get tired of hearing you say that, Smile Girl, I'm pretty sure I know what it is you should major in."

She frowned. "You do? I'm not even sure."

With a *tsk*, he pointed to her book. "Do you know how much your eyes sparkle when you're reading those books? How animated you get when you talk about ancient texts?"

Elisa tucked a strand of hair behind her ear. "Do they?"

He shrugged. "Heard you talk about library science once."

"Yeah, but there's no money in that." She sighed, thinking about her class. Jules was right, she'd never had so much fun in one of her classes as she was now having in Stringer's, studying up on the Renaissance, and medieval literature. Learning how to properly have intelligent discourse over the merits of Picaresque versus Bildungsroman.

Bildungsroman, like what in the hell was that, right? She'd never even heard of it in high school, and yet now she didn't even need to think about the fact that it was a style of writing that focused on the psychological and moral growth of the protagonist from youth to adulthood. She was barely a month into her English course and Julian was right, she was completely fascinated.

Stringer wasn't really going in depth with the various styles, the course was mainly just an overview of literature through the centuries, but she'd be lying if she said she didn't wish to delve deeper into the subject matter.

"So what?" he signed a moment later. "As long as you're happy, then who cares about money?"

She snickered. "Happy doesn't pay the bills."

Wrinkling his nose, he patted her knee. "If you can make enough to live, then that's all you need. Money can't buy you happiness, Smile Girl."

Scooting into him until her thigh pressed up against his, she brushed her fingers through the feathered tips of his hair, drowning in his sea-green eyes.

"When did you get to be so smart?"

Her parents were probably not going to be very happy about her pursuing such a degree. When she said there was no money in it, she wasn't lying. Elisa would basically be little more than a starving artist, but just the idea of someday traveling to Rome, or London, and getting to tour the great libraries, smelling the musty odor of leather-bound books that rarely saw the light of day anymore filled her body with a jolt of adrenaline.

Snorting, he crossed his arms behind his back and, closing his eyes, rested his head against the cushion. Before getting back to work she trailed her finger down his bristled cheek, tomorrow she'd go to her counselor and officially announce her major.

Gradually they settled into an easy rhythm, and Elisa was happy. Unbelievably, and utterly happy, even if their schedules had become so crazy, stupid busy that they had to schedule date nights well in advance.

"You need to come," Chas said, her voice clearly exasperated over the line. "Luke set this thing up, and he'll totally freak if no one shows."

Elisa sighed. She hated partying. It just wasn't her thing. Every once in a while, maybe, but she was swamped with homework and training for the final meet of the season.

What made this one so much more important to her than any of the others was that Coach had mentioned the possibility of Clive Amsler being there. Clive Amsler was literally one of the best swim coaches in the world of competition. For the past twenty-six years he'd had the distinction of training five Olympians, two of who were multiple gold medal winners.

Just the thought of it made Elisa want to puke. Coach hadn't out and out said that Clive was there because of her, but the intent had been clear enough.

"I'm not sure, Chas."

Julian frowned and asked who it was. For the past two months Jules had been more than a little stressed out. He was just barely scraping by with a low B average in his math course, and he was only doing that good because his nights were mostly spent in the library with his nose in his books.

His eyes were bloodshot and ringed with dark circles. He hadn't been sleeping much. She tossed her leg over his lap and brushed her fingers through his hair. "Chastity," she mouthed.

With a weary sounding sigh, he nodded before taking a bite out of the apple they were sharing.

She felt bad for him. Elisa still couldn't understand why when someone was majoring in the arts, math classes were still such an important requirement, but they were.

This was the first time in seven days that they'd actually had a chance to sit down and eat dinner together.

Her because of her extreme swim schedule, not to mention the twenty hours a week she worked as the campus library secretary, and he because of the major cram sessions he'd been doing just to help him stay afloat in Calculus.

"Come on, Lisa," Chas wheedled. "Your meet's not until next Saturday, you'll have plenty of time to rest and recover before then."

Elisa was the type of athlete who barely left her house during swim season, let alone to party and drink. She really didn't want to go, but maybe that's exactly what she and Julian needed—some time to relax without the stress of books, or meets, or not getting to see each other all piling up.

"Hold on." Setting the phone on her lap, she looked at Jules.

Tonight he only wore a pair of gray sweatpants, and his naked chest full of tattoos and pierced nipples was making it a little hard for her to concentrate. Dressed up or dressed down Julian was the yummiest specimen of male beauty she'd ever seen. Feeling inordinately pleased that he belonged to her, she flicked his left nipple—just because she could.

The latent heat that always simmered between them flared to life in his eyes. Julian shifted on his seat, giving her better access to his body. She smirked.

"Chas, wants us to go to this party thing that Luke's set up for Friday. You free?"

Taking the final bite of apple, he tossed it in the wastebasket and nodded. "I was going to meet the tutor, but I could bump it back to Sunday if that helps." His warm fingers wrapped around her waist, bringing her more firmly on his lap. She nibbled on her bottom lip when he began to kiss the hollow of her throat.

Swallowing a groan, she picked the phone back up. "Chas." Her voice came out a barely audible sound.

"Elisa?" She could practically hear her friend's sudden confusion.

"We'll...ah—" She grunted when his tongue joined in on the assault of her body, and dragging her nails down his scalp, she cleared her throat. She needed to get off this phone now. "We'll go," she rushed out.

Her body became warm and languid when his callused palm slid down the waistband of her sleep pants, cupping her ass.

"What in the world are you... Oh," Chas snickered. "Oh, that's naughty, Lisa."

Stomach quivering when his mouth locked over her still-clothed right nipple, Elisa clicked the stupid phone off and tossed it onto the seat opposite them.

Chastity would understand, and if she didn't, Elisa really didn't care at the moment...

She walked out of their bedroom and then did a twirl holding her arms out to her sides.

"Well, how do I look?" Elisa asked once she faced Julian.

It was Halloween night, and Luke had set up a couples-themed dance for his frat. There wasn't really a set theme so much as a request that if you were a couple you tried to match.

Julian had snorted and said no way in hell would he wear a costume. He had however let her put him in a little bit of color. She'd bought him a dark red plain t-shirt and stylish jeans that were scuffed at the knees. Elisa had also brought him over to the dark side by getting him out of his skater shoes and into black converse sneaks.

She on other hand had gone all out with her costume.

"Well?" She smiled when she walked out of the bathroom, beginning to feel a little awkward the longer he stared. Maybe the wig and makeup had been too much. She patted her head nervously.

But his impassive face soon turned into a large grin. Wiping his palm down his jeans, he signed, "So hot."

Wearing a lopsided grin now, she patted her stomach. The moment she'd seen the Queen of Hearts outfit in the store window she'd been possessed by the need to slut it up a little for him.

Normally Elisa dressed pretty conservatively. Just jeans and a nice shirt, occasionally a dress or skirt, but nothing super racy. This thing stopped short at mid-thigh and puffed out around her bottom in such a way that every time she took a step it flounced up and down, exposing so much of her thigh that at times she felt a brush of cold air against the bottom curve of her ass.

Chastity had tried to convince her to go for the white thigh highs with red hearts lining the sides and garter straps to hold it up. She'd put her foot down with that one and instead she'd gone for the black fishnet, which, yeah, wasn't that much better at covering her up, but at least she could pretend. However, she had taken Chas's advice to get the black suede pumps with the four-inch heels.

Advice she wished she'd now said no to, she was not used to wearing heels at all, and already her ankles were throbbing their displeasure.

Getting up from his seat, he came to her and threaded his finger through her black wig.

Blushing, she snatched the piece of synthetic hair out of his hand. "Feel silly," she signed.

Julian grabbed her fluttering hand and brought it to his lips, giving her a sound kiss on the back of it, before letting her go to grab their jackets out of the hall closet. A knock sounded on the door just then.

Emotions all over the place, Elisa jogged to open the door. Chastity stood on the stoop wearing a red-corseted devil outfit, complete with horns and tail. Her long dreds were piled high on her head in a sort of modified ponytail. The smoky eye make up she'd done made her caramel-colored eyes pop almost like neon.

Julian whistled as he helped Elisa into her jacket, buttoning her up from waist to neck without missing a beat.

Chastity laughed. "Thanks, Jules. And do you always let him dress you like a baby?" she teased, saying it not only in words, but in sign.

Once Chastity and Luke had discovered how serious she and Julian were, they'd decided to learn how to speak to him. Elisa had the best friends in the world.

"Come on, admit it," Julian told her back, "you'd love it if Luke was half as romantic as I was."

"You Wrights were blessed with a healthy dose of ego, I swear." Chastity slapped his shoulder and Elisa couldn't help but chuckle, it was so true.

"Now come on." Chas rubbed her arms. "I'm freezing my ass off in this getup." Turning on her heel, she jogged back toward her still-idling car.

Locking up behind them, Elisa handed Jules the key and gripped his elbow to help keep her steady. Already she was majorly regretting her decision to wear these heels, but she was stuck for it now.

She settled into Chas's passenger seat with a loud sigh of relief. It wasn't horribly cold out tonight, it really could have been worse, but Luke had apparently set the party up to happen in the McCreary Woods. Which was cool, but would mean her nipples would be frozen nubs by the end of the night.

Elisa didn't speak until they were on their way. "How big is this thing gonna be?" she asked, making sure to sign it so that Julian could be included in the conversation.

Chastity shifted gears as she cruised to a stop at a red light. "Um, well, about that."

She frowned. "What?"

Tossing her a tight grin, Chastity gave a self-effacing chuckle. "So apparently once everyone found out where the party was going to be held, well, it got kind of big."

Julian tapped Elisa's shoulder to ask her what had made her suddenly grimace. Making sure to keep a running narrative of not only her conversation but Chas's as well, she asked, "Like how many are we talking here?"

"Umm." She took off again, threading her way through the back roads of the campus that led toward McCreary's haunted woods. "A couple hundred, I'm thinking. Which is good," she was quick to interject, "'Cause you know they were trying to raise money for the animal shelter. And by the way I'm pretty sure the entire swim team is gonna be there." She didn't look at Elisa when she said that.

Tossing herself back on the chair, Elisa shook her head. "Chas," she sighed, "you know I only agreed to go because I didn't want Luke to have a bad turnout. You know how I feel about my teammates, though."

Things had not cooled since the night of the "incident" at the pool. In fact, Ava's hostility toward Elisa had only seemed to increase. She was always careful to never do anything to land herself on Carter's radar, but the last thing Elisa wanted to do was to spend an evening around her and Thomas. For whatever reason, Ava had it in for Elisa and was determined to make her life a living hell.

Chas tapped her fingers on the steering wheel. "Not my fault. Ava came up and invited herself and Luke didn't know about you guys. I'm sorry, babes. You really mad at me?" She gave Elisa a brief, worried frown.

Julian patted her shoulder. He wasn't much of a fan of Ava either.

"No. But don't think it escaped my notice how sneaky you were by not telling me."

She shrugged. "Well, I'm not gonna apologize for that. You know how much I hate crowds, but I had to go cause of Luke and you had to go cause of me. But it's not all bad—Chris and Rome are coming too."

Elisa smiled at Julian as she'd told him. Even though they were all going to the same school, neither she nor Jules had had much of a chance to hang out with the guys. Only about once a month or so could they all find the time to get together. Roman and Christian had done exactly what she'd expected them to do in college: they'd joined a frat, gotten involved in team sports, and basically lived the party lifestyle.

Chastity turned down a quiet country ride, causing them to bounce up and down in their seats. Without streetlamps, the car was suddenly cast in deep shadow, with only the faint light of the moon to see by.

Elisa dropped her hands to her lap.

"Hey," Julian tapped onto her bicep, "we can go whenever you're ready, even if we have to call a cab, okay?"

Smiling, and so thankful she'd fallen for Julian instead of Rome or Christian, she nodded. "Okay, thanks babe," she said, even though she knew he couldn't hear the words.

Chastity frowned and glanced between them for a minute.

"What?" Elisa asked when she said nothing.

Shrugging, she smiled. "Nothing, we're almost there."

Looking up, Elisa saw the lights. Elisa wasn't really sure who owned McCreary Woods, but it was private property that somehow the college campus was able to access.

Only once had she come through the woods, and that had been during the day for a long fifteen-mile jog with Julian. Even in the wash of morning sun it'd felt creepy. It probably had more to do with her imagination than the fact that the trees looked like something straight out of Washington Irving's "Legend of Sleepy Hollow" and it was a known fact that murders of crows nested there, which all added to its spine-chilling allure.

Elisa had never wanted to come back, but she had to admit it was the perfect setting for a Halloween bash.

"I strung up the lights, what do you think?" Chastity asked when she parked the car.

Getting out, Elisa smiled. The white stringed lights that Chas had hung up through the dead branches all over the place, coupled with the strobing pulse of lights from the DJ booth set in the back did make it kind of funky cool.

There were punch booths set up, food tables, and instead of

chairs to sit on, Luke had scattered square bales of hay all around.

Elisa was glad for her friends warning, because she was right, the place was packed with bodies dancing, laughing, eating, and making out. A few faces she recognized immediately.

She spotted Ava and Thomas who looked like they must be a matching Romeo and Juliet snipping at each other at the refreshment stand.

"It's pretty damn awesome, actually," she said, turning and smiling at Chas, who now looked like a proud peacock.

Chas was studying to become a bio-medical engineer, but her passion of late had been design, much to Elisa's surprise. This was the fourth party Chas had set up for Luke, with each one looking a little better than the last.

The moment Chas's eyes began to twinkle, Elisa knew Luke was headed their way.

Luke sidled up next to them just a minute later and instead of wearing a devil costume like Elisa had assumed he would, he wore an all-white suit with a golden halo crown on top.

A very light-skinned black man with unbelievable green eyes that spoke to his Irish-African heritage, it was easy to understand why Chastity had fallen in lust with him the moment they'd met. Thankfully the feeling was totally mutual, Elisa loved seeing them together.

"Hey sexy," he said to Chas, wrapping his arm around her waist and planting a big kiss on her lips before turning to Elisa and Julian.

Freeing his hands, he jerked his chin toward Jules's outfit. "See you didn't get the memo."

Shrugging almost sheepishly, Julian settled his arm across Elisa's shoulder. She wiggled deeper into his warm body, wrapping herself up in his clean scent of soap and mint. No matter how cold she got,

Julian always stayed warm—he was like the world's best blanket.

"Do you want some punch?" he asked a second later.

Nodding, she watched as the two guys walked off to grab their drinks.

Chastity threaded her arm through Elisa's. "So you guys are super serious, huh?"

"I don't know," she said even as her stomach grew hot with nerves.

"Pft." Blowing a raspberry, Chastity led her toward a stack of hay sitting before a large bonfire and took a seat on the edge of one of them. "Yeah, and I'm blind. The way he looks at you, holy hell, it makes my insides want to combust."

"Chastity, you're such a freak. What would Luke say if he heard you?" Elisa laughed, glancing at the guys who were now in the middle of an animated discussion.

Luke and Julian, she'd discovered, had had much in common. Namely, their love of rhythm and blues.

It always astounded Elisa how much Julian could hear without actually hearing. He loved music, sometimes she'd come home to find him lying down on the couch with the stereo turned to full sound and his eyes closed as he'd tap his foot to an invisible rhythm.

Which she was sure drove her neighbors nuts, but since the Ken and Barbie twins liked to blast their music through all hours of the night, she was hardly going to ask Jules to turn his down.

Chastity grinned.

"Anyway, how are things going with you guys?" Elisa flicked her wrist, switching the subject. Not that she was shy talking about her relationship with Julian, but it was just one of those things where what they had still felt so new and intense that she wasn't really sure how to define it.

"Good. I guess." She sighed, slumping her shoulders as she toyed with a thread of hay. "He graduates next year."

Elisa's stomach flopped at the sadness tingeing her girlfriend's eyes. It was easy to forget sometimes that she was now a junior and Jules only a freshman. Next year she'd be the one saying the same thing.

"Oh hell," Chastity said, squeezed her hands. "I totally forgot, Lisa, you and I are pretty much in the same boat, huh?"

Feeling a little like someone had deflated her balloon, she shrugged. "Well, at least we still have almost two years before we have to talk about that."

Just then a hard kiss popped the left side of her cheek. For a second Elisa grinned, thinking it'd been Julian, until another pair of lips popped her right side.

Twisting around, it was to see Rome and Chris—dressed in gladiator getups—grinning back at her.

The guys had begun to look even more alike as they aged. Almost to the point that if she hadn't known better she would have thought them identical twins instead of fraternal triplets.

They'd filled out nicely, and the costume only helped to highlight their now bronzed and muscular physiques. Chris's hair was still slightly lighter than his brother's, and his blue eyes just a little more intense, but apart from that they were almost carbon copies.

It didn't help that they'd bought the exact same outfit. A dark brown pleated leather skirt with wrist cuffs and a leather collar around their necks. On their feet they had leather sandals that wrapped up to their knees.

Leaving their rippling abs and nicely toned biceps on full display. She could admit to having the tiniest of heart flutters.

The Wrights could never be accused of failing to make an

entrance.

"I think you guys got had." Elisa grinned and pointed at them.

"What?" Roman's brows twitched as he glanced down at his body and then at Chris, who was having the same reaction.

Snickering, Chastity nodded. "Yeah, somebody forgot to sell you the rest of your clothes."

"Oh please, you know you love it." Christian made his pecs pop as his eyes gleamed.

Roman sat beside Chastity, and Chris beside Elisa, both guys grabbing their hands and petting it seductively.

"I say we ditch the losers and you fine ladies come and dance."

"Like hell you will." Luke slapped Roman upside the head, which caused him to laugh and hop up from his seat.

"You heard that, did you, damn." He snapped his fingers. "Maybe next time." He winked unabashedly at Chastity.

Elisa knew Luke owned Chas's heart, but the woman had an eye for hotness. And good looking was good looking, no matter which way you diced it.

Julian cocked a brow, giving Christian a knowing look.

Wiggling his own in return, Chris gave her another kiss on her cheek. Elisa laughed as Julian growled, but it was all in fun. Grabbing her hand, he got her to stand so that he could take the spot she'd been sitting at and then patted his knee.

Tossing Chas a silly little grin, she took a seat and sighed when he handed her the drink.

"I think it's sick the way you let her use you like a chair," Roman teased. "But come to think of it..." He pretended to adjust himself.

Julian tossed a clump of hay at his brother's head and he merely chuckled before sitting down on the bale beside them.

The boys were currently single but actively looking for their

Mrs. Wright now.

Taking a sip of the hot punch, she played her fingers along Julian's slightly furred forearm.

"So how are things going, guys?"

Christian shrugged. "It's going. But I'm thinking of switching majors."

"Already?" Chastity chuckled. "You've barely even begun."

He grimaced. "Yeah, but I'm not sure I'm actually that serious about being a horticulturalist."

Julian snickered, signing quickly. "Are you serious? I thought you were kidding."

"It's where all the chicks were, dude."

Roman chuckled, yanking Chas's drink out of her hand just as she was about to take a sip.

"Lord save us," she growled at Luke.

"Hey, babe, you've got some straw between your boobs," Julian tapped out on her spine. "I would get it but…"

Laughing, she glanced down. "Do I really? Oh jeez, how in the world did that happen?" Yanking it out, she released it into the nippy fall breeze before turning and giving him a kiss. "Thanks."

Chastity's mouth opened wide.

Casting a worried frown at everyone else, who didn't seem to be in on whatever kind of surprise Chas had just elicited, she asked, "What?"

"Do you guys just speak by osmosis or what? Y'all are freaking me out just a little bit."

"Oh, yeah." Roman snorted. "You mean that strange Morse code shit they do."

"Morse code." Elisa rolled her eyes. "You guys are crazy."

"Its not even sign." Chris nodded. "It's weird, right? Rome and I always said that shit was weird."

Chastity and Luke nodded.

"But," Luke said, "I see them do it all the time."

"Do you really?" Chas turned to him before looking at everyone else. "I only saw you guys do it for the first time tonight on the drive here, and just now. What are you guys saying?"

Blushing, even a little embarrassed, Elisa glanced at Julian. "Care to explain?"

Nipping her shoulder, he tossed up his hands.

"Oh, gee, thanks. You're such a help, Jules, really."

He tweaked her nose.

Pretending to be annoyed, she swatted him away. "I don't know, we just talk. We can't always look at each other when we do it, I guess we did kind of develop our own style."

"Um, yeah." Roman leaned forward and began doing a dance of fingers across her bicep.

Elisa gave him a perplexed frown. "And just what was that?"

"My point exactly." His blue eyes twinkled. "And for the record, I told you when you get bored of the kid, call me."

Julian flexed his fist, which set everyone off to laughing. But Elisa wasn't laughing. If she allowed herself to think about their relationship too much, she'd almost scare herself—the way she needed Julian, the way she loved him, how they knew each other in a way no one else in their lives did, sometimes it made her feel like heart ache just waiting to happen.

She shivered. Misunderstanding the source of the movement, Julian wrapped his arms around her and gave her a gentle squeeze. Kissing whatever part of his skin she could reach, which just so happened to be the side of his jaw, she decided that at least for the rest of the night she'd stop overthinking things and just have fun.

And she was having fun, sitting around the fire, chatting with friends while being held by Julian, it was a perfect, idyllic night.

Until it wasn't.

Somehow Julian had managed to coerce her onto the dance floor. He was making an effort to have fun. This was his scene about as much as it was hers, she'd like to think it had more to do with her dress and how she looked as she moved, more than the fact that Chastity had mentioned it probably hadn't been fair to create invite them to a dance when Julian couldn't enjoy it the way the rest of them could, but they here they were, slow dancing to a fast techno-pop song. Bumping into bodies and being bumped into.

She didn't care, though, they were under a canopy of stars, tucked away in an eerie forest of skeletal trees and Halloween decorations and it was all so beautiful. Her feet were killing her, though, and she'd managed to take off her jacket for a little bit, but now her skin was pimpling up from the cold and she was just about to ask Julian if he wanted to go back to the fire when something slammed into them.

Shocked, Elisa yelped as she lost her balance.

Even though the fall took all of a second, it was like time slowed to a crawl. Elisa had an almost out-of-body experience as she watched her arms windmilling, as her steps became crooked and her right heel caught on a divot, wrenching her ankle with a loud *pop* and dropping her like a sack of flour to the ground.

Fire bolted up her calf and tears came immediately. Julian was down on his knees beside her, his fingers trailing along her kneecap. She bit down on her lip, hugging her leg to her body as her ankle literally swelled before her eyes.

"Don't think I didn't see that, bitch!" Chastity's shrill voice pierced through the fog of Elisa's pain. "You tripped her on purpose."

"No, no, I swear," Ava's shrill voice rang with panic.

Squeezing her eyes shut, trying to focus on anything other than the stomach churning queasiness of her throbbing right leg, Elisa shook her head. Right now she didn't care if it was on purpose or not, hell, she wouldn't have even cared if the woods were burning down. The only thing she did care about was getting to a hospital immediately.

"Are you, okay? God, Elisa, I'm so sorry."

That voice didn't belong to Julian, in fact the voice was so unexpected that she couldn't help but react to it. Thomas's soft blue eyes stared back at her. He was glancing between her and Julian with a concerned frown marring his forehead.

Swallowing the bile on the back of her tongue, she didn't have the energy to answer him. Elisa signed, "Jules, gotta get to a hospital, I think it might have broken."

Her ankle was already bruising.

Scooting closer to her that it forced Thomas back on his heels, Julian scooped her up. She couldn't help but cry out as another bolt of fiery pain tore up her body. Gritting her teeth, she wrapped her arms around his neck, burying her face in his collar.

The ride to the hospital was nothing but a blur of pain. It was only three hours later, sitting in the emergency room, that she finally felt a little more human thanks to the high dose of ibuprofen they gave her. They'd wanted to give her something harder, but she'd turned it down. Last thing she needed was to fail a pee test because of drugs in her system.

She lay on the cot with Julian rubbing her head softly as the doctor finally came in with her X-ray.

"So it's not broken, that's the good news." He showed her the X-ray photo and pointed to a spot on it.

"Can I swim? That's all I care about."

He grimaced. She did not like that grimace. Feeling like she'd just swallowed a rock, she clenched Julian's fingers hard.

"When's your swim?"

"Next week."

Giving her the look—the one she knew well, as this wasn't her first rodeo getting an injury that forced her to suspend her swims—he shook his head. "I really don't think that's likely. You have what's called a Grade II sprain."

There'd been a girl last year who'd gotten a Grade III from a taking a tumble during a hiking trip. The tear had been so severe it'd caused her to eventually lose her athletic scholarship because of it.

Tears streamed from the corners of Elisa's eyes. Forget the Olympics. How the hell would she pay for college if she lost her scholarship?

"So I'm done?" Her voice cracked.

"Well, you didn't tear the ligament completely, so your recovery won't take nearly as long had you had a more severe injury." He thinned his lips, giving her the "I'm so sorry" eyes that she suddenly hated him for.

Julian, sensing her distress, rubbed her shoulder gently. What was she gonna tell Coach?

The doctor patted her knee and it was all she could do not to slap his well-intentioned hand off her.

"You'll need to make a follow up appointment with an orthopedic physician to see what your options are. For now all I can tell you to do is get some rest, put an ice compress on it, and elevate it. We'll send you some of the good stuff home to help with the pain along with a pair of crutches, I definitely would advise against swimming competitively anytime soon."

With a nod in both their directions, he got up and left.

Julian took the seat the doctor had just vacated. "I'm sorry."

No longer able to contain the tears, she dropped her head into her hands and bawled like a baby.

An hour later, Elisa and Julian were making their way out of the ER when she spotted a familiar face.

It was Thomas, now dressed in a pair of jeans and sweater. He was sitting in the waiting room and he didn't act surprised to see them come out.

She frowned. "Thomas?"

Getting up, he walked over to them. His hands were deep in his pockets and every so often he'd glance at Julian.

The air between the three of them became thick and tension-filled.

"What?" She cleared her throat, trying to fight the nauseous waves of pain as the Motrin finally began to wear off. "What are you doing here?"

Licking his lips, he finally pulled his gaze away from Julian. "I wanted to come and make sure you were all right."

"Yeah." She snorted. "I'm really not." She hated that her voice trembled.

"I broke up with her."

The hand that Julian had wrapped around her waist clenched up. Elisa patted it gently.

"I'm sorry," she said, but mostly because she had no clue what to say to a statement like that.

His blue eyes gleamed intensely down at her. So heavy was his gaze that she swore she could almost feel it brush her flesh.

"I'm not. I should have done it a long time ago. I'll be reporting a couple things to Coach in the morning. Just thought you should know." He caught his lip between his teeth.

And it was such a familiar gesture from him that her heart gave a tiny pang. Thomas was a good guy; he hadn't deserved what she'd done to him.

Touching his sleeve, she nodded. "For what it's worth, Tom, I'm sorry too."

Swallowing hard enough that she saw his Adam's apple roll, he said a quick goodbye and turned and left without saying another word.

She looked at Julian with the heat of tears still shimmering in her eyes.

"That was him, right?" he asked.

Elisa nodded as his jaw clenched.

"Come on, Smile Girl, let's go home." He kissed the crown of her head so gently.

"I love you, Jules. I hope you know that."

"I do. I know you do." But his gentle smile didn't quite reach his eyes.

Julian tucked her into bed later that night, kissed her forehead, and was about to walk off when she stopped him with a touch of her fingers to his wrist.

His eyes looked haunted when he turned back to her.

"Where are you going?" she asked, her thoughts were sluggish, her tears dried up. The doctor was right; the drugs he'd given her were good.

They were probably also banned, which would have disqualified her anyway. She'd tried to go an hour without them, but after nearly throwing up twice from the pain, she'd caved and decided that grinning and bearing it was for the birds.

Bending over, he kissed her gently. "I'm going out."

She frowned, thinking how weird it was for him to want to go out so late at night, but the drugs had taken hold of her and she was helpless to resist its siren call.

Four days later, with the help of Julian and a pair of crutches, Elisa sat in front of Coach Carl's closed office door waiting her turn to go inside and see what her future held.

Julian patted her knee. "You're going to be okay. You won't lose this scholarship."

Giving him a weak grin, she signed, "But they could—"

"No." He shook his head. "They won't. Season's almost over, you have time to heal before you need to train again."

Wiping nervous fingers against her lips, she sighed. As much as she wanted to believe his words, she couldn't get the sick feeling out of her stomach that they'd find some loophole to drop her. Something to make them say they refused to waste any more money on her.

The door finally swung open and Ava's tear-stained face caught Elisa by surprise that she gave a gasp of disbelief and clenched her fingers in her lap.

Ava looked like a mess today. So different from her normally slick and put-together outfits. Dressed in a pair of skinny jeans and a baggy gray sweater, her hair was wild, looking as though she'd not combed it in a day or two, and her nose and eyes were red.

"Elisa," Carl's grumpy-sounding voice rang out from the office, "you can come in now."

In the shock of seeing Ava, Elisa hadn't noticed how tense Julian had gone. She turned to him to ask him for help getting up and noticed his eyes glaring holes at Ava's head.

"I didn't do it," Ava whispered in a broken voice. Tapping a fist against her thigh, she shot a glance at Julian quickly before repeating herself. "Whatever you might think of me, I wouldn't have done..." She shook her head. "I wouldn't have done that."

"Why did you hate me so much, Ava? What did I ever do to you?"

Ava's jaw clenched, and for a moment Elisa thought she wouldn't answer her, but finally she said, "Because he never wanted me the way he wanted you."

Elisa didn't need to ask who the "he" was. For a second she felt the guilt all over again for what she'd done to Thomas. Julian's fingers were gentle as he grasped her elbow and helped her to stand.

"Elisa," Carl called again, startling her.

Glancing quickly over her shoulder one last time, Ava turned and walked away.

Carl's blue eyes were cold and aloof as Julian helped her to her seat. Arranging her crutches on her lap, she jerked her chin in Jules's direction.

"Can he stay here with me?"

"I don't see why not." He shrugged and pointed to a chair sitting beside his large trophy case.

Carl looked tired today. There were heavy bags under his eyes and he was rubbing his brow as though he were battling a headache. Sighing, he tapped his finger on his desk. The silence was deafening and made her feel even more sick to her stomach with each second that ticked past.

"So how are you feeling?" he finally asked.

She shrugged, fighting the tears in her eyes. She'd promised herself she wouldn't cry, there was nothing that could be done. As much as she'd tried to convince herself she'd be good in time for the swim, there was no way. Her ankle was swollen and ached anytime she placed even a minimal amount of pressure on it. Elisa bit her tongue and swallowed hard.

Nodding, as if coming to some sort of a conclusion, Carl looked between her and Julian. "Clive won't be here."

Her fingers clenched. Not that it came as a surprise, but suspecting it and having it verified were two different things.

"Obviously." He pointed at her. "You're out for the final heat of the season."

"And the..." She cleared her throat. "My scholarship? What about that?"

"That remains to be seen. Since this happened at the end of the season we can hold off on making any final decisions until next year. I'll obviously be following your progress, but if it looks like you can remain and stay competitive, I doubt you'll have to worry about that. And as for Ava..." He leaned back in his seat, popping a Tums in his mouth. "You won't need to worry about her anymore."

She turned her face to the side. "Ava swears she didn't do it." Elisa wasn't sure if she was defending her or being sarcastic. Honestly, where Ava March was concerned she didn't feel a whole lot other than quiet antipathy.

"Yeah." He snorted. "Whether she was the cause or not for this incident, there is reason to believe she's done other things."

Frowning, she glanced up at him. "What other things?"

"Thomas and a few others have come to me. Told me about a head-kicking incident a few weeks ago. And regardless of what she now claims there are many who can vouch that what happened to you that night wasn't an accident. There is an investigation pending, of course. But I don't tolerate this type of behavior. Not on my team."

Swiping at the lone tear had fallen out of her left eye with her palm, she made to stand, and Julian was by her side in a second.

"Helluva thing, Elisa. Helluva thing," Coach Carl said. And she supposed that was as close as she'd ever get to hearing him voice any regret.

Smiling through the tears that now fell in waves, she said, "I'll see you next year."

Standing, he extended his hand to shake hers. "Yes, I'm sure you will."

Elisa sighed through the phone as she talked with Chas. It'd been two weeks since that night, and the what-might-have-beens would haunt her for years, she was sure, but it was done.

"That bitch deserved it," Chastity snarled. "I told you I saw her trip you. I'm glad Thomas did the right thing by speaking up."

"She swears she didn't, Chas."

"Yeah, and if you believe that, then I'm a monkey's uncle."

Exhausted from thinking of this, Elisa shrugged. "I'm at the point that I don't really care. Whether she did that or didn't, she's done other things. I'm just glad the whole stupid thing is behind me now."

Elisa frowned as she stared at her still-tender ankle. Julian was probably the best nurse in the world, checking in on her every hour or so, bringing her tea and snacks whenever he felt she might be hungry, but she was tired of lying in bed.

Thankfully the physician had agreed with her that no surgery would be required. Her ankle still ached like nobody's business, but it would eventually heal on its own. Best part of the whole stupid thing, Ava had been kicked off the swim team. Indefinitely.

She hadn't gotten to the school on a scholarship, so, as far as Elisa knew, she would still be allowed to attend classes, but that was currently in review as well.

"You serious? That's all you feel right now? I'd be over at the bitch's place and clawing her eyes out. The Olympics, Lisa, that's what she cost you. Stupid, selfish wench. Not you, of course."

Shrugging, Elisa picked at her pink sweatpants. "We don't know that. I probably wouldn't have made the team anyway. I might be fast for college, but the Olympics are totally different kind of fast."

She said it, but she didn't really mean it. Sometimes if she thought about it too much, she'd still cry. She'd never tell Chastity that she wished she'd never gone to that party, even though for the rest of her life she'd probably regret that decision.

Deep down, she was pretty sure Chastity knew it too; it was a subject neither girl would ever broach.

"Elisa, you always do that. Always try to put a positive spin on life. If you won't hate her, I will. I love you, girl, and you would have made it. We both know you would have made it." Chas sounded disgusted by the whole affair. "But I can tell you that your boy toy was livid that night. He came back to our apartment, banging on my door and demanding I tell him where Thomas and Ava lived."

That was the first she'd heard of this. "What?" Her knee-jerk reaction was to sit up, which caused her ankle to move and made her hiss in response. Dropping back to the pillows and shaking from the runoff of adrenaline and pain, she rubbed the bridge of her nose. "He didn't tell me that."

She laughed. "I'm not surprised. I'm so glad neither Luke or I knew where to find them cause I think if we had he might have killed them. As it was it took us an hour to talk some sense into that boy. I've never seen him so angry. Not for nothing, but damn, he loves you."

Stomach fluttering thinking about what he must have looked like that night, like some avenging angel of death, she couldn't help but chuckle. "I'm glad he didn't go there, but I'm happy he cared that much."

Chastity was silent for a moment. "Hey, I'm really sorry you didn't get a chance to show off for Amsler. I know how much you—"

Waving her hand, she twisted her lips. "It wasn't meant to be. To be honest, Chastity, I wasn't even sure I wanted to be an Olympian—that's so much stress. To be doing school, while competing at that level, I would have never had a life, much less any time for Julian. I think I mostly just wanted to do it to see if I was good enough, but not because it was a dream or anything."

"Well, at least it looks like you'll get to keep your scholarship. I know you were freaking out about that."

Their bedroom door opened a crack and Julian stuck his head inside. "Need anything?"

She smiled, waving him to her. "Hey, Chas, I'm gonna go. I have a paper due tomorrow and about five pages left to write."

Julian took a seat beside her, his fingers fluttered up and down her arm.

"Okay, bye," Chastity chirped and hung up.

Dropping the phone, Elisa opened her arms. "I love you, Jules."

His confused countenance turned into a bright smile as he let her pull his head to her breast.

At least there was still one good thing in her life, and for that she was grateful.

Chapter 14

That year flew by in a rapid blur. Elisa could walk now without any problems. On occasion she'd experience a slight twinge in her ankle if she stepped down wrong, but Julian's freshman year was now nearly behind them. They had two weeks left until summer vacation and now it was just a matter of trying to decide whether they wanted to go with Chastity and Luke to cabin on the lake they'd rented before going home or not.

Elisa wasn't much of a cook, but thankfully Jules never seemed to mind that most nights it was salad. At least that was impossible to burn.

Their apartment door swung open and she glanced up with a smile, but Julian wasn't smiling. He was glowering and tossed his book bag onto the door unceremoniously.

Setting down the head of lettuce, she dried her hands on a dishtowel and asked, "Hey, mister, what's up?"

A muscle in his jaw ticked several times before he answered. "I'm going to fail my fucking art class, that's what." He sat on the couch, tossing his head back and staring at the ceiling with a hard, cold stare.

Shocked to hear him say that, she walked over and tapped him on the shoulder until he'd look at her.

"What do you mean you're going to fail?"

"Final assignment of the year is clay in color."

She frowned. Not that she knew a lot about art, sadly, but that didn't seem so hard. "Jules, I don't understand, that's easy, just put a little color on it."

He gave her a droll look.

Sighing, she arched her brow. "You know what I mean, just pick some colors, it shouldn't matter if—"

"But it does matter. We're supposed to approximate it as close to ancient Greek pottery as we're able."

She grimaced. "Babe, did you tell him about—"

"Of course." He gestured angrily. "But he said if he makes an exception for one, he'd have to make an exception for all. This fucking assignment is worth thirty percent of our final grade."

"What a dick!" She clenched her jaw. "This isn't like you asked him for a damn extension." Angry now for him, she frantically wracked her brain for ideas. "Report him. He can't do this to you, there's the handicap—"

A rumbling grunt tore from his throat. Julian did not consider himself handicapped, and in fact, neither did she. He was more able-bodied than even his brothers. Julian was brilliant in so many ways.

"Baby, I'm not calling you handicapped, please don't misunderstand me, I'm just saying you have avenues."

"No." He shook his head. "I don't know how I'm going to do this, Smile Girl, but I'm going to do this and shove his stupid rules down his fucking throat."

She smiled; she had no doubt he could. Then an idea came to her. One completely and totally so out there it would either be brilliant or stupid.

"What colors are predominant in Greek pottery?" she asked quickly, heartbeat racing as her stupid, brilliant idea grew.

"Reds. Browns. Blacks. Yellows. Umbers. Sometimes blues, why?"

Holding up a finger, she kissed his cheek. "Hold that thought." Then, turning on her heel, she raced for his art room.

Feeling slightly dumb as she kicked off her clothes, she giggled softly to herself. This might or might not work, but at least he'd be happy by the end of it.

Every once in a while Julian would ask her to pose for him, and he'd called her his muse more than once, which she found to be incredibly romantic. So one day while walking past a boutique shop she'd spotted a silky peach-colored robe bursting with exotic printed flowers. She'd bought it on the spot, but had never felt bold enough to actually wear it, as it was sexier than most anything else she owned.

Slipping it over her shoulders, she then grabbed several paint tubes of color—of the nontoxic variety, of course—sticking to the ones he'd mentioned and placed them on the rolling tray beside her. The final thing was to let her hair hang long and heavy down her back.

Just like she loved Julian's longer locks, he too loved hers being long. It now extended to the center of her back. Shoving her fingers through it to give it a sort of tousled, careless look, she nodded and then poked just her head outside the door, beckoning him to her with a smile.

He wore a confused little frown as he came, asking her what she was doing, but rather than answer she took her place in the center of the room and struck a sensual pose—or at least what she hoped would be one—trying to ignore the nest of butterflies swarming her stomach and telling her he wouldn't get it and she was just being weird.

But all her nerves were forgotten when Julian walked through the door and his eyes became glazed with passion. A small, crooked grin slowly tipped up one corner of his mouth.

Never taking her eyes off him, she unscrewed the first tube of paint. It was labeled "Blue Regent." Rarely did Elisa see Julian reach for his colors; usually he preferred sticking with gray and black mediums. It was almost like she could sense how much he wanted to understand color, but how terrified he was of the prospect too.

Dabbing some of it onto her finger she traced a line of that color down from the edge of her eyes to her lower cheeks. Wiping her finger clean on a paint rag, she grabbed the next tube of color. This one was a deep wine red.

Heart racing out of control she sat it back down and untied the knot of her belt with nerveless fingers. The room was silent save for the sounds of their breathing.

His fingers curled by his sides as she allowed the robe to slip in a silken puddle to the floor. Sea-green eyes moved leisurely down the slope of her body, lingering upon her breasts and between her thighs for several tense, breathless seconds before finally meeting her own.

Still fully dressed, Elisa might have felt embarrassed with anyone else, but not with Julian. He had a way of looking at her that let her know no matter what she did or didn't wear, he always saw her. Saw beneath her flesh to her soul.

Smearing the red paint onto her finger she drew a heart slightly off center and partially on her left breast.

He licked his lips and her stomach curled with tendrils of heat as she sucked in a stuttery breath.

There were many different levels of silence in life. This was the type of silence that echoed like the crescendo of drums. Gentle and melodious at first, but slowly rising to a beat and pattern that left one breathless and entranced, unable to look away, to move, to even blink for fear you might miss its climax. That to hear it would forever change you, but to not hear it might just kill you.

Elisa knew as she spread bands of yellow, gold, brown, and black paint upon her forearms and thighs that this was one of those moments in life she'd never forget. That by doing this she was cementing Julian even deeper into her heart, that ten, twenty, even thirty years from now when she looked back on the memories of her life this would be a vignette she would visit often. Regardless of time or distance or what may come for the two of them, Julian Wright was inexorably bound like a string on a loom to the tapestry of her life.

The thought made her hands shake.

He seemed to sense the sudden heavy turn of her thoughts, because his nostrils flared as he took a tentative step toward her, closing the already scant distance between them.

Summoning her courage, she pointed to her cheeks. "This is blue like the tears I sometimes cry." She pointed to her chest next. "Red. My passion for you." Her arms. "Gold. Brown. Black. The different shades of flesh."

She'd made sure as she painted the colors on her body to show enough of a contrast between them that hopefully he'd be able to tell them apart regardless of the fact that he'd never know exactly what he used.

"The point of color, Jules," she continued, "isn't to drown out the art, but to make them have different sensations on the eye."

Elisa lowered her hands then, shaking like a sapling as she

wondered what he'd thought of her impromptu art lesson. She was no teacher, and she knew nothing of art.

It was like someone had suddenly flipped a switch inside of him. Julian grabbed the edge of his shirt and practically ripped it off him. She sucked in a sharp breath at the beauty of his body.

Julian ate like an athlete and it showed. His abs were prominent ridges, tapering into a tight vee that led down to the waist of his jeans. Gaze greedy, she couldn't find just one spot on his body to focus on. Because all of him was so beautiful. From his strong and defined pecs, to his wide shoulders, and his square jaw—Julian would have made Michelangelo weep.

If she could have dreamt up her dream man, she doubted she could have done better. Never in her life could she have imagined falling for a guy with pierced nipples, a pierced lip, and with gages in his ears. Julian was the antithesis of everything she'd ever thought she'd wanted. And yet…he was everything she wanted now.

She even loved his tattoos that now crawled up the sides of his neck. He didn't move, letting her study him as he'd studied her. When her gaze finally reached his again, he must have seen in her eyes that she wanted more. Undoing the buttons of his jeans, he shoved them down his legs and then shucked them off to the side.

He wore no underwear beneath. She bit her bottom lip at the sight of his jutting erection. His legs were long and strong, and covered in a fine dusting of black hair.

"You're so beautiful, Jules," she signed.

Julian took two big steps, lifting her easily into his arms as he strode over to his sliding stool, refusing to release her when he took a seat.

She pushed at his chest. "Jules, I'll make you dirty."

But he didn't seem to care. His lips claimed hers almost

punishingly and she melted into his body, wanting nothing more than what he was offering.

Elisa wrapped her short legs around his waist, rubbing her aching center along the length of his erection, moaning with relief even as her eyes burned with heat. Fearful, but not because she was unhappy.

She'd never been happier in her life.

His fingers tapped out words on her body, talking to her even as he slipped deep inside.

Elisa hugged his head to her breast, undulating and writhing on top of him. Closing her eyes she lost herself to the sensation of his body. The springy hairs of his thighs tickled her own smooth ones. Pressing her toes into the floor to gain better leverage, she took her time, easing slowly up, before moving down, increasing her pace as their breathing grew more ragged.

She was lost in his smell of soap and mint, in the words of love he painted upon her skin. So focused on the feel of his thickness inside her that she could hardly make out what he was saying.

All she caught was smile and falling, but it didn't matter, because her soul understood. Elisa wanted to get lost in this moment. In the feel of their bodies coming together, their sweat mingling, the smooth sensation of his tongue dragging from one nipple to the other. Shuddering from the exquisite agony of his fiery touch, she tilted her neck back and smiled into the colors of light that burst behind the darkness of her closed eyelids.

She saw blue, and red, bursts of brilliant gold, and the hypnotic sea green that she loved so well.

"Are you close?" he tapped out on her spine.

Nodding, needing him even closer than he already was, it was her turn to take his mouth. Dipping her tongue between his lips like she was lapping at the sweetest of honey.

He made the most adorable mewling noises in the back of his throat as his fingers dug hard into her hips. Julian hadn't been her first, but he was the best.

And even though she sat on him, and had the position of dominance, he reversed it by digging his fingers into her hair and jerking her head back, exposing the long line of her neck.

Desire built like a tightly winding coil inside her he licked and nibbled the hollow of her throat. Her orgasm came swift and furious, and his followed soon after...

Summer went by in a blur. They spent every waking moment together. Recognizing that this was their final year. Elisa was determined to push the thought of that truth to the back of her mind.

She didn't want to think about what would happen once the year was done. It was agony to even consider it. Sometimes she'd wake up in the middle of the night with her heart pounding violently in her chest, woken up by a dream of them living on opposite sides of the world. She'd be pining and miserable and he'd be laughing and clinging onto someone else's body, worshipping someone else's curves, and feathering words of love upon someone else's skin.

Elisa hadn't shared with him what her dreams were about, but he'd wake up and reassure her with kisses and tender affection and for a time she'd forget. But now the year was half over and she felt the desperation of time slipping through their fingers.

Soon she'd be graduating, which meant she'd need to start a job search. There were a number of prestigious libraries she could apply to, but none of them were even remotely close to campus.

The closest one was in New York City, which was still several hours' drive away. She'd do it, though, just to make sure she could at least see him, but there was no way she could put all her eggs in just one basket either.

Julian came up behind her as she sat at the breakfast table and massaged her shoulders.

Huffing, she gave him a weak smile. "Trying to decide where to send applications."

Taking a seat beside her, he grabbed one of the apple slices off her plate and took a bite. "All of them."

She loved how he looked when he first woke up in the morning. Sleep tousled, his hair feathering out every which way, and his yummy abs completely on display for her.

Shoving her laptop aside, she lifted one of her legs on her chair and shook her head. "They're far, Jules. All of them. So far."

The smile he wore slowly dissipated as he sat the apple slice down. A faint wash of morning sun hung over his head like a golden halo. In the year in a half she and Jules had been together, they'd gotten in their fair share of arguments. He was stubborn, and sometimes left messes around the apartment for her to clean up.

He was prone to getting quickly irritated and annoyed by things he couldn't quite understand, but he was also one of the sweetest, most selfless guys she knew. Especially when it came to her.

Drumming his fingers on the tabletop, he gave her a pointed look and then said, "What do you want to do?"

She frowned. "I want to stay with you."

"I want that too," he said slowly, but they both knew she couldn't.

The campus already had too many on staff as it was, and he knew very well, because of how often she'd talked of it, that her dream was to work at a prestigious library. Someplace in Italy or England or Rome... Basically any place in Europe would do.

But how could she leave him?

Shutting her laptop, she frowned at it, feeling torn by her desires to both stay and go.

From the corner of her eye she saw his fingers move.

"What?" she asked.

"Let's go out tonight. Finals are over, let's just get out of the house and relax. What do you think? I can invite my brothers and you can invite Chas and Luke."

She smiled, but her heart wasn't really in it.

Noticing, he got up from his chair and came around to her side of the table, holding out his hand to her.

Taking it, he lifted her from her seat and pulled her tight into his body, rocking her gently back and forth.

Feeling the brick in her gut ease just a little, she tapped words onto his lower back. "Where do you want to go?"

He shrugged, but then said. "Luke is going to be playing at the Blue Moon next week."

She knew what the Blue Moon was, it was the only blues club for several miles in any direction. Elisa's brows lowered.

"Music? You'll be bored."

Tipping her chin up, he gave her a tender kiss before saying, "I can hear more than you think."

Laughing, she shrugged. "Okay then, I'll call and see what they say."

Chastity and Luke were excited to go. Roman and Christian, however, couldn't make it. The guys had opted to hit up a gentleman's club instead. Considering all three of them had just turned twenty-one, Elisa wasn't terribly surprised by their decision.

Because Chastity had told Elisa that the place was a kind of throwback to the smoky elegance of a fifties club, she'd decided to go shopping. She'd gone to the mall with the hopes of finding a sequined flapper-style dress, because it just seemed like the right sort of dress to wear to a place like that, but the moment her eyes had landed on the floor-length, spaghetti-strap, form-fitting dark red gown, she'd known she had to grab it.

It wasn't often that Elisa got to dress up; she and Julian were well beyond proms at this point. Chastity had promised that everyone went in their best duds to this place, so she'd bought Julian a few items she'd found on clearance.

Julian wasn't a suit kind of man. He probably never would be. So she'd gone with black slacks, a steel-gray short sleeve, button-up shirt, a pair of suspenders, and a funky striped tie that she thought would look fun on him.

Running the flat iron through her hair one final time, she applied a thick coat of nude lip gloss and then walked out of the bathroom only to come up short when she saw him.

Julian hadn't styled his hair, but he looked almost like a different man. The black tattoos trailing down his arms and up his neck made her heart thump violently against her ribcage.

He rubbed his own chest before slowly offering her his arm.

Remembering the last time she'd dared to wear heels, Elisa had decided on a pair of buff-colored chunky-heel pumps that she had to strap on. Last thing she wanted was to fall and break her foot this time.

"You look beautiful," he said and then trailed his knuckles down her cheek.

"You too, Jules. How did I get to be so lucky?"

"Beauty and the beast," he said with a snort.

Kissing his cheek, she shook her head. "I love the way you look. Now," she said, grabbing her purse, "let's go before we're late."

The club was packed by the time Julian and Elisa made it there, but thankfully Chas and Luke had gotten there an hour ago, and, because Luke was friends with the owner, had managed to snag a choice booth by the stage.

Elisa smiled as she slipped into the booth, taking a seat beside Luke, who leaned over and kissed her cheek before shaking Julian's hands.

She was so glad she'd dressed up the way she had, because Chastity hadn't been lying. The people inside ranged from her age to over the hill, but all of them were dressed to the nines.

The dress she thought might make her stand out like a sore thumb seemed sedate compared to some of the gaudy dresses parading around. Men were either in suits or at least dressed semi-formally.

Chas herself was dressed in an eye-catching sequined mid-thigh gown. Half black and half white, it had a sweetheart neckline that showed off the ladies very nicely. Luke wore an all white zoot suit with a black tie and even had the hat on his head.

Her friend's eyes bugged. "Holy crap, you look so much like JLaw now—doesn't she look like JLaw?" Chastity smacked Luke's shoulder, and he just gave her an indulgent smile before nodding.

Chastity was currently into all things Jennifer Lawrence, not that Elisa minded one bit being compared to her.

"You're so crazy, Chas, and you look gorgeous too," she said as Julian slipped in beside her, placing an arm across her shoulder.

"You found it okay, I see," Luke said a moment later and spread his arm wide. "What do you think?"

The smoky ambience of the place was what got Elisa, especially considering she didn't actually see anyone smoking. The room was low lit, the tables covered in white table cloths, the booths so high as to give it a private feel even though the place was crowded, and the house band had her tapping her feet already.

"It's awesome," Julian signed quickly, which made Luke beam.

A waitress came by a moment later for their drink order, wearing a Playboy bunny-style outfit, complete with the black bow tie; the only things missing were the bunny ears and tail.

Elisa smiled, already enjoying herself. She'd so needed this night and she was grateful now that Julian had suggested it.

"So what are your plans for graduation?" Luke asked, signing it at the same time.

Unlike her and Chas, he'd graduated the year before, but had managed to find an accounting job within twenty miles of the campus, making it possible for he and Chas to continue living in the same apartment.

Chastity's lips thinned as she patted Luke's chest, as if to say, *Don't ask that.* His eyes widened and he glanced between her and Julian with a wide-eyed "sorry" look.

Shrugging, Elisa leaned into Julian's side. "It's okay. It's obviously the elephant in the room."

Julian kissed her cheek, running his fingers lightly up and down her goose-pimpled bicep. Not talking, just touching.

The band switched to a more up-tempo song, one with a strong back beat to it. Couples started getting up and going to the center of the floor to sway to the music.

"I don't know what we're going to do," she said a second later. "There aren't many options for my career field around here. A few places in Massachusetts and New York, but yeah." She ended on a sad little sigh.

The drinks arrived a moment later and the conversation soon turned to other more neutral topics. But now Elisa couldn't stop thinking about her and Julian and what they would do when the time came.

"Hey, I want to dance." Chastity grinned and, sliding out, held out her hand for Luke. Giving them a wink, she turned and sauntered off with Luke into the crowd.

"I think she did that to give us some privacy," Julian said a minute later.

"I think they did too," she agreed, giving him a sad little smile.

"Smile Girl." His beautiful sea-green eyes gazed at her tenderly. "Don't think about this."

"Jules." She scooted deeper into him. "It's all I can think about lately. I try so hard to remember that we still have several more months before this becomes an issue, but it feels like time is just—"

Grabbing her hands, he kissed her fingertips. It was what he did when she refused to switch the subject. Shoulders slumping, she leaned deeper into his touch.

"Close your eyes and listen to the music with me," he said, smiling deep into her eyes.

"How do you do it? I see you all the time with the headphones, how do you hear it, Jules? Show me."

Sliding his hand over her throat, he placed his other palm flat on the table. The song playing now was slow with a smooth, and easy back beat. He didn't move a muscle, as if waiting for something.

Elisa sat perfectly still beneath him, her excitement growing as she waited to hear the world as he did. Then the song switched over, and the drumbeat was a forceful cadence.

His finger moved on her throat, mimicking the beat just a half a second later on her skin. Her eyes widened as tears burned the back of her throat.

She didn't move, and barely took a breath as she lost herself not to the sound of the song, but to the rhythm of it playing along the column of her throat.

Julian had closed his eyes, his whole body one of intense concentration as he focused. When the song finally ended, he looked up at her, and she framed his face with her suddenly cold hands.

"You're amazing, Julian Wright," she said, his eyes immediately moving to her lips. "So amazing. How can I ever leave you?"

When he kissed her, a quiet tear slipped out the corner of her eye.

Chapter 15

Julian walked into the Adrians' kitchen, sitting down beside her as he took a sip from their shared coffee mug.

Elisa had graduated and since she'd no longer be back at campus, she and Julian had moved out of their apartment and back home for summer vacation.

The job search had become less a source of sadness and more a source of frustration as the weeks rolled by and one library after another wrote back with the dreaded "Thank you for considering blah, blah, blah, but we regret to inform you that..." nonsense.

She had, however, been invited to two libraries for interviews. One in Massachusetts, and one in Dublin—it'd been a cluster flying to Dublin just for the weekend to do that interview. The jet lag had been horrific, but Julian had been with her and his presence had settled her nerves enough to give a professional sounding interview, she hoped.

The moment she'd stepped foot into the Trinity College library she'd just about had a heart attack. The place had been a nerd's paradise, polished marble floors, bookshelves that seemed to run on for miles, and the book of Kells prominently displayed behind a glass case. Her fingers had gone cold, almost numb with a desire to hold it. To read it.

The Boston Public Library had been nothing to sneeze at either, but if she had her choice, Dublin won her heart. Problem was, while she loved the idea of working in Dublin, she did not enjoy the idea of being so far away from Jules.

"What's the plan for today?" Julian signed. "Want to catch a movie, or—"

Her cell phone rang. The song wasn't one she was familiar with. She programmed different songs for different people, and this was her "stranger" ringtone. Eyes shooting immediately up to Julian, she froze.

Frowning, he clipped his head, staring at the screen.

"It's Ireland."

She nodded. "I know."

Each ring pierced her heart, made her feel like she wanted to puke.

"Pick it up," he said and then scooped it into his hands, answering the call before shoving it into her face.

"Hel...hello?" she mumbled.

"Yes, hello," a pleasant female voice that didn't sound at all like the one who'd interviewed her said. "May I speak with Elisa Adrian, please?"

Shaking the cobwebs free, Elisa nodded her head. "That's me. Yes, hi."

"Hi." She could hear the smile on the other end. "We've had an opportunity to look over your packet, and we're all in agreement that should you still desire to work here, the job is yours. We would also be very glad to assist you with finding an affordable flat in the city center."

Heart racing out of control, she gave a silent nod. She'd not yet heard back from Boston—what if they said yes?

She already knew from her inquiries that Dublin wouldn't pay half of what Boston would. Though she had no doubt she could find a roommate if she needed to help float the cost. But by no means would she be rich. All this she told herself, even as her internal little girl bounced up and down in exhilaration that she'd gotten the offer from the one she'd wanted most.

"Can I have time to think about it?"

"Oh yes, absolutely. Though we will need a firm answer by week's end, I'm afraid."

Holding on to her chest, she nodded forcefully. "Yes, I understand, thank you."

When she hung up, Julian's smile was broad, but it didn't touch his eyes. "They offered you the job."

It wasn't a question.

Biting onto her bottom lip, she nodded. "They did."

"You seem surprised." He traced her cheek softly. "I knew you'd get it."

Grabbing hold of his finger, she felt suddenly sick to her stomach, but tried to put on a brave face. "It was probably because of the way I kept gushing about their Strachan collection."

She swiped her fingers along the kitchen table, as if dusting it off.

"You didn't say yes."

Closing her eyes briefly, she sighed. "I need to hear back from Boston first. Besides, they pay more."

Giving him a weak smile, she got up from her seat. "I think we should go see a movie—give me a sec to go get ready."

She felt Julian's eyes follow her out the kitchen like a hot brand searing into her shoulder blades.

Two days later she got the call from Boston while Julian was out of town with his brothers.

She hung up only to spot her mother and father looking back at her from their spots at the kitchen table. As one, they stood and walked to her side, taking a seat on either end of the living room couch.

"So what's the news?"

"They accepted me, too." She turned to her dad, but it was her mom who threw an arm around her, and with no warning whatsoever, Elisa began to cry big, fat, ugly tears. "I don't know what to do."

Her father's large, warm, and comforting hand rubbed up and down her spine as her mom petted her hair. "Baby girl, that's the beauty of having choices, you can decide."

Sniffing, she wiped at her nose, wishing like hell she was ten again and back at the beach with the boys before they moved away, before Mr. Wright had died, before things with Julian had become so much more complicated.

But she wasn't ten. She was twenty-four and life was complicated, it was messy, and she had a huge decision to make.

"You'll make the right choice, Elisa Jane, you always do." Her father's deep voice brought a tiny smile to her face.

Pulling away from her mother, she tried to get herself together. "I know what my heart wants."

"And that is?" Her mother took her hand, patting it gently as her father got up to putter around in the kitchen.

Looking deep into her mother's brown eyes, so similar to her own, Elisa envied her in a way she never had before. Mom had gotten it all. She'd married her dad straight out of college, found her dream job in her dream place, bought her dream home, and had lived the fairytale life.

She closed her eyes. "I want to work in Dublin, but I want to live in Boston."

"Yeah," her mother chuckled, "but we both know that's not possible at all. So let's weigh the pros and cons. Dublin?"

She shrugged. "Pros. It's probably one of the top three most prestigious libraries in all the world. I'll have access to their rare and special collections department that literally makes me want to weep with joy. I'll live in a new and exciting place."

"Now cons."

Her father came back in then and handed her a warm mug of chamomile tea. Elisa took it with a grateful smile. With a kiss to her forehead and one for her mother, he turned and walked out the door, heading out for his daily twenty-mile bike ride.

Dad tried, bless his heart, to support her, but he'd never been very comfortable with heart-to-hearts. Especially after how she'd reacted when Mr. Wright had passed.

"Cons." She sipped from the tea. "It will only pay half of what I'd get at Boston. But more than that, the distance between Julian and I might as well be planets apart."

Agreeing with a gentle nod of her head, her mother plucked at her shell-pink capri pants. "True. And as much as I wish it were otherwise, long-distance relationships rarely work out."

"Really?" Elisa sat her mug down and turned her body fully toward her mother. "Don't they sometimes, Mum? I mean, I've heard of it happening. I've heard of people making it, and Julian and I, what we have, it's magical. I'd like to believe that if I choose Dublin we'd be able to make it work until he graduated and could come out to me."

"Ha." She gave a surprised laugh, her blonde brows reaching up into her hairline. "Honey, that's assuming an awful lot. Just because you want to go there doesn't mean he would."

Her mother's words made Elisa's heart bleed. Deep down she knew it was true, but her desire to get it all beat strong inside her. "But he's an artist, he can work anywhere."

"But baby"—she patted Elisa's knee—"the quickest way to make someone resent you is to force them to live the life you want. If Julian decided he'd like to go, that's one thing, but don't pin all your hopes and dreams on that."

"Even if I choose Boston, we're still several hours apart. It's long distance either way we go."

Elizabeth shrugged. "Yes, that's true. But one doesn't require you to save thousands of dollars a year just to fly out to see you."

A tear leaked out the corner of her left eye. "Mom, I don't know what to do. I applied at Ashe College, but there was nothing available. I applied everywhere I could think of... Do you know how improbable it was for me to get asked to not one, but two of the top libraries in the world? The odds of that are astronomical. I'll never get this chance again."

Her mother hugged her hands to her breast in a Saint Mary type of pose. "Honey, I know. And I also know that he will understand no matter what you choose."

"So why is this so difficult?" She licked her dry lips, hating that she couldn't even be happy right now. Either choice would take her far away from Julian. For a time their age gap had ceased being a problem, but now here they were again in the same situation as high school. She couldn't afford to stay and he wasn't able to leave.

"Because you love him desperately, and he feels exactly the

same way about you, and I'm going to be the bearer of bad news, Elisa, as much as I don't want to. Two years is a long, long time. You could stay, get a job at a local Wal-Mart, bag groceries, flip burgers, whatever"—she flicked her wrist—"but as the weeks rolled by and turned to months, then years, and you're stuck in a dead-end job with no prospects you'd grow to resent him for it. You'd think about everything you lost by choosing him and you'd grow to hate him."

The way she said it, with an emotionless tone of voice, gave Elisa chills. "You sound like you're familiar with that."

Her mother had been staring off into space, but now turned her gaze back to Elisa. "Why do you think your father walked out of here? Elisa, if you think he and I have always had it easy, you couldn't be more wrong. Your dad and I made it work, because we love each other, but there was a time..." She closed her eyes and a small shudder worked its way across her shoulders.

Elisa cocked her head; she'd never heard of this. "Mom?"

Smiling softly, she shook her head. "Doesn't matter. Point is, you have to make the decision you can live with. Be fair to him and be fair to you, that's all you can do."

A knock sounded on the front door, one Elisa immediately recognized as belonging to Julian. She sucked in a sharp breath, giving her mother a terrified, wide-eyed look.

"It's okay, honey. Things have a way of working themselves out the way they're supposed to be." Then, getting up, she walked to the door and greeted Julian with a big smile and hug.

He looked delicious today. As always. Julian could walk in wearing a potato sack and Elisa would think he'd never looked better. It was sick how bad she had it for him.

He walked toward her with his hands in his blue jean pockets, his hunter-green shirt making his tats and eyes pop, and her heart trembled with an even greater, even deeper love.

He seemed to sense immediately that something was wrong with her because when he took a seat, he didn't kiss her as he normally did. "What's wrong?" he asked.

She was going to break his heart either way.

"I got the call from Boston."

He wiped his palms down his lap. "Where are you going, Smile Girl?"

"Where do you want me to go?" she asked, knowing what her mother had said, but she needed to hear from him. He was part of this too; she could lie to herself and say this was her life and her choice, but it wasn't, Julian was her partner. And that mattered to her.

Taking her hands, he kissed her fingers and then placed them gently onto her lap. "Don't ask me that. I knew when we got together that someday you'd have to leave me again, and I prepared for it. No matter where you go, I'll be there. Even if it means I have to fly."

Bottom lip going wobbly again, she tossed her arms around his neck, tapping words between his shoulder blades. "I will love you forever, Julian Wright."

The day before she flew to Dublin, Elisa joined Julian at the Ink Blot—the tattoo parlor where he'd gotten nearly all his ink from since the age of fourteen. His buddy, Ray—also deaf—gave them matching tattoos.

On the spot of his arm where there'd been an empty space Julian tattooed the word "Destiny." She'd gotten words printed on the inside of her wrist, words that resonated with how she felt when she thought of her and him.

"Destiny may decide who touches my life, but only my heart can decide who touches my soul..."

She flew to Dublin the next day, and even though Julian had hugged her and swore nothing would change, Elisa knew that everything had.

Chapter 16

One Month

Elisa squealed the moment Julian's image displayed on the screen. He looked exhausted. There were tired lines around his eyes, but otherwise he looked as gorgeous as she remembered him.

"Hi," she signed quickly.

Julian leaned over and his finger flitted over the screen and for a moment she could almost feel his touch. Her heart twisted in her chest as she leaned into the screen.

"I wish I could really feel you," she said.

Sighing, he nodded. "I miss you, Smile Girl."

"If there were some way I could crawl through this screen, I think I would."

He frowned. "What's wrong?"

Giving him the type of smile that consisted of nothing more than a muscle spasm, she sighed. "I don't know. Just lonely I guess."

"No friends?"

She shrugged. "I guess so. One. Meredith. I tell her about you all the time. I think she's getting sick of hearing about my awesome boyfriend."

He grinned. "It's going to be okay, baby."

"Really? You don't regret this already?"

Julian was sharing the apartment with Christian and Roman now. It panged Elisa to see that their couch that used to be there was now gone and in its place was a foosball table. There were empty pizza boxes strewn on the counters. Julian was living like a bachelor and it made her skin prickle with goosebumps to see it. It was no secret that Christian and Roman hadn't grown out of their whoring ways, not that she doubted Julian would stay faithful to her, but if she were honest with herself, she didn't like to think of what he might be seeing.

Which was silly, of course, but she was fiercely protective of what was hers.

"I don't regret it, because it makes you happy—"

"I'm not sure it does anymore, Jules." She huffed, trying to dry her tearing eyes before he saw it.

But he must have, because he tapped his chest and then said, "You'll shatter me if I see you cry."

"Just promise me we're going to be okay," she signed it quickly.

"I promise, Elisa. These last two years will fly by and then nothing will keep us separated again."

Biting a corner of her lip, she gave him a brave smile. "I love you," she said.

"I love you too."

Three months later

Elisa laughed as she stumbled through her front door, Meredith trailed in behind her, lifting a bottle of half-drank wine high and chirping, "Here's to all the galas in all the world, may they all rot in hell."

Tossing her keys and purse to the counter, Elisa toed off her shoes and snort-giggled. "I think I might be a little drunk," she said as she lost her balance and had to grab hold of the support pillar in her kitchen to help keep her upright.

"Oh, I'd say so, just a little." Meredith tossed herself onto the couch. "Did you see the way that pompous, officious little man looked at me all night?" She kicked off her bright red sling backs and closed her eyes.

Covering her nose with her hand, Elisa chuckled. "I do believe the Dean might be a little star struck with you. Which isn't entirely bad; maybe next time you see him you can offer to show him the goodies and get us a new copy machine."

She snorted. "I'm no one's trollop. Though I'll do much for a proper copy machine." Meredith glared at a curl of brown hair that'd slipped over her shoulder. "I hate brown hair. Have I ever told you how much I hate brown hair? I must change it, but first I need to close my eyes for a minute. I'm so very, very tired..." Her words slowed and by the time she said "tired," a soft snore escaped her parted lips.

In two more minutes she'd be dead to the world.

Elisa opened her mouth, ready to tease Meredith back, when her laptop buzzed with an incoming call.

Frowning, it took her a minute to realize she was over an hour late for her Skype call with Jules.

"Oh crap." She tripped over Meredith's shoe as she ran to her desk and accepted the call.

Julian looked more than a little upset when he popped up on the screen. "Are you okay?" he asked quickly.

Grimacing, feeling like the world's worst girlfriend, she took a seat. "Honey, I'm so sorry. I totally spaced on the gala we had tonight. Needed to raise funding for the library and Mere"—a loud snore punctuated her friend's name—"asked me to tag along as her date. I'm so sorry. I thought I'd be home in time, but we got stuck in some pretty awful traffic coming home. Please don't be mad."

Knowing Julian the way she knew him, he didn't seem mad so much as disappointed. In her. It just about broke her heart.

Picking up her laptop, she tilted the screen to the side so that he could see Meredith lying on her couch.

"That's her," she said a minute later when she put the screen back on her face.

But rather than it appeasing him, he said, "I should go. I just wanted to make sure you were okay."

"You still coming next month?"

She itched to shove the lock of hair that'd fallen over his eye back.

"Yeah. I am. But...um..."

She frowned, heart going still for a moment. "What?"

Christian and Roman bent over Julian's shoulder and waved like idiots into the monitor.

"Hey sexy." Chris's deep blue eyes twinkled. "You miss us?"

She loved joking around with her brothers, but right now she was fighting a pit of anxiety working through her stomach. Julian wasn't smiling or laughing, even though his brothers were trying to get him to loosen up.

"You know I do," she said softly. "But I'm really tired, Chris."

"Oh yeah, well." He shoved his fingers through his hair. "Kind of feel like I've interrupted something. Just wanted to stop by and say hi." He clapped Julian's shoulder.

Roman leaned in. "Real quick—Mom's trying to figure out how many are coming back for Christmas this year, can you make it?"

As much as she wanted to, she doubted it would be possible. At least not this year. "I wish I could, Rome. But tell her I said hi and sorry I'm taking Julian away this year."

Roman frowned and looked as though he meant to say something else, when Julian shook his head. They both said something, but Julian had his back turned in a way that she couldn't read what he said.

Turning back to her a second later, Roman shook his head. "Okay then, girl, I'll leave you guys alone. Love ya."

"Yeah, me too."

Julian came back on the screen and wiped a hand down his jaw.

"What was that about?" she asked once Roman was gone.

"Nothing. Don't worry about it. I've got to go, I've got classes."

She'd forgotten that it was already Monday morning there. "Julian, I'm really sorry. Don't be mad at me."

His look was tired as he said, "I love you, Elisa. Glad you're okay."

They hung up a minute later and when she crawled into bed she couldn't stop wondering what in the world had been going on between him and Roman and why she suddenly had the worst feeling of foreboding.

Five months.

Five long, agonizing, excruciating months since she'd physically seen Julian last. Elisa tapped her heel on the marble floor in a nervous, methodical rhythm as her stomach churned with excitement.

Meredith peered up from her workstation wearing a smile on her painted red lips. "Do try to contain your excitement, Elisa Jane." She winked, her British accent sounding all proper and Jane Austenesque, which they both knew was nothing like what she actually sounded like.

Elisa snorted. "Oh, bite me."

Meredith lifted a brightly painted purple brow, but chuckled beneath her breath. She'd recently gotten rid of her brown and Elisa thought she looked a million times better. Of course the boss hadn't been exactly thrilled by it, but Mere worked behind the scenes so he'd not fired her for it either.

Meredith was originally from Manchester; she was hip and trendy and basically Elisa's polar opposite in every way.

Elisa was tanned and blonde (well, considerably less tanned now than she'd been when she'd first arrived) while Meredith now had lavender and navy blue hair. Elisa dressed like a preppy librarian, replete with the cardigans, pencil skirts, trendy Mary Janes, and pearl necklaces, and Meredith was pure modern mod, or, as she liked to call herself, a modern-day Twiggy.

They'd formed a friendship over their love of Austen, Shakespeare, and blues.

Elisa glanced up at the clock again. In three more hours, she'd see him. In one more she'd be walking out the door to her flat to change and hail a taxi to Dublin airport. Running her finger beneath her necklace, she began to tap her foot again.

"Good God, Eli, you're driving me insane. How can I properly restore this binding with you carrying on as you are?"

Growling, she threw her friend an evil little glare before sticking out her tongue. "I'm not carrying on. But I am excited."

A twinkle gleamed in her friend's bright blue eyes. Setting

her work aside for a moment, she turned and leaned against her desk, tapping her gloved finger on its edge as she studied Elisa. "I can't wait to meet this boy. I have a feeling I'm going to be terribly disappointed in the looks department, though."

Elisa gave an exaggerated gasp.

"Oh yes." Mere nodded, causing her slicked bangs to spill into her eyes. "I think you've been toying with my imagination. There is simply no way a man such as you've described could actually be real."

"Is that a bet?"

She shrugged. "Might be. If I'm wrong, I'll pick up the tab tonight, if you've lied, you will."

Elisa grimaced. She'd forgotten all about the pub-crawl.

"What?" Meredith narrowed her eyes. "Please don't tell me you plan to bail again. You did it last time. I won't let you toss me to the wolves."

"Toss you to the wolves." She laughed. "You're so crazy. It's not like you don't know them all."

"Ha!" She rolled her eyes. "Tobias with his filthy, dirty jokes. And Angelica and her 'I'm so rich and you are not' superior attitude, and let's not even mention Callum and his—"

"Callum and his what?" A deep male voice caused both women to emit low pitched shrieks, turning toward the door as one as the thirty-two-year-old former Calvin Klein model and now full-time nerd leaned against its frame with a large, Cheshire grin on his Adonis-like face.

Short brown hair with a soft wave to it that he styled in such a way as to make it look sexy but still scruffy, a very neat, full beard, and piercing brown eyes, Callum Dunn had set many a hearts on campus to fluttering. Even Elisa had felt her cheeks grow warm the first time she'd met him.

He reminded her a lot of slightly beefier version of Jamie Dornan. Oh whom Meredith currently had the biggest crush.

Dressed in his typical fashion of dark jeans and a steel-gray cardigan, Callum was definitely easy on the eyes. And the fact that he originally hailed from Northern Ireland, Belfast to be exact, made his accent even a slightly bit more exotic than the norm out here. Which in turn made it sometimes hard for Elisa to talk with him.

Mostly because she found his accent to be one of the sexiest she'd ever heard in her life, much as she hated to admit it.

"Hm?" He lifted a brow. "Callum, what? I do believe I heard my name."

Snorting, Meredith batted a wrist. "How long were you waiting out there just to hear your name? You've quite the ego, Callum Dunn."

His smile was nothing but straight white teeth and dimples, which Elisa pointedly ignored. She was on the hunt for a Jacobite scroll and had found little in the past two days of searching to lead her to believe she was any closer to sussing the thing out.

"You are coming to the pub tonight, eh, Elisa?"

"Mm." She didn't glance up at the shivery sound of his voice. "I don't know." She clicked on a new screen. "I'm picking up my boyfriend from the airport today."

"Elisa," Meredith whined, "you have to come. I'll not go without you."

"There, see?" Elisa could practically hear Callum's smile. "You must come. And bring him too." Then with a nod in her direction, he turned and walked back out.

Meredith jogged over to her a moment later and shook Elisa's elbow, forcing her to glance up. Her friend's face was a bright cherry red.

"That man is so fuckin' beautiful I just want to take a bite out of his arse."

"What?" Elisa's face scrunched into a half-grimace, half-laugh.

"Yes." She reached out her hand and pretended to grab something from mid-air. "Just sink my teeth into and shake it. God, he's lovely."

"I'm just, yeah, wow, I'm not touching that one with a ten-foot pole."

"Oh, hush, I know you have a boyfriend, but if you cannot see that man is fine, then you're blind, Elisa Adrian."

With a huff, Elisa began to power down her laptop. "I'm never going to find that scroll today. I think I'm just going to go, I have to get ready for Julian."

She hopped off her stool and grabbed her purse.

"Bring him to the pub," Meredith said in a high falsetto. "I demand it, I must see the glories that is Julian Wright."

Giving a finger wave, Elisa rolled her eyes. "I'll think about it. Later!"

If it hadn't been for the heels, Elisa would have run the entire two miles back to her flat. Hopping into the shower, she washed up quickly, before moving on to her closet and choosing her sexiest outfit. Which wasn't really all that sexy.

Not skanked-up sexy, as Meredith would put it anyway. It was just a floral-print strappy dress that came to just above her knees and cinched at the waist. She paired it with dove gray heels, and applied just a little bit of makeup. Something she'd been getting into more and more lately, thanks to Meredith's assertion that to not wear makeup was nothing short of criminal.

Putting a touch of smoky eye shadow onto the corners of her eyes, she curled her lashes and applied a light tint of shell-pink lipstick. Thankfully she had great hair that didn't require much in the way of upkeep. A quick blow dry and a little bit of gel gave it a tousled, just-woke-up-from-bed feel.

Biting onto the corner of her lip, she raced around the small apartment and picked up the bras she'd allowed to collect around her living room and bedroom. Realizing she was starting to stall, she rang for a taxi. They got to her within ten minutes. The drive to the airport felt hideously long and short all at the same time. By the time he dropped her off, she felt like she might puke.

They'd been keeping up by Skyping whenever possible, and of course emails when one or the other wasn't free for a face-to-face chat. But that all felt so impersonal, Elisa was almost desperate to see Julian.

She ignored the swivel of men's heads as she walked through the doors to the waiting area.

What if Julian had changed? What if he didn't love her like before? So much time had passed.

But the moment she saw his smiling face coming down the escalator, she forgot all her nerves, all her what ifs, and, with a happy squeal, raced over to meet him.

Dressed in dark, distressed jeans and tight-fitting CBGB black print shirt, Julian was causing his own set of heads to turn. He'd cut his hair—it no longer fell as long as it had—but he'd also lost all traces of his boyish looks. There was a light dusting of scruff on his jaw, and Elisa flung herself into his arms, wrapping her legs around his waist, not caring that she was probably showing off all the goods to the world.

"You're here," she tapped out on his arm and then kissed him passionately.

He tasted like Julian. Like mint and candy. He smelled like she always remembered, clean soap, and his touch...his touch was strong and powerful and intoxicating.

"I'm here, Smile Girl," he danced the words down her spine and she nodded in return as a single tear slipped down her cheek.

The moment they stepped foot inside her flat it was like old times. Elisa peeled his shirt off, dragging her nails down his abs as he sucked and nibbled his way along her neckline.

She was just about to kick off her heels but he shook his head no. Instead, he scooped her into his arms and laid her down on the couch. Then without tearing his gaze from hers, began to slowly take her clothes off.

There were no thoughts of anyone or anything else in her head when Julian stared at her as he now did. Like she was everything good and lovely and perfect.

He took off everything except the pearls and the heels.

Giving him a smirk, she drew a finger down her thigh, and then laughed when he attacked her like a feral jungle predator.

And when he moved deep inside her, feathering words upon her sensitive skin, she remembered all over again why it was that they'd vowed to remain loyal to each other. Because no man on Earth could ever make her feel a tenth of what she did when she was with him.

Three hours later they were just about to fall asleep in each other's arms when her phone rang.

Holding up a finger, she kissed Julian's nose and then reached over his body for her purse where she stored her phone.

"Hello?"

"Tell me, duckling, exactly where you are, because I am certain I told you there'd be no getting out of it tonight."

Groaning, Elisa shook her head. "Not tonight, Mere, seriously. I just want to hang out with Julian, but I promise that I'll—"

Julian's fingers were waving in the air and he was frowning at her.

"Hold on," she said, and glanced at him. "What's the matter, babe?"

"Is that your friend?" he asked after he'd disentangled himself from her arms.

Nodding, she watched as he put his clothes on roughly.

"Yes, what are you doing?"

"Did you have plans already?" He turned to her.

His hair was all rumpled and God he looked so sexy, she just wanted to bring him back to her side and have him be naked again. But there was something in his eyes that didn't feel right—an energy was there she'd never felt before with him.

It made her feel suddenly shy. Sitting up, she covered her breasts with her arm and dragged her dress over with her foot.

"No, not really. They wanted me to bring you out to the pub tonight and introduce you, but I didn't think you'd want—"

Brushing his fingers through his hair, he gave her a grin. But it didn't quite reach his eyes. "I'm fine. I told you before I came that I didn't want you to change your plans because of me."

"Jules." She slipped her dress on and stood, reaching out for him when the static of a loudly buzzing voice rang through her phone speaker. She glanced down at it.

Picking the phone up, Julian handed it to her, and then turned on his heel and walked toward her bathroom.

What the hell had just happened?

Feeling slightly numb, she placed the phone back to her ear.

"Hello!" Meredith's sharp trill made Elisa realize she'd probably been yelling for the past minute.

"Hey," she said glumly, staring at her bedroom door, listening to the rush of water from her sink and growing more and more worried each second that ticked past that something wasn't right.

"Whoa, what's that tone for? Problems with the mister?"

"No." She frowned, shaking her head almost violently. "Of course not."

"So are you coming or not, love? We've been saving two seats for ya, but the natives are growing restless."

Julian stepped out a second later, and, taking one look at her on the phone, gave her the hand motioning gesture for her to continue.

"You sure?" she asked.

He nodded. "Of course, Smile Girl."

Feeling a little bit better because he'd used his pet name, she agreed. "Fine, we'll be there in about an hour."

"Thirty minutes tops. Bye, babes!" Meredith hung up with a sharp burst of laughter.

The cab ride to Turk's Head felt long and stressful for Elisa. At one point Julian tossed his arm across her shoulder and gave her chaste kiss to the crown of her head, but it didn't feel natural.

She pushed a hand into his chest until he looked down at her.

"Are you breaking up with me?"

Scoffing, he kissed her fingertips. "No. Why would you ever think that?"

He said no, but she didn't feel good about it. The sex had been great, but the warmth they'd always shared was gone and it was terrifying her.

He sighed. "Baby, I'm just exhausted. I flew halfway around the world. And, I didn't get a chance to tell you yet, but I can't stay the full two weeks."

"What?" she shrieked and signed at the same time. The cabbie looked back at them with a tight-lipped scowl. "Why are you just now telling me this? When do you go back?"

"Day after Christmas." He wouldn't look at her as he said it.

"What? Why?" She turned his face with her finger. "Why are you leaving me this way? What's the matter, Julian? If you think I don't know something's up, then you're crazy. I know you like I know my own soul."

He grimaced. "I couldn't get out of it. Mom begged me to come back early."

But again he wouldn't meet her eyes when he said it and his jaw was clenched too tight for that to be the total truth. Having a sudden flashback to the day he and Roman had been signing off-screen, she wondered if that's why Roman had looked shocked when she'd mentioned stealing Julian away from the family.

That would mean he'd known he wasn't staying for two months now and hadn't bothered to tell her. She'd be furious if she wasn't so terrified of just what that could possibly mean.

Feeling a heaviness centering in the middle of her chest, she turned her face to stare out the window, watching in a daze as the bright lights of the city center flashed by.

Julian paid the fare once they got there and it was one of the hardest things Elisa had ever had to do when she walked into that bar to pretend like all was right with the world.

Turk's was as busy as it usually was, with bodies lining the bar and seating area. But the mood was congenial. Elisa hoped the lighthearted atmosphere would help snap Jules out of whatever funk he was in.

Meredith bum rushed her almost immediately, looking up and down her body before giving a wolfy whistle. "Somebody cleans up nice and—" Her jaw dropped when she glanced at Julian. "Bloody hell, I guess I'll be picking up the next round. You're hot as fuck, Julian Wright."

His lips tipped just briefly. At least he was being nice to her friend. Maybe things weren't all lost. Wishing they had time to talk properly, Elisa cast him a very quick glance before Meredith took her hand and whooped.

"Look what the cat dragged in," Meredith cried out from their table. Causing all heads to turn in their direction as they walked over to join them.

Giggling, Elisa covered her mouth with her free hand and gave Julian a quick glance of apology. It was obvious to her that Meredith had already had a beer, or maybe even two; she was never usually quite so blunt in front of males unless she'd taken a shot of liquid courage.

"Elisa." Angelica gave her a tepid smile before her pretty green eyes zeroed in on Julian's body like a laser.

Angelica was edging close to forty and at one point must have been a serious beauty. Her skin still held the luminescent quality of youth, but her hair had silver in it, and there were lines framing her mouth and eyes. She was a pearl losing its luster and not enjoying the process one bit.

She dieted almost obsessively to keep her slim, statuesque figure, and wore nothing but black. Elisa couldn't convince her that rather than making her look modelesque, most times she looked emaciated, washed out, and in dire need of a good hamburger or twenty.

Angelica sipped at her whiskey neat. "And who is this?" The faint trace of a French accent made her just a little more bearable to be around.

Callum pulled the stool from beside him out, and patted it. Indicating Elisa should sit. Elisa was just about to shake her head no and go to sit at the one beside Meredith, but Julian was already sitting down.

Feeling suddenly anxious and awkward she took a seat, staring at faces she'd only just begun to know, wondering what Julian was thinking now.

"So Julian." Meredith waggled her brows. "Elisa tells us you read lips. So read mine." She took a huge swig of her beer.

"No," Elisa shook her head and chuckled. "Don't read her lips, whatever comes out of there is going to be humiliatingly raunchy."

"Speaking of raunchy..." A ruddy-cheeked Tobias grinned, which caused the entire table to groan.

"Well, if you aren't going to listen to me, you certainly don't want to listen to Tobias," Meredith wailed.

"No, no, now hold on a moment." Tobias whipped off his cap, wiped his sweaty brow, and then grinned. "This one's funny."

"Oh, piss off, the lot of you!" Meredith glowered before taking another large swig of her beer.

Callum snorted and then cast a quick glance at Elisa before taking a sip of his own beer.

"Mickey Mouse stood before a judge waiting for the verdict on his divorce case—"

"Mickey!" Elisa laughed. "Oh no, don't you dare denigrate the mouse, Tobias."

"What?" he chuffed, took a large swallow of his beer and winked at Julian. "It's the most American joke I have. Now stop interrupting me."

"Anyway, as I was saying. 'Mickey,' says the judge, 'I cannot grant you a divorce. Although you claim she is crazy, the court has found Minnie to be mentally competent.' 'But your honor,' says the mouse, 'I never said she was crazy. I said she was fucking Goofy."

Groans and giggles erupted from the group, even Angelica

laughed at that one, but when Elisa turned to Julian, he wasn't smiling. He had a sad look on his face, haunted, and almost distant, and the fears she'd felt back in the car came back with a vengeance.

She tried her best to engage him the rest of the night, he was kind and sweet as ever, but he was different too.

The week flew by, and unable to bear their strange silence another second, she erupted the night over dinner the night before he left.

"What's the problem? You tell me now!" She slashed her fingers through the air.

He smashed his fist onto the table and she jumped in her seat, eyes wide and looking at him in a way she never had before.

Clenching his jaw, he squeezed his eyes shut. "You want to know what's going on with me, Elisa, really?"

Sick to her stomach, she grabbed at herself, nodding her head even as inside she screamed, preparing herself to hear the worst.

When he looked at her again, there wasn't any of the anger or fury, but there was an overwhelming sadness that brought tears to her eyes.

"We don't see each other. We talk online and all you talk about is this place and these people and I'm glad, I'm glad you're making friends, I'm glad."

The pause was so lengthy that she had to urge him on to continue. "But?"

It was rare to see Julian cry. He'd only done it once or twice in front of her, and now he wasn't out and out bawling, but his eyes were teary and glistening.

"But I'm stuck back there. And you're moving on. Just like we always do. Do you like that guy Callum?"

"What?" She jerked and then shifted in her seat. "Of course not," she said defensively. “Why would you even ask that?”

Had she been making eyes at him that night? She didn’t think so. Elisa had made every effort to keep Callum at bay, not giving him eye contact, not laughing at his jokes, she loved Julian—he had to know that.

His touch on her cheek was so gentle it stirred memories of what they’d once been. She leaned into it desperately, but all too soon he pulled away.

“Because I saw how he looked at you. You have a life here, Elisa, and I’ve got no part of it. I’m so happy to see you thriving, but it kills me too, because I feel you slipping away and I’m not sure you’re even aware of it.”

“I’m not slipping away. I love you, only you. So what if I think someone else is attractive?” She fessed up to it. He wasn’t stupid after all, nor was she to believe that Julian wouldn’t see other girls and not find them beautiful. “But attraction is only skin deep. I don’t know him, he doesn’t know me. You mean everything to me.”

“But we still have another year and a half before I graduate. Are you telling me you think this can work like this for that long?”

Taking several panicked, deep breaths she shook her head. “Don’t tell me you’re breaking up with me.”

“Of course not.” He sighed, and then getting up, he held his hand out to her.

She took it and shuddered into him when his large, strong arms wrapped around her waist.

He kissed the crown of her head and tapped out his words on her body. “But I feel like I see the writing on the wall, Elisa, and I’m terrified of what’s going to happen to us. I’m sorry if I get moody, but when it comes to you, I’ve never been really good at pretending.”

Finally understanding the source of the strain, she wrapped her arms around his neck and walked with him backward to her room, wanting to prove to him with her body just how much she truly belonged to him, mind, body, and soul.

But the next morning when she walked him to the airport the tension was back, and as she turned for home she admitted to herself what she'd been unable to say to him.

How could they survive another year and a half of this?

Visits came and visits went, and some of them were better than others. Elisa and Julian grew as busy as they'd been before and the online chats became less and less.

The emails became more impersonal and before she knew it, it started to feel a lot like she was hanging on to something that'd died a painful last breath months ago.

Elisa stared at Julian's latest email.

"Don't worry about coming to graduation. I'm actually finishing my classes early and will be done here in two weeks. Mom's pissed I'm not walking, but I just don't feel like it. I found a studio in New York I think I'm gonna buy. It suits me. It's in Chelsea, I think you'd like it if you saw it. I miss you lots.

Love,

Jules"

Elisa debated not answering, but decided to anyway.

"So you don't want me to come? Julian, I can't help feeling like something..."

Staring at her words, she swiftly deleted it and powered down her laptop. Anything she said now would come out too needy and make her sound pathetic. Did Julian want to break up with her? It would be so much easier if she could just talk to him face to face, but he was probably already asleep and the last thing she wanted was to wake him up to have a serious, relationship-defining sort of talk.

Her phone rang. Sad and not wanting to talk, she debated whether or not to just let it go to voicemail, but eventually picked it up.

"Hello."

"Well, there you are." Chastity's familiar voice made Elisa smile.

"Chas, oh man, it's so good to hear a friendly voice. How's married life treating you?"

"Oh, you know, good, and by the way we're having a baby in two months."

"What?" She sat forward. "You didn't tell me this. Congratulations! Boy or girl?"

"Well, I didn't tell you and I am sorry for that, but I had a sister who had about three miscarriages so I was a little anxious about spilling the beans to you until I knew it would stick. And it, by the way, is a girl!"

They squealed and laughed together.

Elisa had flown to Luke and Chas's wedding last summer. Chastity had made a beautiful beach side bride. Even Julian had been in high spirits for it. It'd almost felt like he and Elisa had fallen in love all over again as they'd danced beneath the stars on the cold sand by the light of several lit tiki torches.

That memory seemed like a lifetime ago now.

She swallowed hard. "Chas."

"Yeah?"

Elisa picked at her thumbnail. "How's Jules?"

"Girl, I can't believe how busy that boy is. His art is really starting to go mainstream. I wouldn't doubt if in a few months he becomes the next *it* artist. He's been making the rounds in the New York art scene and rubbing elbows with the hoi polloi. Yeah, he's moving on up. But don't you guys talk?" She sounded genuinely confused and it almost made Elisa want to cry.

No one knew how strained things now were between the two of them, mostly because she felt that to own up to it would make it real. But it was getting beyond the point that she could simply ignore the obvious either.

She sighed, and stared out her window. "Not like we used to. When we see each other, things are great, but this distance, I don't know. It's just not good."

"Hm. I'm sorry to hear that. But he's not seeing anyone else, if that's what you're worried about."

A wave of relief hit her hard enough to make her realize regardless of how little they now talked, Julian was still important enough to her that it mattered.

"He's super busy. Luke likes to check in on him whenever he can, and sometimes he'll come over here for dinner and whatever, but I don't think I've ever seen someone more driven to be a success than he is."

"I always knew he would be." Her grin wobbled, her vision suddenly blurred, and she wiped at her nose swiftly. "Anyway, it's late, and I have work early in the morning so I should probably go."

Chastity sighed. "Yeah, I figured you might. I just wanted to say I miss you lots. You still planning to come back this summer?"

A few weeks ago the answer would have absolutely been a yes, but now, everything was just so confusing. It wasn't like she was going home only to see Julian, and it wasn't fair to her parents to not go home just because she wasn't sure what kind of a reception she'd get from him, but she'd never really been good at holding it together where he was concerned.

"I don't know, it just depends on if I can get the time off of work. I love you. Kiss Luke for me, okay?"

Chastity said her goodbyes and then they were off. Elisa had to drag her body away from the desk to her bed, feeling weary and more exhausted than she had in years.

Coming to Dublin had seemed like the right thing to do, she loved her job, she loved her friends, but none of it was keeping her happy.

Rolling into bed, she did what she'd done for the past several months. She sniffed Julian's pillow. The one he always slept on whenever he came for a visit. He'd taken to dousing his cologne on it before he would leave, claiming that by the time it faded he'd be back and able to do it again.

But it was fading quickly and he wasn't coming out this summer.

She could barely smell the warmth and spiciness of it, and sometimes she could swear she'd even forgotten what his scent of mint and soap smelled like. She was losing him, or she'd lost him, she wasn't sure which.

Either way, Elisa was miserable.

Chapter 17

Elisa glanced at Meredith over her laptop screen at work the next morning. "Hey you, got a favor to ask."

Meredith lifted a lavender brow. "And just what might that be, luv?"

Grimacing, she gave her friend woebegone eyes. "My mother's shipped me a stack of boxes, and by stack I mean stacks. Each box is probably going to weigh about twenty pounds, or umm..." She blinked doing the math in her head. "One point four stones—I think that's right."

"One in a half stones? Bloody hell, Elisa, have you never heard of an e-reader?"

She laughed. "Leave me alone. It's just two boxes, but there's no way I can move those up my apartment stairs and I don't want to have to pay to do it—"

"And what makes you think I could, eh? Do I look like the a girl who plays around with weights?"

Meredith, dressed in black tights and a bold red and white-striped knee length dress, did not in fact look capable of lifting much over five pounds.

She sighed. "Well, I figured between the two of us we could make it happen."

"Or you know," Callum's deep voice broke into their conversation, "you could ask me. I've nothing to do today." He stepped into their room wearing a large, sexy grin.

Elisa's heart beat a rapid tattoo in her chest.

Meredith bit her bottom lip and had a devilish glint in her eyes as she said, "Hm. I think yes, suddenly I seem to have found the time after all." She winked and with a laugh, flitted from the room like a drunken, little butterfly.

Elisa rubbed her arm. "Thanks, Callum, but seriously I'm sure Mere and I can handle it."

"Aye. I'm sure you could."

Her stomach bottomed out every time his accent came out. His voice was actually very refined and cultured, she wondered if sometimes he did that on purpose just to get a rise out of her. Taking a deep breath, she pretended to fiddle around with her laptop, willing the heat in her veins to slow down a little.

"But I do believe that if I don't go, neither will your little helper." He winked.

She had to fight to keep her mouth closed and not hang open like a fish out of water. The man completely threw off her equilibrium.

"What time should I be there?"

Forced to look up at him, she steeled her nerves and gave him a small smile she hoped would pass for gratefulness and not anxiety and said, "Six. If that works for you."

"It does. I'll bring some beer, you order the pizzas."

She frowned. There'd been no intention of this turning into an all-night thing, but he was already out the door and Tobias came waddling in a moment later asking her to jog over to collections for him.

Sighing, she got back to work.

That night she had a belly full of nerves. Meredith had cancelled on her at the last minute, claiming that her brother had planned an unexpected visit and was waiting for her to pick him up at the airport. Judging by her tone of voice and the multitude of invectives she'd let loose, Elisa was inclined to believe her friend was none too happy about her sudden change of plans.

The night air was brisk and a little chilly as a storm cloud rolled in. Elisa stared at the boxes on the sidewalk, wishing her mother hadn't sent the stupid things and placed her in this type of situation. The carrier had looked perplexed when she'd instructed he should leave those enormous boxes on the sidewalk—he'd been willing to take them up.

For an exorbitant fee, of course. She rolled her eyes.

Hugging her arms to her body, she waited for Callum to arrive. He did so about ten minutes later, and, just as he'd promised, he had a case of beers with him.

Walking directly up to her, he wrapped her into a warm hug that smelled strongly of good clean soap and cologne. Thrown off by his show of affection, she awkwardly patted his back.

"Hey," she said after a second.

"Hey," he repeated. "Where's the fae?"

Chuckling, she tipped her chin in the direction of the airport. "Brother called last minute, said he needed to be picked up from the airport, so, unfortunately, it's just the two of us."

"Well." His unusually light brown eyes gleamed. "I wouldn't say it was unfortunate."

"Oh," she said dumbly, because she had no clue what to say to that. Was he flirting with her? It seemed like it. But they worked together and interoffice romances were pretty much forbidden. He'd know that, of course, so maybe this was just Callum's way. Some guys were horrible flirts; in fact, she knew two of them very intimately.

Feeling slightly better by that thought, she took the beer from him.

"And these are the boxes?" he asked, shrugging out of his cardigan and handing it to her too.

He wore a fitted black shirt beneath that sculpted beautifully to his chest. There could be no doubt that the man had once modeled; he looked like some airbrushed god straight out of the pages of *Vogue*.

Several women, young and old, turned to stare at the two of them. Elisa's cheeks heated, though she wasn't sure why. Hefting the cardigan so that it lay over her shoulder, she nodded.

"Yup. If you just give me a second to put these down upstairs, I'll come back down and help you with them."

"Elisa," he snickered, "I've no need of help, just guide me to your door is all."

"But they're heavy."

With a wink, he knelt and lifted the enormous box like it weighed no more than a feather. And for a quick second she found herself hypnotized by the flex of his smooth, tanned, bulging biceps.

"Typically I wouldn't mind the ogling, but this is heavy." His lip twitched.

"Oh God, yeah." She jerked, turned on her heel and raced up the stairs. She couldn't believe she'd been caught staring like that.

Of course she'd just left a box hanging out on the sidewalk all by itself, tempting anyone to take it if they wanted, but that was the least of her worries right now.

Opening her door, she held it out for him. Callum was breathing just a little heavy when he walked through. Setting it down in the middle of her flat, he then turned and walked back downstairs to lug up the second box.

He returned about ten minutes later, and, apart from a little sheen of sweat on his brow, looked no worse for wear.

Sitting down on her couch a second later, he sighed. "Bloody hell, woman, you do love your books."

Laughing, and feeling some of the tension easing up between them, she shrugged. "Of course. I doubt I'd be working in this job if I didn't."

Elisa eyed the cheese pizza on her counter. She'd ordered it when she'd still thought Meredith would be showing up, it seemed silly to kick him out when there was no way she could finish off a whole pizza by herself.

The root of her entire problem with Callum was that she felt guilty because of Julian. Not that she planned to do anything with Callum. Men and women could be friends, if the relationship was well defined from the beginning.

Rather than being scared of him, maybe she just needed to get to know him better. Maybe if she did she'd find her silly little crush would cease to be.

Squaring her shoulders, she turned back to him.

Callum was sitting up, with one of his hands dangling between his thighs, looking at her in such a way that she was pretty sure he knew exactly what she'd been thinking.

"Elisa?"

He said her name like a question. But she heard not just one question behind it, but several.

Should I go?

Are you okay?

Is there more?

Giving him a big, brave smile, she pointed to the pizza and beer. "You hungry?"

Laugh lines framed the corners of his eyes and mouth as he said, "I'm famished. Haven't eaten all day."

"Yeah, so I suppose you don't count the entire bag of grapes and that bit of turkey sandwich you stole from Meredith as food then?"

Snorting, he ran a hand through his hair. "Well, I did forget about that."

"Hm." Shaking her head, feeling a million times better, she grabbed two paper plates, slid a slice of pizza onto each of them, and then, taking two beers, went to join him.

"Thank you." His fingers grazed hers as he took the plate and drink.

Stomach curling with fronds of heat, she nodded mutely.

But Callum seemed determined not to let the conversation get tense and stilted again.

"So how are you enjoying Trinity?"

Taking a delicate bite of her pizza, she nodded. "I like it a lot. In fact, I love it. It's everything I'd hoped it would be."

Crossing his leg over his lap, he smiled. "I'm glad to hear you say it. It's always nice to work in a place you love. Doesn't quite feel like work then."

He took a big man-bite of his slice, chasing it with a swallow of beer.

"You've always confused me, Callum. You were a big name in the modeling industry..."

He groaned. "I wondered when we'd get around to that part of my life."

Taking a tentative sip of her beer, she gave him a wondering look. "You can't tell me that that wasn't exciting too? You got to see the world and meet all the prettiest people and—"

Snorting, he shook his head. "Travel the world, I'll give you that. But even at its most fun, it's wearying. To always live out of suitcases, to have to deal with the stress of that lifestyle and the people that live in it. To be so in demand that your life is not your own." He shook his head. "Trust me when I say, it's highly overrated. As to meeting the prettiest people—"

His brown eyes gleamed with a look she recognized clearly, because she'd often seen it burn through Julian's eyes. Feeling like her skin would suddenly combust, Elisa cleared her throat and scooted just a little farther away from him.

He must have noticed, because he gave his head a little shake and took another bite out of his pizza.

Throat tight with nerves, she said, "So you threw it all away to pursue your true passion. Books." Elisa laughed as she said it, but his look was totally serious as he nodded.

"I'm a man of great passions, Elisa. I know what I want, and modeling wasn't it. That was merely a means to an end. I had massive college bills to pay off and that was the easiest way for me to do it, but it was never my intention to remain there."

"Must have caused quite a media circus. Mr. Golden Abs turning down millions to pursue his true love of academia."

His lips twitched. "Doesn't happen often, I'll grant you that. But, I think you'll find the stereotypes that live in that world are often quite exaggerated."

"Well, you have me there, Callum. Though I never was the type of girl who bought into the myth that all models are dumb."

"No." He looked at her intently as he said it. "No, I don't suppose you would be."

She nibbled on her bottom lip, forcing herself to break eye contact with him. Staring at Callum for too long felt a lot like looking into the sun, not something anyone wanted to do for any amount of time.

"You know my hobbies." He smiled. "What are yours? Although I suppose you've as much of a passion for the written word as I do." He stared pointedly at the boxes on her floor.

Laughing, she said, "Guilty as charged. But I was also a competitive swimmer."

"Aye?"

There went that shivery burr again. The man was totally doing it on purpose. "Will you stop that?" She took a giant pull of her beer.

"Stop what?" He gave her a look that said he knew exactly what she was talking about.

"Being so…" She flicked her wrist at him. "Being so you."

"Me?" He chuckled, a deep-bodied sound that shivered through her flesh and made her blood sing. "But okay." He nodded gallantly. "I'll stop."

"Thank you."

"As to your swimming." He took another bite of his pizza, finishing it.

"It was no big deal. Well, okay, I guess it was kind of a big deal. It paid for my college."

His brows rose. "That's a big deal indeed. Just how good were you?"

"Good enough that an Olympic scout came out to see me." She sighed.

"Wow." He actually looked impressed, which made her feel good. "I take it by your sigh you didn't make it?"

Lips thinning, she sighed again. "No, the sigh is because I'll never know if I was good enough or not. I suffered a really terrible injury the week before and wasn't able to swim the race."

"He couldn't come back later?"

"Sometimes we only get one change at things." As she said it, her voice lowered and her memories veered not toward Clive Amsler, but Julian.

Drifting off she stared at the wall, wondering what he was doing right now.

"Well then." Callum clapped his hands on his jeans, startling her and making her jump in her seat. "I should go."

It was on the tip of her tongue to ask him to stay, but nothing good could come from him staying longer.

"Okay, thanks for helping me with the boxes. I don't think I could have done it myself."

Chuckling, he stood and made for the door. Grabbing his cardigan, he slipped it on and then stood in the open door staring at her for a long, intense few seconds.

"Callum?" It was her turn to ask questions just with his name.

Screwing up his face, he patted her shoulder. "I...uh...well." He sighed and then gave her a tight smile. "I'll see you later, Elisa."

Nodding, she waved goodbye and stood there watching him go silently. He never turned back to stare at her, but she sensed that if she so much as cleared her throat he'd be back up the stairs in a heartbeat.

"Oh my God," she whispered when she knew he was well out of earshot, "what the hell is happening to me?"

"Okay, okay." Meredith held up her shot glass. Her lavender hair was now longer, hanging in a shaggy bob around her long jawline. "My turn." She glanced over at Elisa and winked, her brightly painted lips turned up into a half smile. "Either you A, tell us how you'd rather die, or B, you take the shot."

"Die? How morbid are you?" Angelica sniffed and rubbed at her nose, fluttering a hand over her slicked bun.

Meredith stuck out her tongue and downed her shot of whiskey aggressively before pouring out another one. "Then take the shot, 'Gelica."

Tobias chuckled, shoving his glasses back up his nose. Normally he wore contacts, because he always said that if he didn't he looked a lot like a nerdy hobbit, but Elisa found him more charming with his tweed jacket and thick framed glasses on than off. He looked just like how a proper Keeper should.

Elisa grinned. The gang had been at Turk's only an hour, but already most of them were drunk off their asses. At one point Meredith had even tried to crawl up on the bar to dance.

It'd taken both Elisa and Callum to drag her down from there.

A foot kicked at Elisa's underneath the table. She glanced up to see Callum's glimmering brown eyes smiling down at her. "So what say you, Elisa, how would you rather die, inquiring minds wish to know." His shot glass played along his full bottom lip.

Stomach fizzing with a case of nerves at his sudden playfulness, and the fact that she hadn't had a thing to eat today—other than half of Meredith's chicken sandwich at lunch—she shook her head, tucking a curl of hair behind her ear.

"Jaysus," Mere snorted. "It's not that hard, duckling, here let me show you. If I had my way I'd rather die in the arms of my lover as we drank from a bottle of poison. Together. Forever..." She clutched at her chest.

"Good God," Tobias groaned. "Why am I not surprised you'd prefer a Shakespearean end?"

Rolling her eyes, she gave him a pointed look. "Well then, if my death is not sufficient for you, how would you go?"

"I'll likely meet my end in the loo, after a violent and very painful bout of—"

"Do you mind?" Angelica turned in her seat to glare at him, and then eyed her amber-colored whiskey with a wrinkled nose.

Tobias chuckled heartily, and, with a shrug, downed his shot anyway.

It'd taken Elisa months to figure out the slang in Ireland. WC, she'd learned, was short for "water closet," also known as the loo, also known as a bathroom. At least to Americans anyway, they'd teased her mercilessly that a bathroom should have a bath in it and that they never could understand Yanks and their backward ways.

Her lips twitched as she pictured a pantless Tobias sprawled out on a toilet, with his mouth gaping open, dead from a heart attack.

"My imagination is so vivid that I'm having a very hard time not picturing this," Elisa said with a chuckle.

He winked; his normally pinkened cheeks were now an even deeper shade of red. He and Meredith had been hitting it hard. It'd surprised Elisa how unpretentious academia actually could be.

She'd expected before arriving that everyone would be buttoned-up snobs, only interested in expounding the virtues of whatever priceless rare collections they'd been recently working on. And they were, to an extent.

Tobias seemed to take almost orgasmic delight when reading through the *Book of Kells*, as one of the U.K.'s premiere authorities on it, he was the man to ask if you had any questions on the matter. But he also enjoyed a ribald joke or two, he loved his beer, and the weekly get-togethers had been his brainchild. A place, he'd said, where they could go to relax and not talk about work for just a few hours. Elisa had come to look forward to their Saturday nights.

Callum smiled at her again, and she glanced away.

"Well, I know how I'd like to die," his deep throated voice interrupted Mere and Tobias's squabbling.

"How?" Angelica asked with a raised brow.

Elisa was convinced that Angelica only came to these get-togethers because of Callum and her hope of someday making him husband number three, but that was just a guess.

"Alone on a secluded island, with a good woman beside me." He grinned at Elisa as he said it. "And a stack of books that reaches toward the heavens."

"How utterly Hemmingway of you." Meredith chuckled.

"Never go on trips with anyone you do not love." Callum smiled, tipping his glass toward Elisa.

She swallowed hard, feeling slightly anxious by his obvious attentions tonight. Apparently she wasn't the only one to notice because a moment after Callum excused himself to the bathroom Meredith shielded the left side of her mouth with her hand so that neither Tobias nor Angelica could see her mouth, "Wow."

He'd gotten friendlier with her since the day he'd helped her with the boxes. It was nice to have finally broken the ice, but now she was scared that she might have done more than broken the ice with him.

There were moments where her mind would drift, wondering what he was doing, where he was at. It unnerved her that she couldn't seem to control those thoughts. She still loved Julian, but it was so easy sometimes to imagine what it might be like if she was free and so was he. As much as it pained her to even think it, all signs were pointing toward their relationship heading in that direction.

Shushing her friend, Elisa waved her off. "I think I might go."

"Oh no," Meredith cried, "not yet, I haven't even gotten properly drunk."

Laughing, she got up, feeling a little lightheaded, but not too bad. She'd only had two beers and a shot. Her tolerance for liquor was growing since meeting the rowdy bunch.

"No really." She pretended to yawn, accidentally bumping into a bar patron as she did. "I'm tired, I haven't slept much the past few nights and I'm exhausted."

"Oh, come on," Meredith wrapped an arm around her neck. "You can sleep in tomorrow, there's no rush."

"No." She looked up as Callum sat back down, giving her a strange look as she slipped some cash onto the table. "Really. Angelica." She gave the French beauty a nod of goodbye. "God of Books," she then said to Tobias, who gave a hearty chuckle at her nickname for him and reached his arms up for a hug.

He was quite touchy when deep in his cups. Elisa would never tell him so, but in the pub he was a happy drunk, unlike the strict taskmaster at work.

Giving him a quick hug, she nodded at Callum. With a quick kiss on Mere's cheek, she gave a final wave and headed for home.

She'd walk tonight—it was a distance, but she wanted the fresh air.

The city was alive with the sounds of laughter and lights, she loved Dublin, loved everything about it's Old World charm, so unlike Maine. She felt like a different person, a new woman here.

Though she'd spent the majority of her life on U.S. soil, she found it almost too easy to settle into life in Ireland.

Deep in thought, she didn't hear the pounding footsteps coming up behind her until they were right on top of her.

"Hey you." Callum's deep throaty voice made her whirl on her ballerina flats.

"Whoa." She expelled a long breath. "Oh my God, you scared me." She gave a weak chuckle and grabbed her chest.

His hair looked windblown from running, he'd shaved his beard weeks ago, but he now had a fine dusting of dark shadow on his jaw. Her fingers twitched.

"Where are you off to?"

Nibbling on the corner of her lip, she glanced forward and then back. "Did you just chase after me?"

Sticking his hands into his jeans he shrugged and with a coy grin said, "And what if I said I did?"

Pulse thundering so hard through her ears she was afraid he could hear it, she turned on her heel, confused whether to stop and chat or keep walking for home.

"Did I leave something there?" she finally asked in confusion.

"Elisa." He grabbed for her hand, threading their fingers together just briefly. "You must know by now."

The touch of his skin on hers sent shockwaves through her arm. Jerking away from him, she shook her head. "You...you..." She cleared her throat. "You shouldn't touch me that way."

Grabbing her elbow, he pulled her to a stop.

His deep brown eyes mesmerized her.

"How long are we going to play this game?" he asked and she frowned.

"What game?"

Cocking his head, a thick lock of his wavy hair slipped over one eye, and she had to curl her hand into a fist to keep from brushing it back.

"The game where we pretend that we don't feel this."

Clenching her jaw, it was everything she could do to turn away from him. "I have a boyfriend," she said; bringing Julian up made her feel a little braver.

"You mean the man who rarely comes anymore?"

"Hey," she snapped and twirled on him, "what we do is none of your business."

Holding out his hands, he gave her a calm look. "I'm not trying to fight, believe me. I admire you. I have almost from the moment we've met. But I would be a fool to not let my feelings be known. To not fight for any sort of a chance."

Anyone else and she wouldn't even have a second's doubt. But Callum was beautiful. Beyond beautiful, he was the type of unattainable male most women only got to dream about and admire in magazines. He'd modeled for some of the most elite designers in the world and he was telling her he liked her.

Her stomach heaved.

"I love him," she said and meant it with every fiber of her soul. Regardless of how strained things were now between her and Julian, she'd never be able to just move on to a new man. Even one as beautiful as Callum.

He brushed his knuckles over her cheek and for the first time in years Elisa felt the type of sensations that could only spring from new love.

What she felt for Callum wasn't anything close to what she had with Julian, but there was definitely attraction, which made this so much harder.

"I've lived a lifestyle of ease and women, money, and everything it could buy. But none of it made me happy. I'm the kind of man who when I see something I want, I go for it. And I want you, Elisa, I'm intensely serious about that."

He stepped into her, crowding her space. And even though she'd been drinking and could blame anything that might happen on that, she knew she wasn't really that drunk.

Though Callum smelled of books and wine and cigar smoke—smells she loved now—and his looks could make even a saint stop and stare, she turned her face to the side.

"I really don't think this is appropriate," she said.

But he was already swooping in, and she turned just in time for his mouth to graze her cheek instead of her lips.

Her entire body lit up in a blaze of heat, her skin tingled where he'd touched her. It was all she could do not to brush her fingers over the spot where he'd kissed her.

Stepping way back and out of his reach, she shook her head. "Don't do that again."

"I want to see you tomorrow. Just you and me, wherever you'd like. Tell me you'll come."

Each word out of his lips weakened her resolve further. Needing to get away from him, right now, she said, "Callum, I—"

Lost for words, confused, and shamefully excited, she sidestepped him and ran straight to her flat.

The run was exhausting, and by the time she got to her flat she was coated in a layer of sweat, but it'd also helped to clear her jumbled thoughts. She needed to talk to Jules. Running to her laptop, she called him, trying to Skype. But it rang and rang and rang. Either he was asleep or out.

Wanting to leave him a message, she clicked on her Gmail, but stared at the screen as too many words crowded her head.

He'd graduated almost two months ago. They'd just talked last week, but things were so different now. So horribly, terribly different.

Sniffing, she shut her laptop and shuffled into her room, stripping her slacks and shirt off, then stumbling into bed with nothing on but her bra and panties. Yanking Julian's pillow to her, she lay down and stared at the painting of her and him in the hospital room hanging up on her wall.

Was it really possible that after everything they'd gone through, it could be over just like that?

But as her eyes closed and her mind began to drift, it wasn't Julian's sea-green gaze she saw, but a pair of sensual brown ones.

"I want you, Elisa, and I'm intensely serious..."

Chapter 18

Elisa smiled as memories of her pseudo-date last night crowded her waking thoughts. She really didn't even know what to call it. But Callum made her feel things she hadn't felt in years, alive, excited, happy.

She winced into the rare sunniness of a bright Irish morning and pulled the sheets up over her head one final time. Her head ached from one too many beers and her mouth was dry. The idea of eating anything right now didn't appeal, but if she didn't at least have a coffee and some dry toast she'd regret it later.

Thank God it was Sunday and she had the day to recover—Meredith had kept pushing those beers on her last night. Granted, she could have said no, but Callum's teasing smile had made her feel stupidly brave.

He'd asked to see her again today. Her stomach dove to her knees. They'd been drunk and silly, what if it was nothing more than just words? She'd tried hard not to encourage him too much last night. But that kiss on her cheek right before she'd run away...

She worried her bottom lip thinking about it. Why did everything have to be so complicated?

Rolling over, she buried her nose into Julian's pillow, breathing him in before she started her day, but then froze as it felt like she'd just been sucker punched.

Elisa sniffed again.

Nothing.

Eyes going wide in an instant, she shook off her sleepiness and sat up, snatching the pillow up as she did so. But no matter how many times she buried her face in it, his smell was gone.

Numb, she stared at the crimson pillow case with tears blurring her eyes as the finality of what that meant began to wiggle itself through her brain. She and Julian hadn't out and out broken up. But their talks were less, their need to see one another was less, they had their lives, and somehow—without her even being aware of it—they'd begun to move on.

With an inarticulate cry she picked up her phone and called her mother. It would be very late there, but she hoped her mother was still awake.

She picked up on the second ring. "Elisa, honey?" She sounded anxious.

"Mum." The moment she said it the floodgates poured open and the tears began to fall. "Mum, he's gone."

Elisa smashed the pillow to her chest, rocking back and forth on her bottom.

"Baby girl, what's the matter? Who's gone?"

The tears were choking her voice, making her words come out garbled and stuttered.

"Honey, honey, slow down," her mother crooned. "Baby, what in the world is the matter?"

Wiping her face on the pillow, she shook her head, feeling the loss of Julian in a way she'd not felt it before. "His scent," she finally managed to say. "It's gone, Mom. I went to smell it today like I always do and I can't anymore. He's just not here."

"Oh." Her voice drifted off knowingly. "Oh, baby. Did you guys break up?"

"I don't think so. But..." She sniffed and scrubbed at her cheeks with the back of her wrist. "We don't talk anymore like we used to. Sometimes it's barely ten minutes a night. He's so busy and so am I. Our lives are just moving on, but I think we're both terrified to be the one to say it's actually over."

Cradling the phone between her ear and her shoulder, Elisa stared at her tattoo.

Destiny...

She rubbed it slowly. It'd felt so true the day she'd gotten it on her. Inevitable even, in her mind it'd been impossible to even think an ocean could break them apart.

"I met a guy down here," she whispered slowly, admitting out loud what she'd tried so hard to deny to the rest of the world.

"Have you guys—" she began hesitantly.

"No." Elisa shook her head hard. "In fact, up until last night I haven't been encouraging him. But I feel electric when I'm around him. Alive, even. He kissed my cheek," she said, smiling sadly, "and it was like the first time with Julian."

"Hm."

That was all she said, no more, no less.

"What, hm? What does that mean?" Elisa asked, desperate for some pearls of wisdom to be thrown her way. She was so confused. Everything was just wrong and upside down. "I don't know what to do, Mom."

A long sigh sounded and then her mother said, "Elisa, do you love him?"

That was an odd question to ask. She barely knew Callum; true, they'd been working together for two years now and she liked him a great deal, he was sexy, and brilliant, and his accent was to die for, but...

"I don't know, I feel crazy, passionate things when I'm around him. I feel like I can hardly breathe when he smiles at me, and like his mind, he was a Calvin Klein model and—"

"But that's not what I asked you. I asked you do you love him?"

She sighed. "Of course not." Pinching her nose, she said, "So I assume you're getting at the fact that if I don't love him, I must love Julian, and you know that's true. But sometimes I'm scared that the passion is gone."

Elisa could almost hear her mother shaking her head. "I'm going to share a secret with you, honey. One that most romantics will never own up to. Love is not an emotion, it's a choice."

Elizabeth laughed and Elisa frowned.

"Do you honestly think that after twenty years of marriage I wake up next to your father and still get the sensation of fireworks?"

"To be honest, I'd rather not think about you and Dad having sensations at all." She chuckled, sticking out her tongue.

Elizabeth ignored her teasing. "What you're describing, that's what we call the puppy dog stage. We call it that, Elisa, because it's short-lived and intense, but it's not made to last. No matter how many men you date, or how long you keep searching, or how many times you think you've finally found 'the one' it will always, *always* go away."

"Well, I know that."

"No, dear, I don't think you do. Because if you question whether what you and Julian have is still relevant than you're failing to see my point at all. True love is so much more than sexual chemistry or attraction. True love is finding a mate who is as devoted to you as you are to them. Who will hold your hand through the good and the bad. Who will love you even though you've begun to age, started to wrinkle, when your looks are no longer what they once were. Does this man in Ireland know you at all?"

The more her mother spoke, the harder Elisa dug her fingers into Julian's pillowcase.

"Not really," she squeaked out.

Callum knew her fondness for apples, and her love of blues music. He knew she was a featherweight when it came to her alcohol, and that she loved to swim. But all of that was just superficial.

Surface-level stuff anyone who knew her even a little would know. He didn't know her well enough to have told her which major to pursue. If he decided tomorrow that he was over her, it would sting, but would she be devastated?

A year from now, would she care?

"Let me ask you this, consider your life ten years down the road. Who can you live without? If you can answer that honestly, you can make your choice."

With her mother still on the line, Elisa searched her heart.

When she'd dated Thomas, she'd tried to turn him into a replacement for Julian. She didn't want to do that with Callum. He was Julian's opposite in almost every way. A nerdy Irishman who loved a good beer, making people laugh, and being the center of attention.

She liked his style, liked his manners, she liked everything about him really. Then she thought of Julian. His quiet contemplation of the world around them, the intensity with which he lived life, the way he loved her...

Her heart raced.

How he'd held her when she'd cried devastated tears at knowing her one chance at the Olympics had slipped her by. How he'd brought her that apple back in high school and set it on her tray. How he'd listened to her. Really listen. Julian knew her soul inside and out, and the fact of it was she knew his too.

Callum liked British rock. He had a fetish for all things cardigan sweaters, an obsession with American movies, and a love for medieval literature.

But if she were asked to name ten things he loved, she'd be lucky to get to five. With Julian her list was endless.

Julian was a fighter, always had been. He moved and lived in a world that did not cater to his particular needs and he thrived. Julian might not be able to see color, but when she saw him it was like her world exploded with an intense miasma of it. Maybe the fireworks were gone, but what remained went far deeper than superficial lust.

"Oh my God, Mom," her voice cracked, "what if it's too late? What if I messed up? I don't think he's planning to come back here again. Last time he came, it was hard. He said I'd moved on and I got so angry at him, I denied it all." She clenched her fist, digging her nails into her palm. "But he was right. What if he's already moved on?"

Just the thought of it made her want to vomit, to imagine another Mandy in his life, loving him and touching him and seeing the gift of Julian for what he really was.

She covered her mouth with shaking fingers and shook her head.

"No, baby girl. Julian would never do that. When he moves on he'll tell you."

"But I feel it already, a separation between us. He barely calls me now."

"Elisa Jane, how often do you call him first?"

She blinked, blinded by her hot tears, feeling the impact of those words to her very soul.

"That boy has chased you for years, but he's a man, and we all have our limits. He still had college, you had to get a job, I think he understood that, but there is nothing standing in either one of your way now except for you guys. I told you in the beginning that long-distance relationships can kill even the strongest of love, and it's true. Neither one of you would be to blame for it, but it will happen. Humans are creatures in need of affirmation and love. And if he's not around to give it to you, your heart will look for it elsewhere."

Crying ugly tears now, all she could do was shake her head. Elisa didn't know if it was an agreement or not, but everything her mother said now struck a crippling chord.

"I love him so much, but he's not here, and I've been faithful to him, but I'm so lonely."

"As I'm sure he is too. Fact is, Elisa, there's a choice to be made. Your job and your life in Ireland, or a new life with him. You don't have to decide today, but you do have to decide, and once you do you need to let him know. It's the only fair thing to do."

"But what will I do? I can't just quit? I don't have a job lined up, I wouldn't know what to do." She punched her mattress in frustration.

Giving a sad little chuckle, Elizabeth said, "Honey, believe me when I say these things work themselves out the way they should. Don't panic about what tomorrow might bring, you can't walk a thousand miles in a day, the only thing you can do is decide to take that first step."

They hung up a short time later, but for Elisa her whole world changed. Picking up the phone she made one final phone call.

"Lisa?" Chastity asked a minute later, her voice sounding sleepy, and Elisa knew she'd woken her up. "Hey, girl, you okay?"

"I'm sorry, Chas, I know it's late there, I just..." She pulled her bottom lip between her teeth. "I just have a quick question and I need you to be totally honest with me."

"Of course I will," she said then smothered a yawn, making Elisa cringe. She felt bad, Chas probably wasn't getting much sleep thanks to being a new mom now, but Elisa couldn't go the rest of her day without knowing.

"I know you guys still hang out with Jules sometimes. Be honest, has he moved on?"

She could have heard a pin drop, her apartment suddenly seemed so silent. For a moment she thought she might throw up as Chastity's silence seemed to take hours rather than just a few seconds before she finally said, "You haven't been around for a while. He's been quiet, like always, but..."

"But...but what?" She gripped the phone until her knuckles turned what. "Has he met someone else?"

"No, no," she was quick to assure, "at least I don't think so. I mean, you know if he wanted to he wouldn't have a problem, he's incredibly talented and good looking, but he's grown distant with us, Lisa, like he's withdrawing little by little. I wasn't going to tell you this, but since you asked, Luke and I were actually talking about it last week, in fact, and he said it's what guys do when they're ready to let things go. They start to cut out the things that remind them of you."

It was like being cut open and someone yanking her heart from out of her chest, and stomping it to the ground. Grabbing her throat, she couldn't make a sound.

"Oh, shoot, Lisa, I'm sorry. Maybe I shouldn't have told you that, I mean, I don't know for sure, we were just talking and—"

"No," she croaked, cleared her throat, and then tried again. "It makes sense. He told me the last time he came that he felt like we were so different now. But I didn't see it." Squeezing her eyes shut, Elisa had the sick feeling that even if she flew back now it was way too late. "And now I do, and it might be too late."

"Call him."

"I can't." Her laughter was full of bitterness. "What would I tell him? I'm still stuck here, but I love you, don't move on with your life, and by the way there was a guy here who for just a second made me second-guess all the years we had together? What the hell would he think of me then?"

Feeling more miserable than she'd ever felt in her life, Elisa hugged his pillow to her chest.

"I love him so much, Chas, and I let everything else get in the way of that. I want to go home."

Chastity sighed. "I'm going to play devil's advocate here for a second, but...do you really want to come home? Or are you having a hard time letting it go? Maybe...maybe, Elisa, maybe it wasn't meant to—"

"Stop it." She shook her head vehemently. "It might not be meant to be, and that's fine. I mean, it's not fine, if he tells me we're over I think I might actually want to die."

A memory of what had happened after Julian had bailed on her after the night of his eighteenth birthday burned its way into her memory banks. The tears, the utter despondency she'd felt when she'd thought they were over forever, that would be nothing to the desolation she'd feel now.

Because this time she knew what her life could be like with Julian. It wouldn't be perfect, but when she imagined her kids, when she imagined whom she should be with ten years down the road, there was only one face she saw.

The image of her future children, they didn't have brown hair with gentle brown eyes, but black hair with eyes the color of a tropical ocean.

When she imagined hands trailing down her body, they weren't soft from years of studying books, but callused and muscled. And when her mate said he loved her, she didn't hear it; she felt the words dance upon her skin.

"He's got a show in two weeks. Won't show Luke and me the paintings, but they must be damned good for him to be included as part of the Museo's Artists in the City exhibit."

Elisa exhaled a long breath. He hadn't told her about that. Museo was one of the hippest and trendiest art galleries in all of the meatpacking district. For him to have gotten in there was a huge, huge deal.

"I didn't know that."

"Well, if it makes you feel any better, I saw the invitation for you on his desk."

She clutched her heart. "I'll see you guys in two weeks. But Chas?"

"Yeah?"

Elisa stared at her room that had one time begun to feel so comfortable and warm and now only saw it for what it was. A mirage, a reflection of a life she no longer wanted.

"Don't tell him, okay? I know a lot can happen in two weeks"—she thinned her lips as her heart trembled—"but I want to know that no matter the outcome, it's supposed to happen as it should."

She sighed. "Are you going to call him?"

Julian hadn't called in over a week. Elisa wasn't stupid. He was evaluating their relationship too, and he deserved to have that time to do it. Julian had always been patient with her; the least she could do was give him the same courtesy.

"No, not if he doesn't call me first."

"Elisa, I wouldn't recommend that."

"Chastity, he stayed with a girl once because she refused to let him go. As much it kills me to think he'll tell me no—"

"You want him to be sure of his decision. I get it. I think it's dumb as hell, but I get it."

"For the record, I think it's dumb as hell, too."

Dropping her transfer request to her boss had been the hardest part of leaving Ireland behind. Saying goodbye to Callum had been one of the hardest and easiest things to do.

Easy, because she finally knew herself. Hardest, because had circumstances been different, she knew she could have been happy with him. Maybe not a forever romance, or maybe it could have been. He'd been a fork in the road of her life, one that could have possibly brought her a lot of happiness.

But she could not undo Julian, and the fact was that she had no desire to pretend he wasn't a giant part of her soul.

Callum had nodded, and his look had been intense—maybe even a little sad—as he'd said, "I understand. Be well, Elisa."

With those words, he was gone, and for just a second she felt a breathless twinge of what might have been. But it was easy to walk away when she knew the potential of what was hopefully waiting for her.

The only person she'd really truly miss would be Meredith, but they'd promised to keep in touch whenever possible. There'd been many tears, hugs, and kisses when they'd said their goodbyes.

Thank God Julian lived in New York; it made the job transfer infinitely easier. For better or for worse Elisa had left Dublin behind forever. Whether Julian wanted her in his life now or not, she had a job and a new life to build in New York City.

Exiting the JFK terminal she hugged Chastity's and Luke's neck and then slid into the back seat of their black SUV.

Chastity was little rounder, a little softer in the face than Elisa remembered her. But motherhood looked good on her. She'd cut her dreds short, and now they hung to her shoulders, and no longer was she wearing bright dyes, but warm earth tones. Her beautiful friend had turned into an even more beautiful mother.

Luke looked the same. With his gorgeous green eyes and his café au lait skin, he turned heads wherever he went, but his eyes were still just for Chas.

"Where's the baby?" she asked, staring at the empty car seat.

Luke was the one to answer as he slowly maneuvered them onto freeway traffic. "With her grandma."

"She's super colicky, we figured it might make it a little less stressful of a ride if you didn't have to hear her squawking." Chas turned in her seat, giving Elisa a soft smile. "It's good to see you back, Lisa."

She grabbed her friend's hand and gave it a gentle squeeze, not talking much on their drive into Chelsea.

The old redbrick buildings reminded her so much of their apartment in college, that Elisa experienced a pang. Chelsea was a hip, young person's scene, and perfect for Julian's artistic lifestyle.

If there were any place in the world Elisa could envision him living, this would have definitely made the top ten.

Luke snorted. "Julian's making his way into the world. Mama must be a serious moneybags." He tapped his fingers on the steering wheel.

Chastity thinned her lips and swatted his shoulder. "You know his art is selling like hotcakes. Julian's deaf and colorblind." She swiveled around to Elisa. "He can also paint his ass off; it's pretty much a recipe for instant fame."

They pulled up to a curb and Elisa stared at the brownstones in front of her. They were all uniform in size and color and shape, but the stoops had a definite flair of distinction, attesting to each individual's personal style. Some bore potted flowers, others brightly painted doors.

Julian's stood out from everyone's.

His door was white, and hanging on it was a dynamic piece of metal art. It was a large circle with a tree of life carved out from inside of it. She smiled.

"His?" Elisa pointed to it.

Glancing over, Chas nodded. "Yup. He works in all kinds of mediums now. He's really pretty amazing." Digging into her purse, Chastity pulled out a key and handed it to her. "He still hasn't gotten that light system set up yet, so he gave us a key to just come in when we needed to for now."

Elisa palmed the key in her hot hand. Her stomach twisting and diving on itself so violently, she shook her head. "What if he's got company over? I should have texted him, huh? I should have—"

"No." Chastity gave her a lopsided grin. "He doesn't leave his house the day of a show. Sorta goes into one of his funky trances. He won't be leaving here for another two hours."

It bothered Elisa how much Chastity knew about Julian now that she didn't. Chas must have noticed, because she briefly touched her cheek. "You were gone, hun, and he's our friend. We kept tabs on him, that's all."

"Yeah," she snorted, "I was gone. This is probably so stupid. After this long."

"Elisa." Luke glanced at her in the rearview. "I know you and me aren't as close as everyone else, but just from a guy's perspective, there's a lot I would have done for Chastity. When it's the real thing, you can't just move on and pretend like it wasn't."

"Aw, honey." Chastity grinned and pecked his cheek. "Just for that you'll be getting desert tonight."

His eyes gleamed and Elisa couldn't help but chuckle, which did help release some of her tension.

Tipping the key toward them, she nodded. "Well, I guess I should go face the firing squad now, right?"

"Hey." Chas winked. "Cheer up. It's gonna be fine. Do you want us to keep the luggage in our car?"

"Yeah, for now." She opened the door slowly. "I'd feel like a real ass if I took that stuff in and he asked me to go."

"He's not gonna ask you to go."

She stared at his door with her heart in her throat. "I wish you could really read the future, Chas, 'cause then I'd feel so much better."

Giving her friends a finger wave as they drove off, Elisa turned on her heel and made her way up the steps. By the time she grabbed hold of the door her palms were sweating and her hands were shaking so bad that she had to squeeze her eyes shut, lean her forehead against it, and take three deep breaths to steady herself.

She was terrified of what she might see. Terrified of finding him in there with someone else. And even if he wasn't with someone else now, that didn't mean there wasn't someone else already in his heart.

Elisa had always loved Julian, but she was ashamed to say there were times in their relationship that she'd definitely dropped the ball, failing to show him just how important he actually was to her.

Behind this door lived the only man she knew, with every fiber of her being, had been made just for her. If he said no, she would move on, and maybe someday be lucky in love again. Elisa had never bought into the soul mates thing—there wasn't just one person in all the world capable of making you happy—but she also knew that there was no one else in all the world who understood her on a molecular level.

Destiny...

She stared at her wrist. She had to know.

Steeling her nerves, she shoved the key in and opened the door.

Her heart beat so hard she could almost taste it on her tongue as she took first one step, then another, then another into his home. The walls were white, the wooden floors painted a deep-hued brown. There was a pale colored coach in the living room, a small dining chair and tables that could only seat four, but there was life pulsing through his apartment.

Canvases stretched from his high ceilings down to the floor and they were all done in amazing splashes of color.

She recognized scenes from her life, their life, on all of them.

A glistening red apple on a black background. So lifelike and realistic that she felt if she could only reach into it she'd be able to grab it and take a bite. In another there was water.

Nothing was around the water, but the way the waves almost seemed in motion, and the ripples that surrounded it, her skin tingled with a sudden rush of desire to dive in.

There was McCreary's Woods with the Queen of Hearts hidden behind a skeletal tree.

Awed by the beauty of his artwork, her mouth hung wide open as she walked around the place that seemed like a museum of her life. She walked up the stairs, knowing she shouldn't, that she'd likely be intruding on his privacy, but she'd caught sight of an image she could hardly believe was real.

There, in the stairwell, was a painting of her. She was nude and covered in paint. Blue dripped from the corners of her eyes, a red heart had been painted over her breast, her arms and thighs were banded in yellow, and gold, brown, black, and red.

Encircling her entire image was a thick stripe of black words.

"Every time she laughs she hopes he's watching... not so that he sees she's happy, but that maybe...just maybe, he'll fall for her smile just as hard as she fell for his..."

A floorboard squeaked.

Screaming with both fear and shock, she clutched at her chest, and then stood stock still as a halo of light surrounded Julian Wright's very nude body. His skin sparkled with drops of water as though he'd just stepped out of a shower.

She was like a woman drowning. Her gaze roamed his body, her heart thundered as she saw him again, almost as if for the first time.

His body was lean and sculpted and its own work of art. There were tattoos scrawling down Julian's thighs now. He stood before her unashamed and she clutched at her breast, feeling like it might gallop straight out of her chest.

Finally it dawned on her that he wasn't saying anything. Swallowing hard, the fear returned with a vengeance, and she didn't want to go through with it, she didn't want to know that he didn't feel the same anymore.

"What are you doing here, Smile Girl?" he asked tentatively.

Smile Girl. That meant something right? He hadn't called her that for a long time. That was his pet name for her, and he wouldn't have used it if he didn't still feel for her.

Right?

But no matter how hard she worked at convincing herself that this wasn't one-sided, she couldn't quite get over her queasiness.

"Elisa?" he asked harder.

Jerking to attention, she stared down at her sandaled feet. Maybe she should have worn a dress, put on makeup.

Blinking and biting onto her bottom lip hard she couldn't look at him as she asked him, "Am I still the one?"

It took her several tense seconds before she could look back at him. When she did, it was to find him still not moving. If he'd answered her, she'd missed it.

Terrified that it was over, that any minute now he'd kick her to the curb, she rushed to get it all out, knowing she might never get this chance again.

"Destiny. That's what I wrote down on my wrist when I left. Because that's exactly what it felt like. But I was dumb to think that destiny was enough. I got over there, Jules, and I forgot myself. I forgot so much." She frowned and then sniffed.

God, she was so sick of crying.

"You came and I saw you and it brought it all back, but I still didn't get it. Life got in the way, and I got busy, and I forgot the things that really mattered."

"What mattered?" He finally got involved in the conversation.

Feeling a minute spark of relief, she took a brave step up.

"You. Us. This." She gestured between them. "You told me once that you would love me forever. I couldn't understand how you could believe that when you were still so young. But for the past two weeks I've been examining my heart and..." She took another step up, now only three steps separated them. It felt like a bridge to eternity.

"You're imprinted all over me. I see my life and you're always there. When you were born, when you moved away, and my world became nothing but shades of gray. Then you came back, and I didn't understand then like I do now why I suddenly came back to life. The first night we kissed, the first night we made love." She took another step, excited to note the rapid rise and fall of his chest, two more steps. "Living with you, loving you. Jules." She shook her head and dropped her hands, unable to say it any other way than with her voice. "It's always been you. *Will always* be you."

The air grew thick with tension and she wanted so desperately to drop her gaze, too scared to see what he'd say to that.

He took one step down.

Only one step separated them. Just one. So close. They were so close she could feel the wash of his heat brush against her. Her nipples puckered in response, her skin tingled with a fiery wash of desire.

How could she ever have believed things had cooled? How could she ever have imagined that something this meteoric could just wither and die?

"My life is here in New York, I've got no prospects in Ireland, Smile Girl. Could you really leave?"

Smiling broadly now as the tears blurred her vision, she grabbed his hands and clutched them desperately to her chest. Those words had definitely not been a no.

Placing one of his palms over her throat she looked him straight in the face as she said, "I choose you."

His eyes widened and his fingers twitched.

She nodded, daring to slip her arm around his waist. His skin pebbled underneath her touch. Speaking to him in the language only they understood, she tapped out her words on his body.

"I've moved to New York."

With a desperate-sounding moan, he crushed her to his chest and claimed her lips. He kissed her like a man drowning, like a man thirsting for oxygen, for hope, for strength.

And when she kissed him, it was like the first time all over again. The passion, the spark, the knowledge and rightness of Julian, it all came back to her with a vengeance. Tears spilled, and she didn't know whether they were hers or his, but for the first time in a long, long time she knew exactly who she was and who she wasn't.

She was strong. She was independent. She could survive without Julian. But she didn't want to. She loved him. And probably always would.

His large, callused hands framed her face and they stared at each other with the intense look of lovers who didn't need to speak to understand what the heart said.

Julian needed her as badly as she needed him.

When he took her hands and threaded their fingers together, she knew he would lead her to his room.

She smiled.

And when he laid her down on his bed, and she was as naked as he, and he traced the lines of her body with an artist's delicate stroke, she knew she was home.

Julian slipped deep inside, not only her body, but her soul, and when it was all over, and all they could do was hug and cry tears of joy and relief, she knew she'd made the right choice.

"You once told me," she tapped out on his back, "that I was the only one for you."

He nodded.

"It's the same for me. You're the only one for me, Julian Wright, you always were. It just took me a while to really understand what that meant. I can live without you, but I never want to do that again."

She hugged him tight when he shuddered against her.

"Smile Girl," he said after a minute.

"Yes?" She smiled up at him, framing his beloved face, loving him more now that she ever thought possible.

Rolling to the side, he pointed to the corner of his room. Taking a peek over his shoulder she saw a packed suitcase resting against the wall.

"What's that?"

Now it was his turn to smile. "I was going to fly to you tonight after the show."

Her heart felt like it literally had just taken a pause. "You were?"

"I'm so sorry, Elisa. So sorry for not fighting harder, for letting the pain of our separation get to me as it did. But I never, never stopped loving you. All my life I've wanted you, and that hasn't changed. I love you. I always have. And I always will."

Epilogue

To say that life was one giant fairytale ending would be a lie. It wasn't easy for Elisa and Julian to find their way back to each other. So much pain had built up between them in those two years, but they were committed to making it work. And slowly but surely, they found their way back to one another.

Two years later Elisa stood on the sands of her and Julian's favorite beach and turned to stare at her father. "How do I look?"

When she'd gone shopping for her dress Elisa hadn't known what to pick out. She'd gone between buying the princess gown she'd always dreamed of as a little girl. The one with ribbons and sequins and a huge bustle and train. But that wasn't who she was now and Julian knew it.

So she'd gone simple. A sheer white flowing dress with spaghetti straps. She'd walk barefoot to him—in fact, she'd required the entire wedding party to go without shoes. It was who they were, unique, eccentric, and that's how she meant to start their married life together, marching to the beat of their own drum.

The sun was shining, and there wasn't a single cloud in the blue, blue sky of that beautiful Maine morning. The waters were calm, and the gentle strains of Pachelbel's "Canon in D" flitted in on the salty breeze as her maids of honor—Meredith and Chastity—walked down the aisle first.

Dressed in a slacks and a pale Hawaiian shirt with tans flowers on it, her father gazed down at her lovingly. Tears gleamed in his eyes as his knuckles delicately brushed along her cheekbone.

"It's been a long and bumpy road for you kids, but I knew the day I saw you two kissing..."

She blushed remembering that night. Julian had still been underage and she'd been mortified to have her father discover her secret. It seemed silly now. As things often did when looking back on them with time and age behind you.

"I knew I would lose you to him, honey, and I'm glad for it. And you look so beautiful."

She smiled, feeling so happy she thought she would burst with tears. "I do love him."

"I know you do, baby. I know you do." He patted her hand gently.

Elisa was hidden within the shelter of a tent. The music shifted yet again, this time to the wedding march, and when tears came to her eyes it wasn't out of fear or anxiety, but because their dream had finally been realized.

Latching tightly to her father's forearm for support, Elisa walked toward Julian.

He was dressed all in white, just like his brothers—who just so happened to be doubling as his groomsmen—were. His hair hung haphazardly around his face, feathering out around his jawline and, just like it always did, her heart warmed at the sight.

The female pastor smiled at them when she came to stand beside him. Julian shook hands with her father before turning back to her and signing, "Beautiful, Smile Girl."

Smiling from her heart, she signed back, "I love you so much. Am I still the one, Jules?"

In answer, he stepped into her, framed her face with his hands and laid a loud, hard kiss on her lips. The audience, comprised of mostly family and friends with a few work colleagues in the mix, erupted into cheers and applause.

The pastor gave a soft, snuffling sound of laughter at his antics. Elisa had chosen her for one very important reason.

The red haired, middle-aged woman was not only a pastor, but she was, herself, deaf.

"Julian Eli Wright, do you take Elisa Jane Adrian to be your lawfully wedded wife?" she signed.

Elisa hopped onto the balls of her feet when he enthusiastically said yes.

"And Elisa Jane Adrian, do you take Julian Eli Wright to be your lawfully wedded husband? To have and to hold, in sickness and in health, till death do you part?"

With tears streaming down her eyes, she signed and said back to him, "Yes, with all my heart."

When the vows were exchanged and cake cut, and all the guests had had a chance to dance and chat with the bride and groom, they snuck off. Julian had asked her where in the world she'd wanted to go for her honeymoon. She'd thought it over long and hard and in the end decided there was only one place she really wanted to be.

And that was wherever he was. The rest didn't matter.

He'd decided to take her to Rome.

That next night, in their hotel room, she wrapped her arms around his neck and smiled.

"Do you still feel like you made the right choice?" he asked and then traced a finger down her cheek.

Sighing, she tapped out her words on his back. “I married the very best, sexiest man in all the world, of course I made the right choice, and I’d do it all over again. I’m pretty crazy about you, Jules.” She turned her wrist up so he could read her tattoo. “You know what I think about destiny, Julian?”

Chuckling, he asked, “What?”

“‘Destiny is no matter of chance. It is a matter of choice. It is not a thing to be waited for, but a thing to be achieved.’ A wise man said that once a long time ago and I so agree. For so long I kept waiting for it to happen, but now I know”—she framed his face—“that when you want something bad enough, then sometimes it’s up to you to make sure it happens.”

“I’ll love you forever, Elisa Wright.”

She shivered when he said it. “I’m gonna hold you to that, Jules. You’re never getting rid of me now.”

And when he kissed her, she tasted eternity in it.

Author's Note

A big fat thank you to my Street Team, Hatter's Harem. You all were instrumental in getting this book realized. Your constant support and enthusiasm, you guys are so much fun and I'm so happy to have met every single one of you guys! Keep rockin' on, Harem!

Many of you might be wondering if there will be more Wright Brother books planned, the answer to that is, yes. I'll be releasing a book from Julian's pov next, and possibly even a book for Roman and Christian down the road, although that's entirely dependent on you guys, my readers.

About Marie Hall

Marie Hall is a *NY Times* and *USA Today* Bestselling Author who loves books that make you think, or feel something. Preferably both. And while she's a total girly girl and loves glitter and rainbows, she's just as happy when she's writing about the dark underbelly of society. Well, if things like zombies, and vampires, and werewolves, and mermaids existed. (Although she has it on good authority that mermaids do in fact exist, because the internet told her so.)

She's married to the love of her life, a sexy beast of a caveman who likes to refer to himself as Big Hunk. She has two awesome kids, lives in Hawaii, loves cooking and occasionally has been known to crochet. She also really loves talking about herself in the third person.

Visit Marie Hall online at mariehallwrites.com

A Moment:

A Moment...

I killed myself tonight.

Or at least I tried. But a woman I don't know refused to let me die. Liliana Delgado wrapped me up in her slim arms and told me things would be okay. But she doesn't know the demons I live with. The things that have happened to me. Every morning is a struggle just to get out of bed, and the nights are even worse. But the way she smiles at me... I feel something I've never felt before. Hope.

...will change our lives

I should not have gone to that burlesque bar on Valentine's Day, but I did. My life isn't easy. I had a child when I was only fourteen, now I'm in college and things should have been easier. But they aren't. My life is spiraling out of control. Then I see Ryan Cosgrove sitting at a table with an empty, broken look in his beautiful blue eyes and something inside of me feels like he knows. He understands what it is to hurt, to struggle. So when I bump into him later that night, bloody, broken, and dying I know I'll do everything in my power to save him and maybe in the process, I'll save myself too.

forever...

Sneak Peek

Rolling my eyes, I finish getting ready, trying hard not to let the demons knocking on my door crash through. Not yet. Tonight I just want to forget. Sink deep into an eighty-proof fog and pretend that for once I'm normal. Just a normal man who doesn't need to do this to feel alive.

My hands shake when I pat my shirt down.

Traffic headed toward Sixth Street is crazy. Like always. But somehow we finally make it there. The street is one big party. Anyone and everyone who lives in Austin knows the only place to party is Sixth. The city closes down the entire section of street after nine. Already college kids are gathered outside the neon glare of the bar lights. Music thumps hot and hard through the door, sounding like liquid sex.

Girls smile at me as I shove my hands into my jeans. I'm not looking to get laid tonight, so I ignore them.

It's obvious when we draw close to the Pink Lady. The techno music is replaced by the smoky strains of jazz and bassy blues. The silhouette of a neon woman in pink decorates the window. The blinds are all drawn.

I've been here a couple times but have never stayed long. This isn't really my scene. If I want to watch a woman dance, I prefer to see her take everything off. Still, when I flash my card, a shot of adrenaline speeds my pulse.

Alex is scanning the crowd; a second later a huge grin splits his face. I frown—he seems really excited. I don't actually recall ever seeing him act like this about a woman.

He isn't exactly a player, but he isn't the domestic type, either.

So I look around, following his gaze, and it's like someone just pulled the floor out from under me. A petite Hispanic woman is walking toward him with an equally large smile on her face.

Her hair is dark and silky, glinting under the dim red lights of the bar. It spills down her back in a graceful wave. Her body is toned and trim, legs a mile long and encased in a tight pair of red pants. A white top accentuates the bronze of her arms.

But her face is the most gorgeous thing I've ever seen. Heart-shaped with a tiny cleft in the jaw, full lipped and a short button nose. She stops in front of us, carrying the scent of flowers with her.

Which is amazing I can even smell that because the bar reeks of scotch and smoke and food.

Turning green eyes toward me, she smiles. "Hi, I'm Liliana."

Made in the USA
Middletown, DE
21 September 2015